D0251361

KWEEN

KWEEN

VICHET CHUM

Quill Tree Books
An Imprint of HarperCollinsPublishers

Quill Tree Books is an imprint of HarperCollins Publishers.

Kween
Copyright © 2023 by Vichet Chum
All rights reserved. Printed in the United States of America.
No part of this book may be used or reproduced in any manner whatsoever
without written permission except in the case of brief quotations embodied in
critical articles and reviews. For information address HarperCollins Children's
Books, a division of HarperCollins Publishers, 195 Broadway, New York, NY
10007.
www.epicreads.com

Library of Congress Control Number: 2023933501
ISBN 978-0-06-322335-6
Typography by Erin Fitzsimmons
23 24 25 26 27 LBC 5 4 3 2 1

First Edition

Always for the Chums. Always for the Queerdos.
Always for the Cambos.

Introduction

Some legends say it was on the coursing sea that a Naga woman led a group of pirates to take on an Indian prince. Some legends say it was on the battlefields where this warrior princess led her soldiers against this Hindu foe. All legends say she WHUPPED him, and being impressed with his courage, she proposed and took his hand in marriage. Their union was believed to be the beginning of the Funan Kingdom, a cultural fusion of Indians and the indigenous Nagas . . . the creation of the Khmer people. Our people.

Some say she was half snake. Some say she was a spirit sent from above. Some say she was a warrior. All say she was: Queen Soma. The First Monarch. The Real One.

Now, we could've called you Neang Neak, the proper Khmer version of your Indian-given name, but we've never exactly been good Cambodian people, have we? And besides, it packs a punch. When you came a week before your due date, wailing like you had something to say, we knew the only thing we could call you was Soma.

I remind you of your namesake because, gkoun . . . life is sometimes much harder than it needs to be. But that's nothing new for us. We were made for this. So, when you're feeling like the future is uncertain, I need you to remind yourself of who you are: Soma. You are a queen. This is your inheritance. And with that is your ability to say, to do, to be whomever you want to be. Don't be afraid. Step into your legacy.

—Your Ba

CHAPTER 1
Self-View

Set on self-view . . .
Like she's even got a clue . . .
'Bout that red light . . .
Flashing hot, bright . . .

Counting up the time
As she's waiting for that rhyme
To find its other pair
Like palms kissing for a prayer

THO she's not sure 'bout God
(Kind of like this tripod)
It makes sense on a look
But have you seen it when it's S H O O K?

It's supposed to put in place
The framework of your face

The depth of your eyes
As the words begin to rise

What's she gonna say?
When she's some kind of way?
What's she gonna do?
After what she's been through?

She's not looking for a tear
From ye avatars out here
Chick doesn't even know
Who's hooked onto this flow

But she's out on a limb
While things are looking dim
And she needs something to do
When her life is feeling new

YOU SEE—
She's got those yellow-brown blues
Those Jungle Asian views
Of not feeling right
When you're always in the fight

To prove your worth
On this stolen earth
That yours are as equal
As the thieving sequel

Settlers, that is, who once made commands
And without regard, took over these lands
And decided—DECIDE who continue to belong
As long as the notes are right for their song

Even if you hear sounds of bombs throughout the night
An inherited memory of a shared historical fight
To escape the war that just seems to keep going
Making it ever so bleak, the endeavor of growing

Ooh, she's touched on a nerve
And now she's looking to *SWERVE*
Because she's trying to work through
What she knows she cannot undo

The feelings are too hot
Even more than she thought
When she put up this phone
To speak on the unknown

What she *does* know is this
That she's looking to not miss
The chance to speak out
When she's wanting to shout:

THOSE YELLOW-BROWN BLUES!
THOSE JUNGLE ASIAN VIEWS!

OF FEELING NOT RIGHT!
WHEN YOU'RE ALWAYS IN THE FIGHT!

And so . . . the time keeps going
Even as her thoughts are slowing
The self-view is waiting
For the speaker to keep creating

The red light keeps blinking
And she keeps on thinking
About the prayer she is making
That will keep her from breaking

What's she gonna say?
When she's some kind of way?
What's she gonna do?
After what she's been through?

Dear self-view . . .
Who's even got a clue . . .
'Bout that red light . . .
Flashing hot, bright . . .

CHAPTER 2
At the Precipice

Soma, put the phone away. Facedown on the bed, and step aside. The deed is done. There's no turning back. Now all you can do is sit and wait . . .

Sit and wait . . .

Sit and—

Turn it back around. What's good? Nothing yet.

One like!

Shut up, you thirst bucket. One like isn't shit.

Two likes!

Oh whatever. It's just Sophat. He likes everything.

Ten likes?

"What the—"

The phone suddenly sank like a weight in my hand. Had I just made a catastrophic mistake? What mess was I getting into by going public in a post, sharing my free-form in the socials? On a Sunday? The lord's day?! And honestly, did any of it mean anything?

Of course it did.

My hype fever was slowly coming down.

No edit: since Ba was deported back to Phnom Penh, Cambodia, five months ago, it was like I'd been grasping for words. I never had that problem before. Ma and Ba said that when I was younger, they'd put on their CDs, and I'd walk around the house shouting all the lyrics to "It's Tricky." I couldn't shut the hell up. Not when Run-DMC was on. I mean, respect your elders, right?

Truth be told, I always liked talking. I always liked words. I always liked putting them together to make some kind of meaning. Or maybe to capture it. As if the right combination could explain the situation. But these last couple of months, it was like . . . clever lines couldn't cover this feeling.

But then—then(!), tonight after dinner, when I got that chaotic email from Ba (the first personal one *ever*), it left me vibrating. Not because he was sharing any breaking news—the guy likes telling me that same old story about my namesake—but because something hit me differently in this timeline, in this context. It felt loaded. Like it was a challenge. Not necessarily from Ba, but maybe from the universe. "Soma" was my legacy. What was I going to do with it?

Okay, so *maybe* Ba was also going straight to inbox because I'd been struggling to respond to his previous modes of communication. When he FaceTimed me, I really didn't want to see him in that place. When he texted me, I didn't want him to make a joke with some not-even-funny SpongeBob meme.

When he called me, he shook me with his awkward silences. I loved the guy, but I couldn't pretend to try to make this new way work. I kept him on read and hoped he wouldn't notice. But this first email was a sign. He wasn't ignorant. The guy was working to crack me, but he'd have to wait. I wasn't ready yet.

Still. His content had me thinking about my content: *Step into your legacy.*

Maybe I wasn't equipped to fire back at Ba, but this instruction tapped a nerve. Before I knew it, I'd plotted out some rough and ragged words, propped up the self-view, and pressed the red button. I recorded a pure instinct.

Stop starving, Soma. Put the phone under the pillow. Out of sight and out of mind.

Maybe this was a good time to start getting into some of Ma and Ba's Buddhist practices. Like relinquishing. I could relinquish. It's not that hard. All you have to do is . . . relinquish—

"RELINQUISH!" With my face buried deep into the pillow, an animal scream escaped my lips and disappeared into the graveyard of dead cells and now . . . dead dreams. Wow. I really needed to change these covers. They were smelling funky.

In this smooshed stank state, I couldn't help but wonder, why the hell had I just done that? Why had I posted that video—unfiltered, unedited, and very unrehearsed? Instincts be damned. I'd never done anything like that before. Sure, whenever I was with Sophat, I'd goof around some, or when I'd listen to a track in my room, I rattled off, but this was the first time ever I was offering out my own verses, exposing my insides like I got a soul or something. Was I being found out? Or was I outing myself? What was I getting into, actually?

Yeah, no. This stench was getting me twisted. This wasn't going to work, either. This wasn't going to work at all. I needed to *throw* the phone across the room, where it would be impossibly out of reach. That way, I wouldn't be tempted to check my stats as some pathetic reflex.

Thud.

"Well, shit."

"Soma? Hey, Soma!" An unwanted voice barged into my room, as if closed doors meant nothing.

"What?!" I yelled back, unable to conceal my annoyance.

"Not an adequate response, *thank you very much.*"

Sis was dripping with sarcasm, and I didn't have time for it. Since she'd moved back home at the beginning of summer, Dahvy's voice had consistently taken on a more authoritative (some might say, *fascist*) tone that was beginning to grate at my chill. Previously, she'd been living and working in Boston after graduate school, but when Ba's deportation order came up, she insisted on coming back to help. I obviously protested, unsure of why we needed another Kear girl hogging the already sad number of toilets, but Ma said it was a good idea.

Trouble was, Dahvy fancied herself more of a third tyrannical parent than a sister. Every day she was here, the almost-fifteen-year age gap between us felt like it was getting wider and wider. I already had parents, *thank you very much.*

"I'm doing homework!"

"Okay, well, I need your help."

"Can you give me, like, fifteen minutes?"

"But it better be fifteen minutes, instead of you rolling downstairs in an hour like you usually do!"

The unfounded accusation obliterated any chill I had left in my body. I. Was. Hot.

"See you in fifteen minutes. OKAY, BYYYE!" I yelled back, hoping that Dahvy would receive my not-so-subtle tone.

Success. Silence.

I leapt toward the wastebasket and, without thinking, instantly buried my arm in layers of some seriously questionable items: old papers, a plastic boba cup from Sweet Journey (remaining bubbles building their own ecosystems), a pair of holey socks, and . . . my phone, intact. *Thank God.*

"Seventy-two likes?" My eyes squinted to see if they were playing tricks on me. How did the video jump in likes within a matter of minutes?

Before I could even interrogate the development, a model selfie of my puckered best friend took over the home screen. You couldn't make up this timing.

"Who. Even. Are you?" Sophat's voice poked through the phone.

"What. Are you. Even. Talking. About?" I matched his punctuated inquisition.

"Bissshhh."

"Yousabissshhh!"

"Your *video.*"

"I low-key just posted it. How'd you watch it so fast?"

"What do I even do with my life? I legit look at videos all day long."

"Okay, and . . . ?"

"Well, yousabish, Yellow-Brown Blues with those Jungle Asian Views! You have eighty-six likes now—check out those stats!"

He was wrong. The video had . . . ninety-two likes? What. Was. Happening?

This was getting way more likes than that Rebel Challenge I posted last year. Sophat bullied me to do it, and while he tossed his hair back and reigned supreme, I barely did the choreo with a smug smile on my face. To us, that mode was actually hilarious, but to everyone else, maybe not so much. At most, it snagged a sorry fourteen likes. This new video was straight sprinting into unknown territory.

"Let's go!" Sophat shouted, like he was already out the door.

"Is that Sophat?!" Dahvy's voice returned as if it'd never left in the first place. "Soma, come on. You said you'd help me!"

"Meet me, Emceeeee!" Sophat would not be satisfied until I relented.

"Are you listening to me?" Dahvy would not be satisfied until I relented.

I couldn't please them both. I needed to deal with one to get the other.

"At the clock, in like twenty minutes," I instructed Sophat.

"Oh, you are that Beat legacy, loitering on Lowell streets like your ancestors—"

"GOODBYYYE!"

I lodged my phone into my back pocket (shutting down my sweetie), grabbed the nearest hoodie on the floor, and stepped into some kicks. Chick was out of body, of course, and before she could descend downstairs, she needed to take a quick evaluation in the dresser mirror. A pause. I whiplashed for a second glance. Something had me coming back.

My wide, undeniably Cambo nose was always the first feature my eyes caught, a scrunchie held my thick black hair (wispies sparking out like I'd stuck my finger in a socket), and my round yellow-brown face—the one I didn't care for much usually—well, in this moment, it kind of looked . . . right. Or maybe new. Kind of fresh. Sort of wild. Unknown. Definitely unknown. But working it out.

I was curious about this girl. Between two needy people, in this solo space of stillness, at the reflection of myself, I wondered again . . . why the hell had I just posted that?

"Soma?!" Dahvy howled once again, breaking my trance and bluntly reminding me of who and where I was at this exact moment: Soma at the precipice.

Down at the landing, I paused before throwing myself willingly into the kitchen of despair. Unfortunately, there was only one way out, and said kitchen door was currently guarded by a creature that sometimes resembled a troll and sometimes a sister. The distinction was blurry.

I wasn't trying to be hateful, but I knew I was in for it. Not only was I going to be subjected to doing some chore that would take longer than it should, but a lecture would follow. Dahvy couldn't help herself. She didn't have Ma and Ba to go off on. She only had me.

From my vantage point, I could somewhat see her arms awkwardly behind her back, like she was trying to snap something together. It was obvious. She needed help.

I had to face the music: pay the troll the toll.

CHAPTER 3
The Toll

"Motherf—"

Dahvy stood aglow at the center of the kitchen in her traditional Cambodian wedding outfit: a glittery pink blouse with a wide ribbon that floated diagonally across her upper body like some silly pageant sash, and a matching silk sarong that fell perfectly just above her toy miniature princess feet. Everything had gold trimming, making each line of the silhouette sparkle even against the dim kitchen light.

Okay, there was a whole lot of Pepto-Bismol going on, but I couldn't deny the truth. She wasn't a troll. Dahvy was a Disney princess—

"Damn it! Don't just stand there! Get me a Band-Aid!" Dahvy shouted while sucking on her finger like a helpless chaos baby. Never mind. The beauty had become the BEAST.

"What are you doing?" I asked, moving quickly to find her some aid.

"I'm trying to take this thing in."

"Can't Ming Ani do it at the boutique for you?"

"She could, but for some reason she keeps offering me more space than I need. She thinks I'm fat."

"How do you know that?"

"Because she says, 'Dahvy, you fat.'"

Our own self-appointed community tailor was problematic one hundred. Once, Ming Ani made me a dress for this father-daughter dance (barf one hundred), and when I tried it on initially, I remember I could barely fit my head through it. Ming complained I must've gained some weight from the initial measurements, and I cried through the whole fitting. After that, Ma promised she'd always be there to make sure Ming was checked for her hateful, body-shaming ways. Apparently, the terrible tailor was back at it. For however much I enjoyed virtually any joke at the expense of Dahvy, body stuff was off-limits. That was code.

I moved toward the sink in search of a Band-Aid, trying not to offer any semblance of reaction to Dahvy's comment. Best to keep my head low and on instruction. Get in, get out, get the freak away.

Bingo. Ma always stored the box of medical supplies right under the sink. Maybe if Dahvy had tried looking hard enough, she wouldn't have had to call me down in the first place.

Before I could even hand it to her, hoping this would be the end to my sisterly duties, Dahvy slyly intercepted me with a pouch of safety pins pushed against my chest.

"I'll put this on, if you help me." Was it a quid pro quo if you got nothing in return? Yup. I was definitely getting the raw end of the deal. I rolled my eyes, passing the Band-Aid along in exchange for the handful of silver safety pins.

"How?" I asked honestly.

"Just, you know, pull in the fabric as close to my body as possible, and then pin it. But don't stab me."

"Oh yeah, like you?"

"Come on, Soma. I need your help."

With rolled eyes permanently lodged in the back of my skull, I began to grab at the folded fabric around her Barbie waist.

"Dang, this fabric is thick."

"Just a little more."

"Why are you doing this by yourself?"

"Well, I wouldn't have to if—" Dahvy stopped herself abruptly but knowingly, like she was headed this way all along. I knew what she was going to say, so why didn't she just say it?

"Wouldn't have to, if what?" I asked, staring directly back at her.

The truth was, Dahvy's wedding was about a month away, but Ma had to make an unexpected trip to Cambodia to get some paperwork sorted out for Ba. It wasn't exactly her fault. Obviously, Ba wouldn't be able to come to the wedding now, and while there was a lot of conversation about whether we would cancel it or move it back to some undetermined time, Ma promised she'd be back for the wedding no matter what. There was still time for them to fight about whatever ugly table placements each of them wanted. Dahvy just needed to take her foot off the gas a little.

Dahvy's eyes moved away from my question. I'd called her bluff, and she seemingly didn't want to get into it. Not fully, at least. I knew she was calculating her strategy.

"What were you doing up there, anyways? Sounded like you were talking to someone." On to the next tactic! I had to give it to her. Dahvy was masterful at changing topics with zero need for a transition. She confidently moved right along, regaining control over the conversation.

"You guessed it, talking to Sophat."

"Before that. It sounded like yelling. For a second, I thought you might've been talking to Ba—"

"Nope! Just boring Sophat." Record scratch. Why was that her assumption? Was she catching on to me not speaking to Ba? Had he said something? What was the agenda here? Yeah, no, I needed to bury the mention of the old man quickly and divert the attention to my sweet, unsuspecting friend. "Sophat lights me up, what can I say? What, you Big Brother now?"

Maybe she needed the waist to be a little tighter.

"Ooh, too tight. Loosen that one up."

I lessened my grip . . . a bit.

"You think I care? No, it was just loud, so keep it down, okay?"

"There." It was time for this conversation to be done. I snapped the safety pin into place and tried to step away—

"How do I look?" Dahvy reviewed herself in the floor-length

mirror she had propped against the kitchen counter. I looked on, observing two truths: she was drop-dead gorgeous, and if I wanted to leave anytime soon, I had to pay the troll the toll.

"You look . . . good."

"Oh, wow. Was that some kind of compliment?"

"Never mind. You fat."

"I'm kidding! Thank you," Dahvy replied, finally giving me the credit I deserved. She could've left it right there in that vaguely complimentary spot, but no. The beast needed to dissolve any semblance of connection with her next underhanded proposal. "And how about you, maid of honor? Your blouse is getting fixed at the store, but I have your sampot jong gk'bun. You could try it on now."

The cons! It became immediately clear that this was some kind of ploy of Dahvy's to get me to try on my outfit. Sis was trying to fix her problems by positioning herself as some amateur seamstress. Sorry, but I knew my fit wasn't going to be right. Those Cambo bridal outfits were made for bodies like Dahvy's, slim, trim, and flim . . . sy. There would be work to do. I was waiting for the single official fitting, once and only once. We are talking harm reduction here. My eyes darted directly to the second wedding set, conveniently draped across a kitchen chair. Now I *really* had to go.

"Didn't Ma say we were going to do the final fitting all together? She's back next weekend. You know, with Ma there, Ming Ani would talk less sh—"

"Language."

"Would talk less sh . . . izz about your fit. Why can't we just wait?" I began to move toward the kitchen door leading to the outside, but I could feel her eyes locked on to my escape route. She was ready on the offense.

"I just want to make sure everything's perfect, and with Ma cutting it close—"

"She's back next weekend—"

"*With Ma cutting it close*, I just want to make sure we have time for all the alterations. I want to get ahead of it."

"Yeah, and I'm going to wait for Ma." I continued my creep toward the door, but Dahvy moved in fast, backing me up against my only way out. I could feel the doorknob pushed hard against my lower back. This was a sister standoff. There could only be one survivor, and it sure as hell was going to be me.

Without looking, I turned the knob with one hand and readied myself to jump ship backward when a loud knock resounded in the kitchen.

Saved by the Ruben.

"Don't let him in—" Dahvy instructed hopelessly.

"What's good, Soma?" Through the very same door I'd been anticipating ejecting myself from, Ruben bounded into the kitchen with bags in both hands and zero awareness of what was going down. Honestly, this was kind of a neutral stance for him. Where there was some drama, Ruben stepped in, face-plant and all.

"Hold on!" Dahvy shouted back, but there was no way to stop Ruben when he entered a room.

"Whoa, look at you!" His eyes gleamed like a dang puppy at the sight of his fiancée. In this moment, I really wish I had a bucket to hurl into.

"Close your eyes! Close your eyes! Close your eyes!" Dahvy quickly threw up her arms in front of her body to prevent him from seeing her. Ruben followed by mirroring her defensive position. The two looked like some sparring chickens with their heads cut off. It was obvious. The cluckers were perfect for each other.

"What's the big deal?" Ruben asked, as if he hadn't been hanging around this Cambo family since day one. Disgustingly, the two had been sweethearts at Lowell High before they ended up teaching at the same school decades later. There were some lost years in between, but when Dahvy returned home, I guess no one else would have her. Sad.

"It's my wedding dress, genius!" Dahvy shouted back as she ran into the living room.

Ruben waited for a clearing and then opened his eyes again. "I didn't know Cambodians were superstitious like that."

"You been sleeping? We pray for our babies to look ugly, so that the spirits don't steal them." I thought Ruben ought to know what sort of hauntings were coming with this intended marriage.

"Seriously?"

"Seriously." Ba told me about the specific superstition once, and maybe I'm damaged or something, but the image of *really* ugly babies always brought a smile to my face. "Well, now that you have Ruben, I'll be—"

"What's going on, Soma?" Ruben's invitation for conversation was going to keep me captive in this house 4eva.

"Oh, you know."

"Being mysterious as usual?"

"Oh, you know." I'm honestly good with Ruben, but as my future brother-in-law and former freshman English teacher, there was kind of a lot going on there.

"Hey, Mr. Drakos said you dropped a really . . . powerful essay in class the other day."

Okay, so this was actually the problem with having an older sister who was a math teacher who was marrying an English teacher at a school where a history teacher (who'd been there since the dinosaurs roamed the freaking earth) was instructing said sixteen-year-old subject.

Ye Olde Drakos was such a Snitchasaurus. You'd think my dear teacher, knowing that my sister taught at our school, would have some clue about overstepping boundaries, but the surprises kept coming. Ruben was sneaking out some subtext, and I didn't know where exactly he was taking it. Sure, the essay in question was on my mind, but did I want to get into it with Dahvy in the other room? Hell no. Luckily, for the moment, she was still busy changing clothes, warding off superstitions. I had to tell myself to stay cool.

"Yeah. I got essays," I replied, like I wasn't sweating it, even if I low-key was. I hoped he'd just drop it.

"I'd like to read it, if you ever feel comfortable sharing it with me. I mean, I remember the one you wrote in my class about *East of Eden*. 'How come Asians only get one lit hero, and why's he gotta be a Lee?'"

It was true! Why does the entire American literary canon for high school have one Asian character that people barely know about? And why does he have to speak some pidgin English to placate white people's understanding of Chinese people? That was some kind of racist, mental bull crap that Asians have been dealing with forever, but at that moment, it was tapping at the nerve hard.

"I think you're the only one who'd let me get away with that." Unlike Drakos, the artist formerly known as Mr. Diaz never made me feel like my ideas were too much, but that I was actually kind of funny and sometimes on point.

It occurred to me, maybe posting my video wasn't such a bad idea after all. I mean, if my fooling with some words could make Ruben want to hear more about an essay I knew for certain was a powder keg . . . maybe I did have something to say. Too chaotic for the books, but just chaotic enough for the socials? Boom.

One thing was sure: I wasn't about to get into said video or said essay with Ruben or Dahvy in my orbit. I was keeping my business on lock.

Dahvy stormed back into the room, now wearing an oversized Weezer T-shirt that hung halfway over her sarong.

"I still see the skirt! The spirits! *The spirits!*" Ruben yelled, crouching into a defensive position. Dahvy hit him across the chest.

"You're early!"

"You always complain about me being late!"

"A little warning would be nice!"

"I texted you!"

"I was working!"

"OKAAAAY, I'm gonna go!" I yelled over the love/hate birds. Hang out with them long enough, and it was clear to anyone this was their act. Fight, fight, fight, and make out. No need to stick around for that last part, *thank you very much*.

"Where are you going?" There was that real chill tone again. Dahvy just couldn't help herself.

"Out with Sophat."

"And?"

"I don't know. Just, like, get a coffee and chill."

"Smoking some dank on campus?"

What. The. Funk. Why was Dahvy pretending like she knew anything about my life? Home for a few months, and she was on a tirade. She had to be stopped.

"Oh, you don't know me like that."

"I do, because you come back smelling like it."

"Smelling like *what*?"

"You know, it'd be good for me if you weren't smoking out at my new place of employment," Dahvy pronounced, as if she were laying down a perfect poker hand. As if she thought her game had some effect on me. But no way. It wasn't my fault Dahvy had decided to move back home, get engaged to my former teacher, and then teach at the only place I could escape to. Why was it my issue to deal with now?

"It's not gonna get back to you."

"Just because Ma isn't here doesn't mean you don't have one, okay? I'm like your ma and your ba now—"

"Wow, okay, so BYYYE," I shouted back as I reached for the door. I wasn't looking back now, and I sure as hell wasn't taking any orders from her. How dare Dahvy? How dare she think that she could even begin to fill their shoes? It wasn't like they were six feet under. They were just . . . nine thousand miles away . . . for the time being.

With the kitchen door snapped back, the cool air poured into the kitchen, offering some relief from the heat.

"I'm serious, Soma—" Dahvy yelled in my direction, but it was way too late. I was already halfway out the door.

"Careful not to prick her, Ruben. Her blood be boiling! BYYYYE!"

"Before midnight!" Dahvy's blood *was* boiling, and it was sending me right into the night, as far away from her as humanly possible. I didn't care. My blood was boiling too. Dahvy had crossed a line. She had barely said anything meaningful about Ma and Ba up to this moment, and then out of nowhere, she uses them as an excuse for her reign of terror? Nope.

Dahvy might have moved back in, but things were going to stay just as they'd been before. . . .

Before.

Even in the chilly autumn air, the word branded itself on my chest, giving way to some heat on my heart. What was it about that word that felt so painful?

Before.

For once, I'd actually done something—I'd posted that video to try to make sense of what was going on, and now I was wondering if it did anything at all.

Before.

What was before? What was after?

Before.

What is now?

CHAPTER 4
Have You Eaten Yet?

MA (9:01 p.m.):   Have you eaten yet?

The phone glowed the oh-so-obvious question from Ma, who'd probably woken up hours ago and waited to send me her favorite sentiment at just the right moment. Twelve hours ahead, and the woman was always ready to check to see if I had already eaten.

Sometimes it'd hit me wrong, like was she saying something about my weight? Had I eaten too much? Had I eaten too little? But then the calmer parts of my brain would remind me this was how she asked if I was being fed—if I had enough to eat.

Ma and Ba were both survivors of the Cambodian genocide way back in the 1970s, and for a couple of years, the country had been ruled by this evil group called the Khmer Rouge (the Red Cambodians) led by the most monster of monsters, Pol Pot. Families were pulled apart, and people were forced to work on farms. If you were rich, if you were educated, if you sang, if you gave someone the wrong look . . . you'd be murdered.

Ma would tell me stories about when she was a kid in the labor camps and how she'd survive on a little bowl of rice for days. Sometimes, when people were close to the end, their bellies would swell from not having enough to eat. That stuff would continue to haunt her, and even though I wasn't there, sometimes it felt like it was haunting me too. Like my imagination couldn't escape it. I couldn't escape it.

SOMA (9:01 p.m.):	Dahvy ordered pizza earlier.
MA (9:02 p.m.):	Tell her she needs to cook.
SOMA (9:02 p.m.):	But she ALWAYS burns the bigh!
MA (9:03 p.m.):	Practice makes perfect!

Most of the Khmer people in Lowell, Massachusetts, were survivors too. After the war, Cambodians had been sponsored all around the world, and maybe it was because the Khmer Rouge worked so hard to destroy the idea of family that so many landed in this random town. Over time, it became the second-biggest home of our people in the US, next in numbers to a totally different kind of town on the other side of the country, Long Beach, California. I know it's wrong to question our karma or whatever, but sometimes I wondered why we couldn't have been sent to a place with a little bit of sun and a beach or two. Was that really too much to ask for?

I should've worn a coat. It might have only been October,

but I could feel the bone-cold New England winter creeping around the corner. Once December hit, there was no turning back. Winter was coming. Still, the air felt good against my flushed cheeks as I walked down the dark and silent streets.

On the actual other side of the world, Ma and Ba were in full-on monsoon season. It must've been mad hot or raining nonstop. It was funny to me to think about how in the exact same moment, people could have completely different experiences. Hot and cold. Day and night. Beachy and concrete-y. Together and alone.

I crossed through Middlesex Community College, where the view of the Concord River and the Lower Locks Gatehouse always gave me this feeling of being someplace else. Maybe it was the way the city pulsed because water ran through the center of it. Maybe it was that meeting of nature and nurture. Maybe it was just the way it looked at night. Regardless of what the haters say, the glow of the town always felt like being someplace else that was special. Whether it was the massive redbrick walls of the old Boott Mills or the stone Bayon statue welcoming people to Cambodia Town . . . in its remix of cultures, I actually felt at home here. At least, before.

Before.

Now I was beginning to feel like it was just a place. I wasn't so sure where "home" was now.

Now.

Quick detour: across Merrimack Street, past the Green Bamboo Chinese Restaurant parking lot, and arrival at the sacred site of my most spiritual soulmate, Jack Kerouac Park. It was true. The iconic Beat Generation poet was a Masshole too, and in our shared geography and absolute desire to rage, I felt a kind of kinship.

A kind of awe in his work.

A kind of pull into his chaos.

A kind of familiarity in the overlap.

Before Kerouac was Kerouac, he came from a family of multilingual French-Canadian immigrants who settled in our fair town. When he was only a kid, his older brother died of some gnarly fever, and over time, the guy used that inner turmoil to write books like *The Town and the City* and *The Dharma Bums*. He became most known for the company he kept, the generation of San Francisco poets called the Beats.

Okay, it wasn't like I didn't understand the complexity of my affection here. There was a long list of bad behaviors, serious examples of masc toxicity, and questionable crimes to boot (check the Wikis). But I couldn't help but honestly ask: Can you separate the art from the artist? The word from the wordsmith? Because if you could . . . youth, bro.

On the Road was one of the first books of his I read, and I was going "Awww!" at the feeling of it all. In the book, a group of friends can't stay put in their respective homes, so they go searching for something . . . dun dun dun . . . on the road. To me, in his tales of escaping small towns and being fully led by one's achy, aimless wanderlust, Kerouac captured authentically the pure pandemonium of being young. *The feeling of it all.*

Maybe I needed to pack up and go. Hit up someplace else. Even if I'd been fond of our hometown charms before, maybe I was looking for what comes after. What place comes after?

After.

It didn't help that the town was obsessed with its one claim to fame. Everywhere you went, there was some kind of plaque or memorial honoring the literary hero.

With my index finger, I traced the engraved words *Find the true light*, memorialized from his collection of poems entitled *The Scripture of the Golden Eternity*, in the big, brown marble commemorative pillars, standing stiff in the middle of the park. The Stonehenge-like monuments formed a circle around a small bench, where you could sit in the center and take it all in. I jumped up onto it and looked at the two paths intersecting through the pillars to form a cross on the ground. Ruben told us once that the cross cutting through the circle was a nod to Kerouac's Roman Catholic background and his later Buddhist curiosities. Whoever made this must've been smoking that pipe, because it looked like some ancient site intentionally trying to summon some divine, cosmic voodoo.

Honestly, I was into it. Beam me up, Buddha.

Sometimes, when no one was looking, I liked to stand at the center of these overlapping religious ideas, throw my arms out, and spin around like a top. I imagined myself sweeping up all those words, those ideas, that energy, with a couple of epic turns. And when the ground finally felt stable again, I'd open my eyes and walk on. I'd step away feeling fueled by that spiritual curiosity. I'd harness all of it, and maybe it'd make me stronger to deal with . . . whatever.

I took a quick survey of the area. Not a person in sight. It was as good a time as any. I closed my eyes, spread my arms out wide, and—

Round and round and round—

The air around me wasn't resistant but propelled me with each turn—

I thought about Kerouac—

I thought about Dahvy—

I thought about Ma—

I thought about Ba—

I thought about myself—

And stop.

For a moment, I could've been anywhere. Lowell. Long Beach. Cambodia. Dancing on the rings of Saturn. Out on the road. Born into a reincarnated life. A void of nothingness. Everywhere. Nowhere at all.

My head throbbed. My blood was racing. Sweat trickled down my face.

Finally, I opened my eyes, and, still the world was askew. Everything remained a blur, but I somehow felt . . . fuller. Maybe not actually fuller, but like I'd gathered some energy. Enough to get me to my next pit stop. In the darkness, I was still on the journey to find the true light.

CHAPTER 5

One Average Lowellian, Cambodian Youth

As I turned the corner, I could see the old clock jutting out from the wall of the school and levitating above the ground, as if it could come crashing down at any moment. Luckily, it was held up by a mint-green casing hooked on to one side. A light from within illuminated the clockface and the words: *LOWELL HIGH SCHOOL GIFT OF 37 38 39.* A token of past students who'd been there, done that. It looked like some swollen moon, trying to get out of its box, hanging over generations of angsty students in search of a little light and a little time. Beneath it now, one of those students had turned that glowing reflection into a spotlight. This was diva business.

I listened in closely. Obviously. It was Blackpink's "DDU-DU DDU-DU." I mean, it was no match for their debut song "Whistle" or even their global game changer "Shut Down," but as far as K-pop bangers go, this was a go.

I moved in closer, crystallizing the image of this one-of-a-kind creature dancing full-out with that kind of extra energy that only privacy can permit. *Whatever*, though, because he was actually fully outside, available to the public, and still without a care in the world.

I remembered the first time I met Sophat at wat. The Buddhist temple was where all the parents came together to pray to the monks, while the kids chased each other outside with cans of shaving cream. It was a strange hazing ritual that everyone participated in, except, of course, for a couple of unicorns who couldn't be bothered.

From across the parking lot, I saw this gangly, golden-brown kid with perfectly parted hair, impeccably dressed and sitting atop his parents' car without a care in the world. He was plugged into his buds, probably listening to whatever single was next to hit and completely unaware of the animals running around him. We locked eyes. It was love at first sight.

Fast forward to the present: Sophat was still so in step with his music that he had no idea he was building an audience of one. Me. Truth was, I knew the choreo by heart too. We both were Blinks, a term used to describe only the most legitimate fans of the four-person K-pop girl group. I was more on the sly with my fanship (that was just how I approached all things), but Sophat was merch, online news updates, and all. He was unabashed by everything he loved, and I loved that about him. I edited myself until I could barely tell what I liked anymore, and this kid embraced any compulsion he had with a big, cheesy grin on his face. Even now, in his dance, you could tell he had learned not just the moves, but the style. He lived the style.

Still, I thought he might want another Blink to elevate his game . . . so at exactly the right moment . . . with steps on ready . . . and style on flow . . . I jumped in—

"Still got that DDU-DU DDU-DU!" Sophat shouted out as he recognized us moving in perfect synchronicity.

"She stays ready!" I yelled back while staying ahead of the rhythm.

"But can she keep up?"

"In her sleep, SONNNNNNN!"

The track hit the iconic shout-out "*Blackpink!*" and the only thing left now was the big finish.

"*Ah yeah, ah yeah, ah yeah, ah yeah.*"

In the last couple of beats, with sweat slinging off our brows, we went *hard*. Into every movement, every gesture, as if we were headlining a concert at Memorial Auditorium. With a final flourish of double-fisted gunshots, we hit it with that final "*ddu-du ddu-du du*" and *BAM*. Silence. Drop the mics. Hit the lights. Roll up the cables. Pick up your jaws. Wipe your drool. Say a thankful prayer. Feel blessed. Lock the doors. Go home. It's been serviced.

We immediately collapsed onto the cement and into each other, laughing from the deepest depths of our bellies. We were hysterical. Alternating between shrieking like animals to seriously gasping for air, we were a supreme mess in search of oxygen.

"Ugh, I'm gonna throw up." Sophat leaned in like he was searching to be unfriended.

"Please direct your chunks thataway!" I tried to deflect his possible projectile.

"*Thisaway?*" the jokester returned with taunting force. I could kill him. I pushed him back, hoping to fully escape being in the splash zone.

"You're pure filth, you know that?"

"Well, you're pure perspiration."

"Shut up! You know I got a shiny T-zone." Sophat was a hater who must be defeated. I discreetly dabbed my sweaty forehead with my sweatshirt sleeve, as he looked away for a second.

"Must be all that heat from being a rising star."

I pretended not to hear that last one.

As things began to settle, we looked up and out, simultaneously noticing the big, bad sky before us and all its actual stars. It was one of those nights where the lights of the industrial town couldn't grind enough, couldn't work hard enough, to outshine the glow of the sky's constellations. For a moment, we both lay in silence, marveling at it all.

"We should've filmed it." The second it slipped out of my mouth, I regretted it. I immediately pulled out my pipe and began to pack it.

"Aw, man, she's an influencer now. She got those influencer instincts."

"Shut up."

"Seriously, though. Spill it."

"What?"

"Why all of a sudden you posted that TikTok of you dropping beats like you've been doing it all this time?"

"Oh, don't make such a big deal about it."

"It's not just me. You're blowing up. Over three hundred likes, like whoa!" Sophat always seemed to have his phone ready to share whatever nonsense was quaking on the socials.

"Whatever . . ." I leaned in coolly, trying not to look like a tourist searching for a map.

"Three hundred twenty-four likes and . . . seven comments?" I couldn't believe it. It was one thing to mindlessly tap a post, but it was another thing to get into the *discourse*. Who was commenting on these rhymes? And what sort of evil trolling was about to come my way? "OMG, Britney commented, 'Three blue heart emojis.' Dig that ditch and bury me with some daisies."

Yup. Immediately regretted that admission too. Sophat looked back at me with his baby bug eyes, waiting for more intel. I continued to pack the pipe.

"I *knew* you had a thing for her!"

"Whatever. She's cute and all, but I don't know if—"

"She's a lesbian one hundred."

"What, she tell you in choir?"

"In your dreams!"

In my dreams, I was of course talking about Britney Roe, who had just moved into town last year but didn't seem to have any problem getting adjusted. By the end of our sophomore year, she had already joined Student Theater Company, Mock Trial, Student Book Club, and Sound Impressions. In fact, it was at one of the show choir concerts where we were first introduced by their premier star and always vocal king/main visual, Sophat.

Britney stepped out from the group to sing her solo, this Ella Fitzgerald song "Bewitched, Bothered, and Bewildered," and it was like no one else was even in the room. Just her. And maybe me. I had never heard the song before, but there was something in it I recognized. I wasn't trying to pretend like I'd been in love before or whatever, but I did get the sort of deep sadness that fills you up and makes you feel like no one in the entire world understands your situation. You're all alone in that moment.

That night, when I looked up at Britney's face, with eyes as deep as caves, curly hair silhouetted by some seriously angelic backlight, and a voice that had no business sounding as good as it was for a sixteen-year-old . . . something inside of me shifted. I was rearranged inside, and I wasn't so sure I wanted to be put back together. Truth be told, I didn't know much about jazz, but I was definitely bewitched, righteously bothered, and consequently bewildered. By the start of our junior year, I was crushing hard.

"Confess it like a Catholic." Sophat returned me to the land of the living.

"Confess what?"

"Why you posted content like that."

I didn't know how to respond. I was still hung up on Britney's comment, and besides, I'd posted the video like an hour ago. A lot of new things were unfolding in a very short amount of time. I was moving from impulse to impulse. I didn't have a perfectly packaged reason to share. And honestly, I wasn't trying to fold people into my confusion. Not even my Number One.

"Is it because your dad's gone and now your mom? And your sister, though kind of giving up K-pop visual vibes, is actually assuming totalitarian vibes? And the accumulation of that for one average Lowellian, Cambodian youth is like way too much to handle? So, like you had to *do something*?" Sophat looked to me for a verdict. Can you love and hate someone at the same time?

I stared back in wonderment at this aggressive, if not thorough and accurate, assessment. If it was any other human person spouting such nonsense, I would have kicked them off their heels, but no. It was Sophat. The kid had some intuition about what was going on.

"Maybe," I simply replied while pulling out my lighter. I brought a flame to the piece and took in a big inhalation.

Sophat was right about one thing: everything had changed. My dad was gone, my mom said she'd be gone for only a little while, and my sister was absolutely *not* gone. I could've done with mixing up the variables a bit.

"I know you didn't want to get all sad and morose about the situation, but there's one thing that's been bugging me. Wasn't he, like, a citizen?" Sophat inquired harmlessly. I could tell the kid was trying to ask the tough questions, but he knew I was combustible.

"He had a green card. Refugee status 4eva."

"But why didn't he take the citizenship test?"

"He was waiting to, but with his record, things got jammed in the system. Plus, you ever try to ask a Cambodian person to do something when they should?" Even if Sophat had good intentions, I was starting to feel the heat.

"And if it meant he'd be deported?"

"You gotta stop."

"Okay, but—"

"Seriously, just put it on ice."

"Yeah, I know, fuck ICE—"

"*Be done!*" And boom. I combusted. I shoved the pipe into Sophat's mouth, trying to put an end to this bogus line of questioning.

Yes, Ba was a permanent resident, but as it turned out, "permanent" was an inaccurate and flawed description. If one got caught up in a situation they weren't responsible for, if one spent time in jail and a detention center to show the state what a worthy citizen one could be, if one was trying their best to raise a family in a country that constantly makes them feel like foreigners, if one still did all that . . . "permanent" was an altogether lie. Ba had always been a temporary citizen. And now he wasn't even that.

The green wasn't hitting fast enough. I needed a different distraction.

"Oh, I almost forgot to tell you. You're my date for my sister's wedding."

"*I'm sorry, what—?*" That did the trick.

"I said, 'You're my—'"

"Shuduuuuuuup! Life is beautifulllllll!" With his arms wide open, Sophat immediately jumped up and twirled about, proving once again that he was incapable of being subtle about anything. Now he was clearly in his own obsessive thoughts about the prospective wedding. Success: attention deflected!

There was only one problem: I hadn't exactly asked Dahvy yet if he could come. Maybe she'd say yes. . . .

"But I have nothing to wear!" Sophat took a hit and began to talk through the catalog of what was in his fashion inventory. He had *a lot*, but I had a feeling nothing was going to match the moment.

"Well, it's both a Cambo and a Jesus wedding, so—"

"Costume change! I live! Let's go to the mall this weekend!"

"Can't we just order stuff and return it if it sucks?"

"A rom-com makeover movie mome? We serve!" Immediately, Sophat began to vogue, as if he was imagining himself swishing about in whatever wedding couture was waiting for him. The kid was performing for the front, the back, the sides, the mezz, *and* the balcony—shoot, he was performing for the street out front and then some. His skinny limbs twirled effortlessly about like they were made of fabric themselves.

A couple of years ago, after we watched the doc *Paris Is Burning*, Sophat had become high-key obsessed with emulating the dances of the 1980s New York City ballroom scene. Black and brown queens might've been cruelly shunned by society, but they created the house and the rules. They were legendary.

They were also the blueprint for who Sophat could be—
edit—who he already was. It was funny. Even though some of
the signature moves originated as far back as the 1960s, watching Sophat perform them was like watching someone learn the
entire vocabulary of their body. It was an education, and he was
a *fabulous* student. He moved with reverence for these queens
who showed him the way.

"I see that you're burning down the City of Lights."

"And you're burning that blaze . . . Ms. . . . what are you
going to call yourself, by the way?"

"What do you mean?"

"I mean, every emcee's gotta have a name, right? You're acting
like you didn't just start something."

Start something? I looked back at my friend with the question stretched awkwardly across my face. I mean, I wasn't trying
to *start something*. Sure, Ba's spam sent me straight spinning. To
be honest, I knew there was coded messaging in there—like he
knew I was ghosting him and he needed to jump-start communication in a different mode to get me talking. So I guess
it worked in a way. Well, it sparked one side of the conversation, but that was it. It was a solo flash impulse. "Starting
something" implied continuing on. Putting out another thing.
Putting out many things. I was still stuck on the *one thing* I'd
just done. Could I do more?

"Why can't I just be Soma?"

"I mean, sure, but don't you need like a *name* name to . . .
elevate your *game* game. Ooh, I should be a songstress!"

Maybe Sophat was right. The video seemed to be vibing with people. I'd been feeling a desire to control something in my life. Make a change. And Ba's email did feel like a task. Like I needed to step into my legacy or something. Maybe to make things better.

A little branding never hurt anyone. I could mess with some branding.

"Oh crap. I got dance rehearsal this weekend. How 'bout we hit the runway next weekend?"

"That's cool."

"Okay, good, 'cause I can't miss another rehearsal. I've been picking up shifts at work, and Lok Kru's been all pissed. I told him, 'When you start paying me the dollar signs to play these weird-ass monkey characters, then I'll start showing up to every single rehearsal!'"

"You said that to him?"

"He got my vibe."

"Must be fun dancing with them, though." "Them" being the famed Angkor Dance Troupe in town, where Sophat was on the ready to be one of their biggest stars. The kid was in everything. If there was a chance to express himself, he was there, monkey tail and all.

"Fun doing what? This?" Sophat's voguing transformed seamlessly into the traditional moves of classical Cambodian dancing. Dang. The kid had two sets of vocabulary for his body-ody. Selfish. His fluid hands evolved perfectly from a seedling to a plant, a plant to a flower, and an ascending flower to the heavens, with this kind of mad elegance I couldn't locate in my own body, even if I tried.

"God, you're so good."

"Who, me?!" With a flourish of his hyperextended fingers, Sophat showed off just a little more for the back.

"Yeah, when I go to one of your concerts, everyone seems so confident. It's just, like, stone-cold concentration and . . ."

"Presence! We have presence."

"Presence . . ." I whispered the word to myself. For some reason, it felt magical and almost godlike. Who had it? Did I? Was it something you could acquire? Or work on, develop to become better at? Or was it just anointed to those few magical people who were destined to do dope things in this world, like Sophat? What was this thing called "presence"?

"Earth to Soma!" Sophat's nagging voice pulled me out of my fog. "I guess the dank be working!"

"Oh, shut it."

"Where'd you go, sis? You sort of went blank."

"I was thinking about stuff."

"What, 'presence'?"

"Yeah, you got some to give?"

"You have it too."

"Not like you."

"TBH, what does 'presence' matter when we're stuck in this old mill town?"

"It's not *so* bad."

"Are. You. Kidding. Me?" Sophat dropped his dancing and began to flail wildly, overemphasizing words like they. All.

Mattered. Under the influence of skunk, this was his usual pro-
gression: dance, dance, *rail*. I knew he was peaking. My job
now was to sit back for the diatribe.

"I mean, *look at those mills*. Ooh, we love our mills. We love
our industrial city. We make it so quaint. But those things represent a lot of horrible stuff. That cotton came from plantations
picked by slaves. That cotton was turned into fabric by poor little
girlies like you and me. Not to mention, *rewind*, those factories
sit on Pawtucket, Massa-adchu-es-et, and Pennacook land. And
um, no one wants to talk about any of that. We just want to keep
telling the same abridged history. It's like, what even changes
in this town, this country, this universe? What ever changes?
Hello, Universe: *I'm talking to you!*"

"Would you hit the brake a bit?!" Honestly, as Sophat was
hitting his philosophical stride, I found him entertaining and,
most importantly, historically accurate, but the fool's decibel
levels were going to get us into trouble. He needed to be taken
down a notch.

"Hit the brake?! Ah, HELL no. I'm having a real talk with
the universe. I'm channeling our Beat forefathers, who once
rolled around these very streets with wine in their blood, hearts
in their hands, and the audacity to ask some GD questions.
And I have one! A really important one, you're gonna need to
answer, Universe! YOU HEAR ME? Okay, here goes. . . ." At
the end of his rant, Sophat waited a prolonged beat for full
dramatic effect. I wondered which way this was going. With
Sophat, it could go anywhere. . . .

"*Whatcha gonna do with all that junk inside that trunk?! Tell meeeee!*" Sophat immediately dropped to the ground, laughing at himself like he had no self-respect whatsoever. For a second there, he almost had me wondering what sort of all-important question he might throw to the universe. But no, this friend was just a fool singing that retro song "My Humps" by the Black Eyed Peas. He was my fool, no doubt, but absolutely a fool.

"You are so extra. Universe: GET ME A NEW FRIEND." I joined Sophat in shouting into the void.

"Soma (I'm speaking as the Universe now): too bad, bish. *Bish. Bish. Bish . . .*" Sophat pulled away his voice as if the universe was echoing back.

Now the weed had officially done its job. We returned to the stars, feeling warm, settled, fully inside our bodies, just hoping this strange moon looming above us wouldn't come crashing down. At least, not this very second.

A beat passed in silence.

"My dad sent me this email earlier."

"Yeah?"

"He's been texting and calling a bunch, but I haven't really gotten back to him because . . . well, whatever. It's been weird, right? Honestly, I just don't know what to say to him. But I guess this was his way of getting my attention. Ba was telling me about my name, and at the end of the email, he was like . . . 'so what are you going to do with it?' I could almost feel him encouraging me to step into the name like a persona—like the Soma persona, whatever that means. Truth bomb, though— and I know this is supremely weird—but I'm ready for a change to come *from* me and not to me. I kinda wanna step into Soma."

"I kinda wanna too. . . ." Even if he didn't know what I was talking about, I could always count on Sophat to reflect my feelings. Just so I didn't feel entirely alone. Even if I really was.

Now I could feel my lips vibrating and my heart racing. It was the third time this evening I'd blurted something out without thinking about it, but now, I didn't regret it. I meant it. I was ready for a change to come *from* me, and maybe that was what the video was all about.

"She's getting so philosophical." Sophat rested his head on my shoulder, yielding to the stars for the night.

"And maybe she's just trying to find some presence." I yielded too.

Tonight, the moon would not come crashing down. Tonight, it provided us a little light and a little time.

CHAPTER 6
Dig Deep

SOPHAT (7:14 a.m.):   FULFILL THAT LEGACY . . . GLORY
AWAITS U!

I pulled the phone back from my face, trying to make sense of what fortune-cookie nonsense was being texted my way. Did Sophat really need to use all caps to convey his urgency first thing in the morning? OF COURSE NOT.

I rubbed my eyes and noticed the text was accompanied by an attachment. I hesitated. It could be porn. Or some overplayed meme I wouldn't be able to get out of my head for the rest of the day. Sophat was a frequent perpetrator of both offenses, and I promised myself that for the love of gods, I would remember next time.

Do it do it do it. The title of the attachment didn't help any, but it was the morning, and I was hazy. I couldn't be counted on to make sensible choices this early. Maybe it'd be fine. Let the bare butts be seen!

JOIN LOWELL'S LIT LEGACY!

Are you the next Jack Kerouac?
Do you have poems you'd like to share with the world?
Sign up for the annual Jack Kerouac Poetry Competition,
this week only.
Submit an original poem to BecomeJK@gmail.com
by Monday, October 9th. Eight finalists will be chosen
from the preliminary round and notified
by Wednesday, October 18th.

Finalists will then perform a second poem
and compete for third, second and first places.
Winners will receive cash scholarships
to be used towards college.
The Jack Kerouac Poetry Competition Finals
will be held at Lowell High School on
Friday, October 27 @ 7 p.m.
Dig deep and become a Beat.

—Mr. Lozano on behalf of the English Department

"Dig deep and become a Beat." The alliteration buzzed on my lips, as I reread the attachment again. "BBBecome a BBBeat."

Of course, a Beat refers to a group of poets in the 1950s—the group of rowdy, druggy writers in San Francisco (like Kerouac himself) who wrote these (ironically) offbeat poems that were all about jazz and none to do about boxes. Break free from the boxes. It was all about freedom.

Truth was, on the down-low, at a distance, under the covers, without anyone else knowing . . . I'd already freely thought about entering the contest myself. The Jack Kerouac Poetry Competition was held yearly, and I'd always wondered if my own original lines could fit this literary mode. I wasn't trying to be some Kerouac copycat (that wasn't what the contest was about to begin with), but maybe I had some words that might resonate. Could I really go live with my poetical inner thoughts?

SOMA (7:17 a.m.):   you said the guy was septic

SOPHAT (7:17 a.m.):   but you can still get your coin

SOMA (7:18 a.m.):   honestly, I don't know bro

SOPHAT (7:18 a.m.):   Mr. Diaz would be proud

It was true. Ruben wouldn't get off my case about the competition either. I'd done well on a couple of essays in his class, and he was all ready to make me the next Emily Dickinson. He actually made that comparison, going off about how we both knew how to capture grief in our work. But it was so clear I wasn't some mopey Victorian white girl. I wasn't some mopey French-Canadian white boy either. I wasn't sure who I was, so how could I share myself in that kind of way? Posting a video is one thing, but giving the metaverse a real live face, a real live voice with some real live rhymes, was another. Could my nerves handle holding it down in front of a group of real live trolls?

SOMA (7:19 a.m.):   and you're over it?
SOPHAT (7:20 a.m.):   IF I'M SENDING U THIS I'M OVER ITTT

I wasn't so sure Sophat was "OVER ITTT." My Number One had indeed competed last year, and while he stepped up to the mic with some ambitious, melodious renditions (he'd basically assigned his journal entries to his fave pop songs), in the end, he just bitched about the adjudicators being unable to take in *all his style.* As I recalled, the kid, who couldn't stand still if his life freaking depended on it, kept moving away from the mic at the podium, making it impossible to hear what he had to say. At several points, his stylish arms inadvertently knocked the mic, causing thunderous quakes throughout the room. It was a hot mess.

Still, I was impressed with the other student performers. I guess I previously had this image that to compete you had to be a sad, self-obsessed dude wearing a flat cap, but to my surprise, that really wasn't the case. There was range.

Melinda Lopez, star of the field hockey team, delivered this epic poem about how competition made her stronger in spite of some family problems. Everyone knew that Bros Hien was on his way to becoming a Silicon Valley tech wunderkind, but he had the audience belly-laughing from his first impression of his crotchety Cambodian grandma. And I would never forget W.B. Cheng's fierce poem about coming out as trans and being forced to live with their aunt after being kicked out from their parents' house. W.B. won first place, but I knew their performance had nothing to do with the competition. It was more like a manual on survival.

While not everyone was star status, what remained universal was they all *did it*. These students went out on a limb and laid themselves bare out on the mic. I knew Sophat was still feeling soft about last year's performance, so why was he sending this my way now?

I lay back in bed and pulled my video up.

At this point I assumed the likes had plateaued, and the unexpected attention was a total fluke. The itch had been scratched, and now the whole thing could just go crawl into the dark and die. . . .

"Three thousand six hundred fifty-seven likes and fifty-three comments?"

Fluke, say what? I couldn't believe it. Last night I could've convinced myself that sure, this had become a popular social item in my small-town high school sphere, but over a thousand likes and some comments later . . . it had entered the *actual* public sphere—

"Soma? Did you leave for school yet?!" Dahvy wailed from the first floor.

Dang. I looked at the time. DANG. I was definitely late.

If I was going to be on time, I had to forgo a shower and immediately head out the door.

"Do you need a ride? Because if you need a ride, you need to get down here NOW." Dahvy's voice returned with that favorable tone I just couldn't get enough of.

"I'm good. Running over now!"

"You sure? Because I can take you—"

"I said, I'm good!" I did not want to deal with a car ride filled with leftover annoyances from the previous night. I needed to walk—no, *run*—to school without Dahvy's incessant questioning, without thoughts of this competition, and without my phone pulling me back into my newly acquainted, quickly evolving social media self-obsession.

I needed to get to school.

CHAPTER 7
An Inquisition

The rest of the morning was a blur.

In my frenzied sprint to school, I threw my phone into my bag, letting it sink to the bottom, where I would not be tempted to dig for it. For the most part, I succeeded. I only turned it on twice, reprimanded myself on both occasions, and immediately returned it to the bag.

As I sat in my last class before lunch, I could feel my hand twitching again.

Do. Not. Reach. For your. Monster. Box.

What was happening to me? Where had all my self-restraint gone? I wondered if this was what it was like to be a "normal teen"—to post to one's socials with anxiety at max and then to track likes and comments as if one's self-value depended on it. Or maybe the "normal teen" had it all figured out. Maybe I was projecting my own insecurities, and, in fact, one could post without regard for impact whatsoever. You posted as a point of self-expression, and so just, like, chill in your Nike Blazer

Mid 77 Infinite White Kumquat Aurora Green Men's Casuals. Embrace the mode.

As Mr. Drakos went on and on (and on) about the Supreme Court blah blah blah, my eyes began to wander to my fellow teenage clusters of cells. Some were obviously on their phones. Some were genuinely listening to Drakos as he tried so very hard to inspire. Some were fidgeting with their rings and necklaces like they needed to expend their excess energy. And some were just all right.

Maybe I was wrong. Maybe I wasn't so far from them after all, and maybe I was chill—

What was that smell? Did somebody just drop one? Or was it me? Maybe it was the leftover skunk in the fabric? Dang it, dude. I was right! Now I could for sure smell the aura of residual pot smoke deep in the folds of my shirt. I would absolutely not relay this personal discovery to that sister sleuth, who first made me aware of how I was apparently emanating the night before. I should have worn a different hoodie or taken a shower and been late anyways. I was rethinking all my choices in the last twenty-four hours. As soon as the lunch bell rang, I needed to get outside and away from other humans as far as possible.

As I tried my best to burrow deep into my clothes, I accidentally caught eyes with Evie Han from across the room. Her short black hair bounced up and down as she waved emphatically—as if I wasn't mid-class, trying to keep a low profile. The curve of her bob and the curve of the all-caps, all-white letters *LOWELL*

HIGH SCHOOL across her T-shirt curled in perfectly to frame her bright, round face.

I froze, wondering why she seemed *so* excited to see me now. I guess I should've felt some comfort in seeing a reflection of a yellow-brown sister staring back at me, but there were plenty of reasons why we were different kinds of Cambodian girls. She was a prized, straight-A student. I felt real good about myself when I successfully fooled teachers into giving me extensions. She was on the fast track to Harvard, her top pick since she'd popped out of the womb. I was on the fast track out of this classroom, so people couldn't smell the extracurriculars on my clothes. She had the perfect Khmer family with her father, Boo Soriya, being our state representative, the first Cambodian to be elected. Our families didn't even live in the same city, the same state, the same country, even the same continent. Evie and I may have shared the same roots, but we couldn't have been more different.

In ninth grade, we were in Advisory together, and even though our families had known each other for years, it was the first time we'd been in the same class. One of our first assignments was to create some basic presentation, introducing who we were. I honestly thought my idea was money. I went retro and burned a mix CD, explaining how each track shaped a part of my life. It culminated in the most supreme of vibes: Yaeji's "Raingurl," and I swear the minute the track played, the room was *drenched*. Everyone was dancing in their seats. It was some kind of feeling being able to get the energy in sync like that with my own divine powers of curation, but after that, I was totally defeated.

I was followed by none other than Ms. Evie Han, who presented this Google Slides story about her parents' time in dun dun dun . . . the genocide. Sure, there were content warnings, but Evie was unabashed about detailing every sad, scary, horrible moment. She even soundtracked it with a cinematic score, as if to rattle those heartstrings like she knew what she was doing. The story ended in an epic, emotional conclusion with her parents being reunited at the refugee camps in Thailand as little kids. Everyone was crying (me included!), and suddenly I felt totally basic and infantile for what I'd done seconds ago. While I was trying to be clever by bringing us back to the early aughts with my Discman, she was bringing us back to the seventies, unafraid to share our people's history as if it were her own. Maybe it was hers to share, but I couldn't help but be reminded that it was emotional territory I still hadn't developed a relationship with yet. While I knew it was my history too (it was deep in my DNA), I didn't brandish it about for dramatic effect. Her confidence in telling that story made me uneasy.

Now, Evie smiled and then made that little heart sign with her fingers that Korean stars constantly flash to cameras on variety shows or the red carpet. While I thought it was a sort of nice gesture to relay from across the room, I couldn't help but express confusion about what Evie was trying to communicate. My severely scrunched face watched as she pulled up her phone and pointed at . . . the video posted last night.

Ah crap.

I fell back deep, *deep* into my hoodie, trying desperately to disappear for good. I wondered how far turtles turned inside their shells and if they were anything like caterpillars, who just become a puddle of gooey cells inside their chrysalises before emerging as butterflies. I really wanted to find that limit and go freaking further. There was no amount of retreating into my hoodie blob that I could do to hide away 4eva.

I hadn't thought this through. Sure, I wanted people to see my video, but I never imagined *real people*, let alone someone with such rank like Evie Han, responding to it. So what if she had seemingly given it a positive review? She could've just done it to pity me. That's what people do, right? When they're too nice to say something mean? Even when they think it's maybe the worst, most desperate thing ever? But to say that truth would be outright chilly? So everyone lives in a web of lies in the real world, and then when they get home, they spit out their cold truths in hateful anonymous trolling. Was Evie lying to me now, only to take me down the minute she got home?

Okay, maybe I was catastrophizing, but there wasn't anything I hated more than being pitied. At this point I knew my dad's deportation was public news in the Khmer community. People were straight-up asking Ma if she needed help with "the girls," as if we weren't already grown. I was embarrassed by people trying to help us like we were some charity cases. But even worse than that, most recently, Sophat and I were getting gkuh theeuw at the Red Rose when I overheard a pair of women talking about how the Kears must have had some bad karmic luck, that something must've happened in a previous life for so much misfortune to befall them in this one. For as much as I was taught to respect my elders (and their witchcraft), I didn't want any of that—the extra attention, the looking down upon, the being locked into a story we couldn't change. No, I had to believe things could get better. We didn't need anyone telling us otherwise.

I dared not look back at Evie. I was going to stay warm and well in the depths of my Mary Jane fleece. Stay in your pot-soaked self, and no one can pity you. Lunch could not come fast enough.

The second the period bell rang, I was halfway out the door when—

"Ms. Kear, are you running off to track-and-field practice?" The booming yet gentle voice stopped me in my tracks. I could tell there was a particular tone going on. No, this wasn't just a stand-alone question. It was the opening to an inquisition.

"Got my PE credits already, Mr. Drakos, so, no. Why do you ask?"

"Because you were sprinting out of the classroom like you were trying to win a medal." Drakos sat back on the edge of his desk and then smiled, self-satisfied like he was some kind of comedian. Regrettably, the sad punch line trailed off into the awkward silence where all sad jokes go to die.

I looked back at him, a little annoyed and a little sympathetic for his amateur attempt at stand-up. I waited for the follow-up, but he just looked back at me as if I was going to save the moment. We were both helpless.

In his khaki pants, his tucked-in button-up shirt and tie, Drakos looked like your standard-fare old white dude. The kind that had walked these halls long before I even came into the picture and would probably do the same long after I left. The problem with Drakos wasn't that he was a bad teacher or a bad dude either, he just always seemed so unbothered by the reality that his students were decades younger than him. Unlike some of the younger teachers at the school, who tried to relate to their students by diversifying their tactics, Drakos taught American history like it'd always been taught: he spoke, we listened, wash, rinse, and repeat.

I had half a mind to keep on running, but he obviously had more to say.

"Is there something you needed, Mr. Drakos?"

"Well, I'm glad you're no Flo-Jo, because yes, I did have something I wanted to check in on. The essay? Did you happen to chat with your . . . mom about it?"

Drakos was relentless. Couldn't he just leave it alone?

"Oh, I thought that was like a suggestion or something," I lied. I knew it was more of a directive, but feigning ignorance had worked before. The current situation wasn't looking so hot. Maybe this was a moment to actually take advantage of that pity. "Besides, my mom's out of the country right now, so she's sort of busy."

"Of course. I heard she's helping out your—"

"Yeah, my *deported dad*, so I'm just going to have to wait until after she gets back. Like *way* after."

I was laying it on thick. I might've felt bad about the tactic before, but now, I knew I had to sell the sob story to nip it in the bud and avoid the dreaded subject.

This was the essay that Ruben had brought up last night. I knew Drakos didn't share the same perspective about style, but the fact that he was mentioning it again made me feel like it was more of a problem than I had originally thought.

"Well, I understand the *other* Ms. Kear—or should I say, Mrs. Future Diaz?"

"Dahvy's good."

"I know your sister expressed when she took the job here that she wanted to offer you a bit of space, but if she is your guardian now—"

"She's *not* my guardian."

"Since she's helping you out right now, perhaps we could all talk together."

I couldn't believe it. Drakos was blowing up land mines left and right. First, he had the nerve to have a problem with the truth I was dropping in my essay, and secondly, he had the *actual* nerve to think Dahvy had become my guardian. What. The. Hell. I don't know what sort of impression the other nonexistent Ms. Kear was giving him, but it had to be stopped.

"I'll talk to her when I get home."

"To be clear: I need for us to find a time to talk *all together*, so you'll have to let me know when." Through his wire frames, Drakos stared back at me with his beady teacher eyes. I could tell he was for serious, but I was also beginning to smell the faint whiff of pot smoke again and knew I didn't need another thing to build his case against me. I had to get on with it.

"You got it! Okay! Bye! Have a nice lunch, Mr. Drakos!" I lifted my tone to an obnoxious level, hoping that my agreeability would be enough to end this conversation.

"Oh, and apologies for overstepping, but something to consider." With one last plea, Drakos handed me a folded piece of paper I had no intention of checking out until I was far from the room. I needed to get out of there, and not even this last-ditch effort was going to stop me. I turned to go and didn't look back.

As I rushed through the hallway, past the straggling students, I could feel the heat rise again in my chest. God. I knew what he was getting at, and I knew he was worried about what I had written. But was it really my fault that Drakos had assigned us an essay about immigration? Reviewing how the past couple of US administrations had handled deportations? *After* my father had just been deported?

Nope. Drakos was asking for it.

This semester, he had gone on and on about how the government was not just an idea but actual systems that have a direct impact on human lives. He was the one who said it wasn't theoretical but a reality for the survival and dignity of people. I mean, I actually listened to what the dinosaur had to say. So why was he so concerned now about me getting a little real in my essay? I still cited sources. It wasn't like I was writing stream of consciousness on toilet paper. I just happened to get a little personal.

I pushed through a pair of heavy doors and stumbled out onto the side campus of school, knowing there was no way I would approach Dahvy with the topic anytime soon. We were too tangled. I'd wait for Ma to get home, and then I would expertly lead her into consensus. Obviously.

As the sun hit my face, I was starting to feel the oxygen reenter my body and motivate my muscles to step away from the school building. I may not have known who Flo-Jo was, but I was feeling some speed. I had one singular mission: get the funk away.

CHAPTER 8
Khmer Kerouac

Walking along the canal in the open air finally felt like a relief. I emerged from my hooded bubble of pot smoke and was relieved to get wind of less incriminating scents. Still pretty questionable, but none that would get me into trouble.

With the school on the left and the water on my right, I made my way toward St. Anne's Episcopal Church, which was just down the path. This was actually the future site of Dahvy and Ruben's Jesus wedding, but I wasn't searching to preemptively help out in any way. I was just in pursuit of the stone bench across from the building. It was far enough from the main hub of the school where kids congregated but close enough to help out when I would inevitably forget the time and needed to sprint back (only to be late again anyways). You're welcome, future sloppy self.

In my morning rage, I had completely forgotten my lunch, but even if I had it, I wouldn't have been able to eat. My stomach was in knots. Drakos's conversation added another item to my menu of anxieties. This was the kind of buffet I was devouring without even thinking about it. Maybe if I sat here long enough, I might be able to quiet this particular appetite.

I looked up at the ominous gray-stone building before me. My family was Buddhist, but sometimes I wondered if God was really a thing. Like was there seriously an all-knowing, all-powerful force out there answering prayers and whispering sweet nothings in believers' ears? Was there something inside these walls that I didn't get? Just in case, sometimes I would pray to God in the way I had seen my Christian friends do at their own houses, though I opted to make a few adjustments:

> *Our Mother, who art in someplace and beyond,*
> *Shorty got a holy username,*
> *thy money's come,*
> *thy hustle be done,*
> *on earth as it is in someplace and beyond.*
>
> *Give us this day our daily num pang.*
> *And forgive us our funk,*
> *as we forgive those*
> *who funk against us.*
>
> *And lead us not into temptation (unless it's good),*
> *but deliver us from evil (unless we don't wanna).*

> *For ladies and queerdos are the kingdom,*
> *and the power, and the glory,*
> *for ever and ever. A-freaking-men.*

Just a couple of adjustments to the Lord's Prayer.

I honestly felt like the invocation was a powerful concept: this idea that one could just pray to this omnipotent entity, and they had your back. No wonder people were believers.

The one thing I really couldn't wrap my brain around was, if you were a follower and you did something good, it was all attributed to God. And if you did something bad, it was all attributed to you. That all-or-nothing sum felt a little unfair and, frankly, foolish.

But still, in times of need or whenever I was just a little curious, I would say my own private prayer, unsure of who the receiver actually was.

"Dear Mother RuPaul: please make this smell go away."

I kept my eyes closed. I listened to the low hum of students chattering in the distance. I could feel the rhythm of the water sloshing about as it moved down the canal. For however chaotic the day had been, this one spot between the canal and the church centered me. I could feel myself coming back to my body.

Suddenly, I looked down and remembered I had a death grip on the wadded piece of paper Drakos had sent me out of the building with. I began to unfold it to check its contents, hoping it wasn't some other thing I was in trouble for.

"What the . . . ?"

Now, *this* seriously stumped me.

It was the exact same document Sophat had texted me earlier and set me off on this hype day to begin with . . . a flyer for the poetry competition.

Was Drakos being serious? One second the dude was cornering me about his hatred of my essay and the next he's suggesting I enter a contest where I would share my own original work. My neck was sore from the whiplash.

Why was everyone all up in my business? It looked like the deadline was approaching, but between him, Sophat, and Ruben, it was beginning to feel like this was some kind of conspiracy to have me embarrass myself royally. Put her up at the podium and have her tank publicly. That'd be funny!

But realistically, honestly, actually . . . they all probably just felt righteously bad for me. Like when Evie threw unsolicited hearts my way. That's what it was. I could feel everyone dripping in Ba's deportation. Did they think me jumping to the mic was a solution to my sadness? That somehow that expression would solve everything? I couldn't stand that sorry presumption. If I was going to do it, the intention had to be pure, whatever that meant. It had to be for me.

And then it occurred to me . . .

What if I did enter?

What would I even write about?

What did I have to say now?

I'd already snuck out some family history in that video. I

didn't want to full-on exploit our tragic business to win a competition, but it *was* what was going on—had been going on forever. While Evie could talk about it comfortably like some beautiful slideshow start to finish, I was still reeling from the fact that this was where I'd come from, the Cambodian genocide. Sure, from the rest of Cambodian history too, but sometimes, I'd think if one variable had been different, maybe I'd be back there in the motherland now. Or maybe not here at all. But I was. And so what did that mean? Would that be something I would want to talk about in a submission?

I paused. Maybe my thoughts were getting too feral from the surprise of it all.

I knew Sophat. He was my Number One, and he'd never suggest something I couldn't do. Or rather, if he thought I was coming up short, he wasn't scared to push me to be as brave as his neutral. This could be one of those things.

I thought about our conversation last night.

You're acting like you didn't just start something.

After posting the video, Sophat had pinned me down, asking me where I was intending to take all this. Maybe the next step *was* the poetry competition. If everyone around me was telling me to get into it, and I'd already thought about it myself . . . was I then just ignoring the writing on the wall?

Stop. This was too much, all at once. I'd come out here for a little peace, and now I was getting my blood racing again.

I closed my eyes and tried to regain the peace I had found a second ago. I straightened my spine. I placed my hands on my belly. I wasn't some kind of YouTube yogi or fitness guru, but I'd seen people do things like this before, and most of the time, they seemed to be relaxed. Maybe it would help to ground me a bit. Finally, I breathed deep and let the air travel and force itself back out of my nose and mouth. I repeated the actions all over again.

It was working. I was feeling a return to calm. I didn't need to do anything now, and even if I wanted to, I'd do it when I was ready.

Suddenly, I could feel the sensation of my lips beginning to buzz. My tongue was preparing to make itself useful. And then out of nowhere, words began to crawl out of my mouth . . .

I've been thinking about calling myself . . .
Khmer Kerouac
Track that, Jack
All the way back
Yo, let me unpack
And get in this hack
Without any slack
Before you attack
This Lunchables snack
BE taken aback
By this rhythmic smack-

DOWN, down into Mill Town
Your girl's been around
She's not backing down

When she draws the renown
Industrial crown
Making the sound
Of immigrant ground
Don't sleep on this round
Don't get lost, GET found
'Cause it belongs to the brown.

Brown. I wish I could've included "yellow" in there because that was what I most accurately saw myself as. Yellow-brown or golden. But "golden" doesn't exactly rhyme with "brown," and there weren't enough syllables in that line to afford another hue . . . so, yeah, I guess I could claim brown.

Hmm. The lines weren't exactly stage-ready for *Def Poetry Jam*, but they were coming from a place of impulse, maybe need, definitely spontaneity. I had stopped to pause for just a moment, and the words were looking for vibrations to make themselves heard. Maybe it was a sign this was exactly what I should be doing—

"Lunchables snack, huh?" An unknown voice abruptly entered the chat.

Dang it. I wasn't alone. What kind of unwelcome snoop was hovering behind me, and how long had they been there to begin with? Can't a girl just get a single private moment?

"Britney?"

"Lunchables snacks! I love those things. So compact. They're fresh like those lines." Even through her peony Warby Parkers, Britney Roe's eyes twinkled like a social media filter. Actually, that would be an insult to her beauty. Britney's was the kind of face that would launch a thousand filters.

"Sorry, what?" was all I could muster, as I looked back blankly.

Resting just above Britney's glasses, the rim of her bucket hat framed her face perfectly. Her burgundy Docs with the yellow threading looked outrageously mismatched with this bright red (ketchup red!) Muppet jacket. From top to bottom, Britney was a fashion icon.

I was in a static state of shock, and I desperately needed to jump-start my brain to get some words out—

"That was cheesy, right?" Britney was obviously trying to help me out.

"Britney! What's good? I was just working on some rhymes. You?" I was finally able to get something out.

"Coming back from lunch. Are the lines for fun or for something?"

"Oh, just for fun." I shoved Drakos's flyer into my pocket.

"Cool."

"Cool . . ." My eyes shifted immediately to the book she was clutching at her side. "Oh man, you read?"

Britney gave me a curious look and then laughed.

"Yeah. I read sometimes."

Of course she reads, you blob. We are at a school where people read all day long. The synapses were really struggling to make a connection.

"It's called *Parable of the Sower*. It's this sci-fi thing by Octavia Butler."

"Oh, you into sci-fi?"

"Yeah, it's cool. The books came out in the nineties, but the series takes place in like this dystopian version of the 2020s and beyond."

"So, like the normal version of now?"

Britney laughed. Without even knowing it, I had managed to tell a joke, and Britney Roe *actually* laughed. Okay. I wasn't completely hopeless.

"No, sci-fi is cool, because even though these writers make up new worlds, they're commenting on ours . . . like covert analysis on some deep truth or something."

"I like that: 'covert analysis on the truth.'" I had never thought about sci-fi in that way. Honestly, if it wasn't Kerouac, I really didn't read much else unless it was assigned. Most books didn't feature my point of view anyways, so why spend so much time and energy digesting other people's narratives?

"Yeah, and Octavia Butler is seriously dope. During the Jim Crow era, she was like this dyslexic Black girl who was super shy of other humans. But she grew up to be one of the most prolific sci-fi writers ever. That's a journey, right?"

"Totally."

"I love that she writes for people like her and me: Black women. Like it's gotta cost you to share something from your perspective, right?"

I sat in that thought for a moment. What did it cost for me to share *my* perspective? In the video I posted or something like the lit competition, were there consequences for what I had to say?

"Makes me think of your rhymes," Britney followed up, like she had already created this space inside my private thoughts and then let herself in. The intimacy felt surprising and strange. And welcome.

"Sorry, what?"

"Your video that you posted. I really liked it."

At this point in the conversation, I had two options: I could play it cool, or I could throw myself at Britney's feet and offer allegiance to this goddess 4eva.

"Yeah, I saw that you commented! Three blue hearts! I'm always like a fan of the emoji hearts that are not the standard red or the cutesy pink ones. Blue is like . . . bold . . ." Yeahhh so, I chose a third option: ramble about emojis. What. Was. I. Even. Talking. About?

"Yeah, bold is my vibe. What's yours?" Britney stepped in closer, like she had zero understanding of her effect. Or maybe she did.

"What's my what?" My heart clamored inside my chest.

"What's your vibe?"

The game had been inadvertently set by me, and now I had to fess up. What. Is. Your. Vibe. Soma?

"Yeah, so like on a good day, I'd probably say that it's the smiley face with the money sign for eyes and the green tongue."

"Cash money!"

"Yeah, but TBH, on most days, it's more like—"

"Oh wait, you gotta show me, and I'll see if I can guess."

"Um . . ." I had to relent to Britney's request. At worst, I could confirm I was a total clown, and she would never talk to me again. At best . . . well, I had no real idea what the best outcome would be, so I might as well make a fool of myself, anyways.

With one hand in the shape of a checkmark resting under my chin and one brow arched higher than its twin, I went for it: I valiantly portrayed the "thinking face" emoji.

Britney laughed again.

"Ha. That's your vibe?"

"I mean if I had to choose one, yeah."

"It's cute." Britney smiled, as a prolonged silence hung between the two of us like ends of a clothesline. A calm came over me. I suddenly was back inside my body and inside my thoughts. Without knowing it, Britney had given me this gift.

"Sophat says you're still crushing it in Sound Impressions."

"Sophat's the one who's got that star status. The rest of us are backup."

"No way. I mean, don't tell him that, but you all are so good. Like the staging and the harmonies—that's some serious Broadway-level stuff."

"It's a good time. But like honestly between rehearsals, work, and visits to colleges, I'm feeling a little spread thin."

"You're already visiting schools and stuff?" I was in disbelief. Sure, my mailbox had been bursting with brochures this year, but I had hardly been on a college trip. Let alone any kind of trip. The year had been filled with preparing Ba for the worst kind of trip.

"My mom's making me. And I guess it is junior year. You gotta look now, and then just apply next year. Plus, I dunno if I can stay here."

"Oh yeah?"

"I keep thinking I want something bigger, you know? Like I wanna go to New York and write books and be on important panels and stuff and pretend like I'm smarter than everyone else. That sounds so arrogant, right?"

"No, it's like . . . honestly refreshing." I loved how straightforward Britney was. Coming from a family where everyone kept their own secrets, I was grateful that someone could tell me exactly what they wanted. And I knew Britney would get her wish. She was the real deal.

"And how 'bout you?"

"Me?" I immediately felt hot from the attention.

"You don't know what you want?"

"Not really, no." I paused, unsure of how to proceed in answering the question about what I wanted, when I knew it ultimately didn't matter. Recent history had proven that wanting my family to stay together didn't matter, so why even try? "Like even tomorrow seems hard to picture in my brain, so college and the future feel so far away. . . ."

Britney looked back at me with a pair of sympathetic eyes that made me automatically sorry I'd said anything to begin with. This was the theme of my day apparently, and maybe my life. Had I sent out some memo I didn't know about, instructing everyone to feel supremely bad for me? Or was this in fact a sign from the universe via Britney, telling me I couldn't just *not know* anymore? Maybe people would feel less sorry for me if I knew more about what I really wanted. Inside this little existential crack I was finding myself in, the temperature was dropping, and I needed to launch myself out before she went running—

"But lately, at least, I've been feeling like I have some control when I'm putting words down. It kind of makes me feel like I'm getting ready for something." I didn't lie. This was the actual truth, but I knew it was more complicated than that. It was always more complicated.

Another epic pause passed between us, but this time, the line was beginning to slacken. I had clearly failed at picking up the mood.

"Hey, I'm sorry about your dad. I heard through some kids in school. People are always talking, right? But like, that's total shit." *Great.* It wasn't just the Cambos in town. Britney knew about my dad, and apparently so did the entire school. My chances of getting to graduation without socking some town snitch were starting to look dim. It would be impossible to recover from this one.

"Oh, it's all good." It wasn't all good, but I didn't know what to say. How do you even begin to talk about the most trash part of your life?

Britney stared back at me. I stared at my sneakers. Another moment passed.

"Well, I better get going. I have class in a bit. . . ." Britney's voice trailed off like she might have wanted to say something else and was hoping I would intercept. I was too caught up in myself. I had no idea what this moment needed. Britney looked back at me one last time and then began to step away. "See ya around."

What. Is. Your. Deal. Soma?

As I watched my destiny begin to slip from my fingers, I instantly remembered what I had said to Sophat the night before: I was ready for something new. The new that was coming *from* me.

This was it. This was my moment. It had to be. I couldn't let Britney just walk away like that. It was now or—

"Heeeyyy!" I screamed animalistically—white noise replacing any cognitive sense left in my body. Like my wisdom tooth was being violently pulled from my gums. Like I was stuck on an island and saw the first chopper in months. Like a person who lacked any sort of social skills whatsoever.

"Yeah?" Britney turned, fully stopping in her tracks.

"Hey, if you wanna chill or something, maybe we can hang this weekend? Or whatever!" I had no idea what words were coming out of my mouth. Honestly, I had no idea that I was even saying—no, *shouting*—to Britney. All I knew was that I had to keep going. "We could walk . . . and talk . . . and do stuff . . . around town . . . this town . . . that is Lowell!"

Britney managed to smile through the shock of me still *yelling* at her. Without even saying a word, she returned to my orbit, grabbed the phone from out of my stiff hand, added her digits, and returned the device right back before I could even blink. To finish things off, she pressed the call button—

"Now I have your number too." Britney ended the call as quickly as she'd begun it.

"Cool," I replied, hardly even breathing.

"Cool."

Britney turned back around and continued on her way. In silence, I watched her walk the entire length of the path, not blinking even once. I must have been frozen like that for a solid five minutes, just locked into my own fantasy rom-com mome.

The second that iconic shaggy jacket disappeared behind the building, I immediately face-planted right onto the ground. My brain stopped working. The rest of my body was making decisions now. With a mouthful of dry grass and cold soil, I could feel that yes, the ground was still beneath me. I was straight-planking—

"What're you doing?!"

Please don't let it be Britney.

Please don't let it be Britney.

Please don't let it be Britney.

I jumped to my feet like my ass was on fire and turned to the voice looming behind me. What was with people surprising me today? Was everyone hell-bent on making my day a horror story?!

"What're you doing?!" the voice repeated the question again.

God bless, Mother RuPaul Charles. It was only Ruben. I could seriously throw the dude into the canal for scaring me like that.

"What're *you* doing?" I threw it back at him, trying to desperately regain the composure I didn't have to begin with.

"I asked you first."

"Chillin'. You?"

"Same."

"In the church?" I looked back at the building behind Ruben, where it seemed he had just come from.

"If I have extra time at lunch, I like to walk down here. You got a problem with that?"

"Nope."

"And *you*?"

"Yeah, same. It's just . . . nice out here."

Of course, that answer wasn't going to placate Ruben. He stared back at me with that goofy grin of his, like he was expecting some celebrity gossip. Too bad, though. He wasn't getting any.

"Was that Britney Roe I saw you talking with?"

"Oh, was it? I dunno . . . ," I said coolly, like I hadn't even noticed. As if the love of my life hadn't just walked away. As if Britney Roe hadn't just thrown down her digits. No, Ruben did not need to get into my business.

"Uh-huh—"

"Whatever, okay! Why you gotta make it so awkward and shit? Yeah, it was Britney Roe, and we were talking about stuff, so there. Get over it! Are you happy now that you know? Are you?! Why don't you just roll over and DIE!"

"Wow. It's nice to see you too." Okay. Maybe I'd overreacted a bit, and maybe I was unaware of how much my vocal cords really desired to *shout* things loudly this morning, but my body was in shock from the unexpected succession of events. Could you really blame me for just trying to make it?

Ruben looked back at me like some wounded animal caught in a trap. It obviously wasn't his fault that I was a hot mess on display, but the dude surprised me.

"I got hype. Sorry."

"Apology accepted!" And of course, Ruben immediately bounced back like nothing had even happened. Still, I needed to redirect the conversation before he asked me any more questions about Britney.

"What were you doing in there, anyways? What, you religious?" In all the time I'd known Ruben, I'd never known him to be the religious type. I'd never even heard him shout out the holy name in vain.

"Not religious, really, but ever since we booked the church for our wedding, I like going in there for the quiet."

Maybe I was tripping, but my spiritual curiosities had me going. Maybe Ruben would entertain my sudden impulse to get into the clouds.

"You ever like . . . talk to God?"

He looked surprised but willing. This was what I always liked about the guy. Ruben never lied about his reaction, but he had the openness to meet you where you were at. Nothing was too left field to philosophize about.

"What God are you talking about?"

"Well, for me, I like to think of God as Mother RuPaul

Charles, but you know, generally big white dude with lots of facial hair. Like Santa but ripped."

"Yeah, no. But sometimes when I'm looking at the stained-glass windows, I feel like God might be in color."

"Deeeep." I had no idea what he was talking about, but I nodded in agreement. Come to think of it, Britney's Muppet jacket was like the most iconic ketchup-red I'd ever seen, and still the memory of it remained in my periphery. Dang. Britney might be God.

"You know, if you ever go inside, there's this little stained-glass window that's my favorite. Sky-blue, green, this amber that's almost brown, yellow, and a really light lavender. All the other ones are like these epic biblical depictions, Jesus and his crew, and this one is so simple: just some flowers."

"Why is it different?"

"I think it was donated by the Girls' Friendly Society, way back when."

"That a cult?"

"They helped the poor girls in the mills."

"Oh yeah. Everyone's got a story about them, don't they?"

It was true. You couldn't live in Lowell without knowing the basic history of the mill girls. As the story goes, as industrialization was booming, factories opened up here in the 1800s, and poor New England families sent their daughters away to work and live on their own. People always painted a sad, sorry portrait of their lives, but honestly, right now, I think I could hang with the idea of taking a step away from my family—Dahvy, that is. I mean, we were already on that track anyways.

"Some of them were younger than you, you know? They didn't have their parents. All they did was work."

"Maybe I should do the same, just move someplace and work." I didn't mean to pretend like it was something easy to choose, but I thought maybe there was something to being introduced to the harsh realities of life sooner rather than later. Why wait for it when you could deal with it now?

"What about your sister?"

"Dahvy's got you."

"And you."

"Sure." I could tell Ruben wasn't buying my response, and I couldn't blame him. I didn't buy it myself. I knew the difference between me and those mill girls was that I still had Dahvy, but how long would that last? Dahvy and Ruben were getting married in a month, and then what? We hadn't even talked about whether or not Ruben was moving in. We hadn't talked about how often Ma would be going back and forth to Cambodia. We hadn't talked about anything. So who knew what would happen after?

"You wanna walk back with me?" Ruben asked, breaking through my private questioning. I looked over at his illuminated phone he had drawn out, and yes, it was indeed inevitable: I was late to precalc too. I had to face the truth of the day. I was going to be late to everything.

"I'm gonna stick around for just a little longer," I replied, resigned to my tardy fate.

"Okay, but if you're *late* late and your sister finds out, we never saw each other."

"Saw who?"

"Don't be *late* late." Ruben placed a hand on my shoulder and then turned to go. As he walked down the path toward campus, I watched him get smaller and smaller as my thoughts did the same. Eventually, they shrank all the way down to one essential question I just couldn't shake: If everyone goes, what happens to me?

I immediately remembered the flyer burning a hole through my back pocket. Before today, that call for submissions had no relevance to my life, and now it'd been thrusted toward me twice. I unfolded it again and zeroed in on the words: *become a Beat.*

I fixated on the verb. Become. What did it mean to become? Was it about beginning? Was it about beginning to be? Could I become . . . something? Anything?

Relinquish.

I closed my eyes again.

I took a deep breath in.

And started from where I left off.

I've been thinking about calling myself . . .
Khmer Kerouac
Track that, Jack
All the way back
Yo, let me unpack
And get in this hack

Without any slack
Before you attack
This . . . Lunchables snack
BE taken aback
By this rhythmic smack-

DOWN, down into Mill Town
Your girl's been around
She's not backing down
When she draws the renown
Industrial crown
Making the sound
Of immigrant ground
Don't sleep on this round
Don't get lost, GET found
'Cause it belongs to the brown—

LOOK:
I'm trying to have a conversation
About my nation
She's got this reputation
Of declaration
And misinformation
And consternation
About legislation
Of immigration
In process of cessation

Breaking down the foundation

Encouraging ruination

Deteriorating liberation

At the regulation

Of our civilization

And leaving behind migration

For absolute separation . . .

The vibrations were still with me, and they were making a pretty good case to enter the competition. Maybe.

I checked the time. Dang it. I was *late* late.

CHAPTER 9
Captions

Did you know there is a river in Cambodia that is the only river in the world that (check it) flows both ways? That's magic, Baby Girl.

Phnom Penh, the country's capital and your ba's new home, is where two major rivers—the Mekong and the mighty Tonle Sap—connect. Well, the monsoon season brings in so much rain that it swells the Mekong and in effect, forces the Tonle Sap to move northward instead of southward. Did you hear what I said? THE ENTIRE RIVER GOES NORTH INSTEAD OF SOUTH. So when it does this, the people celebrate Bon Om Touk, or as we call it back in Lowell, the Water Festival. See, all that time you've been running alongside the Merrimack River chomping on beef sticks with your friends and cheering on the boats zooming down the water, you were always celebrating the magic of where you came from. You were celebrating the magic of this place.

It's nice to have your ma here. We went down by the river last night, and you know . . . it was almost like being back in Lowell. Almost. There's something about a city that has rivers running through it. They keep its people moving. We keep on moving, gkoun. That's all we can do. And just remember that if we move in one direction, there's always an opportunity to move the exact opposite way. Or even a completely new way altogether.

I promise I won't keep your ma here long, but it does make me think of having all you girls here with me. Just for a vacation. I would love to show you around, take you over to the temples in Siem Reap, make you eat spiders(!), tour the beaches in Sihanoukville, and show you where you're from. But just for a vacation, because eventually we're all coming home. Don't forget that.

—Your Ba

Outside the house by the back kitchen door, I stood frozen, staring at my phone.

Dude sent me *another* email. I couldn't help but be a little shocked. Grateful that he cared, sure, but what was Ba getting at? I hadn't even replied to the first one yet.

He was onto me, and honestly, I couldn't blame him. Ba and I had always been close. When I was at home, we were always talking, he dug at me (cracking jokes at my expense), and when I was out past curfew, he'd send the occasional text like: YOU'RE DEAD. COME HOME. I got that tone because we were buddies. There was no one else I wanted to rag on me like that. There was no one else I wanted to talk to. We got each other. But now, I knew Ba wasn't going to let me not reply. He was going to try to get through.

Reading the second email, it almost unfolded like a magic trick. He was comparing worlds, likening rivers, trying to make it seem like we were basically in the same place. If you squinted hard enough, if he painted the portrait well enough, if he distracted me enough . . . I wouldn't realize that we were so far apart. But the old man couldn't fool me with his sleight of hand. I was here, and they were there. I knew the truth.

If I just kept my silence, Ba wouldn't have someone to help him make this our new reality. He'd eventually have to give up on trying to convince me things would be all right.

Eventually we're all coming home.

Maybe it was the certainty that made me uncomfortable. Were we? Were they? Was he eventually coming home? He was so positive about the whole thing. It almost felt like if the guy who survived a war and was eventually deported back could be so strong about everything, why couldn't I? There was no room for what I was feeling. It was selfish. I should be able to grin and bear it, but . . . I just couldn't.

I couldn't reply. There were no words I could arrange to pretend like I was down with the situation or our intended future. No reply could hold that meaning. In some wild way, I was beginning to feel like that was why I *needed* those rhymes. When I put my mess out into my own words, it was like I was creating a space that could be entirely my own. And even if some of it was getting some public interference, it was still mine to reckon with. I could talk about Ba and not worry about his rebuttal. I could rage with emotions I didn't quite understand without a diagnosis, fear, or the pitying that made me so self-conscious. I could just be me. Ultimately, that was what I worried about if I made the big, bad decision to enter the contest . . . could I still be me? Would that space be even mine anymore?

I wondered if Ba was sending similar emails to Dahvy. I peered through the window of the kitchen, and there she was as always, staking the room as her wedding headquarters. A day had passed since our last showdown, but Dahvy seemed unfazed, tapping away at her laptop next to a large pad of paper with a square drawn at the center and little circles evenly placed about. Her eyes moved from the computer to the pad, and every so often, she'd write down something inside the circles. Her eyes were so focused on what she was doing, they barely drifted up to greet me when I closed the door.

"Heeey . . . ," Dahvy mumbled, not breaking an ounce of that concentration.

"Good to see you too, sis."

"I'm ordering food from Simply Khmer for dinner, *sis*, so what do you want?"

"You know, Ma texted me the other night that you should really practice cooking rice, since you always burn it."

Dahvy's hands stopped moving, and her eyes met mine. Maybe I was being a brat for intentionally stepping into the danger zone, but that definitely got her attention.

"Well, I just got done grading stacks of tests, and I don't really have time right now, so someone else's Khmer food it is."

To qualify as a truly perfect Cambodian daughter, one had to know how to excel at certain domestic things: clean the house thoroughly, keep your hair combed and neat, and cook a moist (not soggy), solid (not burnt) pot of rice. The whole thing was a patriarchal trash fire, but I'd be lying if it didn't offer me a little bit of joy knowing Dahvy couldn't quite hang with that last rite of passage.

"I'll just have whatever you're having," I said while moving across the room toward the stairs.

"You don't want to help me with the table placements? Could be fun. We could decide on horrible combinations— single out the white people and put them at tables with our drunkest cousins!" Dahvy looked back at me as if that seemed like an enticing invitation.

"Yeah, no. I'm good. I got homework."

"Okay, well, here, take these up with you." Dahvy pushed a stack of Ma's old photo albums toward me. "I need you to pick out and scan some for the slideshow for when people come into the reception."

"Of you and Ruben?"

"I already have those, but I want some of the family."

"Why?"

Dahvy looked sternly back at me like, *Are you serious?* And to be fair, it was warranted. Doy. Ba wasn't going to be there, but she wanted to make sure his presence was.

I nodded and took the stack.

"Should I look out for something specific?" I asked with an honest-to-God smile. It didn't hurt to offer a little civility after I stepped into it a bit.

"Just a range of photos is good." I guess I could've been a good sister and stuck around for a wedding activity that had some actual comedic potential, but I don't know, I just didn't want to get into something with the potential to blow up like it usually did. I'd already dipped my toe in the water, and that water was getting hot. I needed to exit before it had a chance to boil.

I began to climb the stairs, when I heard her shout back, "Remember you're coming to the venue with me this weekend! And the weekend after, you will have to try out your outfit with Ma!"

It seemed my cold shoulder didn't have that much of an effect on her after all. I felt less guilty. There was plenty to do, and she would march out orders until the end of time.

Ba's computer and scanner lived in his office, right at the top of the stairs. I'd asked him why he didn't take all his stuff with him to Cambodia, but he said he didn't need it. He didn't want to get comfortable over there. I hadn't been inside since he left, but as soon as I flipped the switch, it was clear that the whole setup sort of spookily remained intact. Like he'd been here this entire time.

Above the desk, this huge poster of Angkor Wat was hung crookedly, with a couple of pushpins to keep it in place—three, to be exact. Ba was a lousy interior designer, and Ma always threatened to get in there and make it look less like a college dorm. Ba objected and said all he needed was this reminder of where he came from. Ma rolled her eyes and said, "Sorry, you were born in that twelfth-century Buddhist temple complex, City Boy?" Ma might be the more serious one, but she knew how to rag Ba for always pretending like he grew up in the rice paddies, when the dude actually spent most of his time before the war on the streets of Phnom Penh.

I plopped down in his office chair and immediately, I could feel him. He didn't wear cologne or anything, but he sort of smelled like that sandalwood incense we'd burn at wat. A couple of his black hairs remained wedged between the creases of the chair. I pressed a few keys to wake up his computer, and there was a picture of us at the Boston Commons—all of us: Ma, Ba, Dahvy, me, and Ba's parents, Thagh and Yay Kear. My vibe was definitely reading perfect, chubby, monster baby, and Dahvy, who'd probably been as old as I was now, was decidedly over the whole thing. With a pink, bedazzled flip phone in one hand, Sis was playing the part of early-aughts teenage nightmare who couldn't be bothered. The picture was miraculous.

Thagh passed from lung cancer a couple of years after the photo was taken, and Yay followed next. Ba insisted she died of a broken heart. They were separated from each other during the genocide, but out of some kind of miracle, they survived and found each again at Khao-I-Dang, a refugee camp on the border of Thailand and Cambodia. Yay loved Thagh like Ma loved Ba . . . or at least that was what Ba would say (I could see Ma rolling her eyes now) . . . like soulmates. Like they were one. With Thagh gone, it didn't make much sense for Yay to stick around anymore.

I dropped the stack of photo albums onto the desk, and dust particles flew everywhere. It'd been a moment since someone stepped in here to clean up. I opened the first album, and right there on the first page was a single picture of Ma and Ba's wedding back in the nineties. Screw Dahvy's cotton-candy-pink palette—Ma was decked out in gold from head to toe. Like royalty. Now, *she* looked like the queen of Cambodia. Her hair (or should I say collection of hairpieces) looked higher than Angkor Wat, and her eyebrows were questionably thin in that nineties kind of way. Like is it fashion, or did you have an accident at the threading joint? Regardless, my mama could survive even the worst of fashion trends. Straight up: Ma was beautiful.

Ba, on the other hand, looked MONEY in his baby-blue suit. I remember asking him once why he hadn't worn the traditional tunic and sampot jong gk'bun, and he explained that back then, he really felt like he needed to fit in—to be and to appear like an American. I mean, the guy was giving "expensive," even if he didn't have that much. Looking at them together now standing side by side—Ma as this golden goddess and Ba as some kind of politician—the two of them couldn't be more the picture of the American dream, whatever that was. In their eyes, they looked so hopeful. So young. So untainted by the future. It was almost too perfect to bear.

Below the picture, there was a caption that read: *Borey and Rachana Kear, 1992; Cambodian wedding in Lowell, Massachusetts, i.e. the Best Day of our Lives!* Ma must've written the description.

I quickly flipped through the rest of the book, and there were captions with every photo. She'd written them all. Some even went into full detail, play-by-play, about whatever ritual was being captured. I mean, I had personally witnessed many of these ceremonies—my parents had dragged us to plenty of Cambo weddings—but I was appreciating this education from Ma now. She was telling stories about our family and our people.

One ritual involved the groom trying to smoke a cigarette in bed aided by the bride, while guests actively tried to blow out the lighter. I assumed this was to help the couple avoid nasty addictions, but I was honestly stunned to see the audience participate in that kind of way. The caption read: *PSA: Married couples don't let other married couples sleep and smoke at the same time.* In another ritual, the cigarettes were replaced with sweet treats, and the bystanders heckled just as they had before. That caption read: *PSA: Married couples don't let other married couples consume processed sugars.* It was starting to make sense why Cambodian people were so nosy. From jump, they were asked to get into people's business, and Ma's narration was getting a kick out of it all.

My favorite was called the Cleansing Ceremony, or Gat Sak, where the bride and groom would sit in chairs side by side, as couples close to them were given a basin, scissors, perfume, and the task to "pretend" to cut their hair. Seriously. It was like a funny, jokey ritual that showed how the community would prepare the couple for their new life together. But Ba said sometimes you had a boo or a ming who'd started the party early with a Heineken or two and forgot the "pretend" part of the ritual. You had to be careful who you were trusting with a pair of scissors.

In the album, there were many action shots of this ritual, but in one in particular, Thagh and Yay were fully committed. Ba was mid-sneeze as Yay pumped some perfume in his face (you could actually see the mist, LOL), while Ma's wide eyes stared directly at Thagh, who was wielding the scissors like one of those hairpieces had done him dirty. This was some high-quality content! It couldn't have captured our family more perfectly: a little sweet, but mostly messy. *PSA: No real scissors at a wedding . . . ever.* It was official: this was my favorite family picture.

In the moment, another thought occurred to me. Like the email, like the photo . . . these would be the versions of Ba I had now. Sure, if I could get around to answering his calls or if I made the epic trip to Cambodia, I might have Ba in the present. But right now, in this place, back here in Lowell, what I had of him were memories—past tense. I suddenly felt kind of sick knowing there would be no way to recreate the Gat Sak for Ma and Ba. Yay and Thagh were gone. Ma and Ba were away. It was just me, Dahvy, and some instructions now.

Even if the modes more than sucked, I was beginning to feel

guilty for not meeting him in the present when I could. Maybe I'd answer the next call. Maybe.

I closed the album, knowing I'd return but also needing a serious distraction from the family archives. I wanted to be reminded of some other kinds of memories, ones that elicited a little less heartache. I grabbed another book, and there on the first page, dead center, was a photo of . . . me . . . standing on a stage. Dang, I looked *right*. I'm not trying to boast, but the truth was the truth. The vibe was *right*. For some reason, I was wearing electric-blue tights and a sparkly silver top, and my makeup was all cat eyes and then some. What could I really say besides . . . I was *right*.

Trouble was, it wasn't me. I squinted to make out the caption. *Dahvy as Mimi in* Rent, *2004*.

Back in the day, Dahvy acted in musicals? Come again? The girl who HATED karaoke and at every party refused to go along with Ma's and Ba's constant nagging for us to jump in? Dahvy would literally sit there with her arms crossed, judging everyone else. You couldn't make me believe she'd performed in a musical, willingly.

I'd seen the movie *Rent* before, and I knew that character was like the go-go dancer/drug addict who almost dies in the end. That character breakdown alone was enough for me to be confused. Did Dahvy have a performance past, or had she hired a doppelgänger to incept our collective memories?

"Soma! Your *unburnt* bigh is here," Mimi's voice bellowed from downstairs.

Huh. Everyone in this family was shy in the streets, and a performer in the sheets. What the heck. Maybe the funky, misshapen apple didn't fall too far from the tree after all.

"Coming!"

I would need to find exactly the right moment to bring up the electric-blue tights. An inquisition was forthcoming.

CHAPTER 10
What's the Point?

3,356 likes and comments like:

Feeling that inner turmoil!

And:

Drop those beats, Jungle Asian Views. #JungleAsians4eva

And:

Heart your rhymes. Why not post more?

I didn't get it. Sure, I'd aimlessly scroll like any other soulless person on the socials. Sometimes I saw something I was actually hyped about and offered an emoji that reflected my energy. On the other hand, sometimes I indiscriminately double-tapped things I barely looked at. But being on the receiving end of that activity, I couldn't help but wonder . . . why? These people didn't know me. Did they expect me to respond to them? And if I did, would something else come from it? A sponsorship? A friendship? A hacking of my account?

It felt sort of existential, wondering what this all was for. Maybe it was the fact that up to this point, all the comments were pretty positive. I posted the video on Sunday, and now it was midweek. It was feeling like the longest week ever, just waiting for the other shoe to drop. I still couldn't believe trolls weren't inside their caves, bringing me down like others I had seen. Could I be free from the collateral?

And then it happened. I stumbled upon a comment I hadn't read before:

She's not even telling us what's up. Like, I like the poem, but what's it actually about?

Dang. That one comment hit different. Hit harder. Yeah, if I were to be totally objective, I couldn't say it was the best set of lines I'd ever written. Also, this person wasn't entirely inaccurate—I'd left out some of the pertinent details of my situation. Truth was, I didn't want to be so confessional that people would be annoyed by me. I mean, I wanted to be confessional, but not like so, *so* confessional.

If I were to be fair with myself (and this anon avatar), I thought I'd been somewhat bold. Pat me on the back, someone! I'd frame the lines in "yellow-brown blues" and "Jungle Asian views" . . . and how America was obviously responsible for the genocide of Native peoples and somewhat responsible for the genocide of the Cambodian people with their bombs and destabilizing of the area during the Vietnam War . . . and how that's sort of ironic now that they're kicking our people out of this country for no good reason . . . and how that ultimately leads to the whole conceit: me as the "self-view." Dang. I wasn't trying to avoid "telling us what's up." I was trying to get there.

Maybe that was why I needed to enter the contest. I'd started something. Maybe I had to keep going.

I replayed the video again just for validation that I was en route to "telling us what's up":

> Set on self-view . . .
> Like she's even got a clue . . .
> 'Bout that red light . . .
> Flashing hot, bright . . .

Record scratch. My eyeliner looked weird. My hands were trying to conduct a nonexistent orchestra. My voice sounded like I'd just learned to rhyme words and thought the whole thing was kind of cute. But no, it wasn't. It was the opposite of cute. It was *ugly*.

This was the first time I'd watched the video since I posted it. Maybe I should have prepared myself a little more (at all), but the experience of watching it now suddenly felt different from doing it in real time. It was a horror story, in fact. It was like looking at myself in a fun-house mirror. The whole image was mad distorted. I was embarrassed by my self-view.

In that discovery, it was like all the other comments immediately evaporated. They might as well have never been there. All I could see now was this solo critique, and it wasn't even the anon troll. I was the troll. The shoe had dropped and straight clunked me on my head. I was left with my own borrowed question:

What the hell was my poem actually about?

"Holy mama, your coffee's on fire!" Sophat shouted while not-so-gracefully dropping the cup and letting a pool of brown liquid ooze around the base.

"Careful, bro!" I shouted back while immediately grabbing my phone from the table.

"What is that? You working on your *rhymes*?" Sophat's eyes got real big and buggy. He'd introduced the idea of the lit competition, um, a few days ago, and he was already getting into my space about it.

"No. Maybe. Sure. But I haven't decided yet if I'm going to do it."

"Why not?"

"And it went so well for you?" I turned it back to my dear friend, knowing there was danger in the topic. If we were going to talk about the possible consequences, I needed to draw from recent history. I wasn't trying to be a brat. I just knew there was potential to fail epically.

"Wow, okay, Soma, best friend, Soma! Why do you have to shade me like that? You know that the AV techie had it out for me."

"And only you?"

"The guy wasn't even changing levels throughout the performance. I mean, do they expect a performer to go monotone throughout the whole thing? The least they could have done was get a professional mixer." Sophat sat back and took a sip from his latte like he was some kind of professional himself.

"For a small-town high school competition like this? Yeah, I don't think they're getting sound designers. And I don't mean to use you as a cautionary tale, but . . . you *are* my cautionary tale." The idea that I could flop as gloriously as Sophat made me cringe in my sneaks. I mean, why would I even do that to myself?

"Look, I royally ate it (like in the bad way), I admit it. I've made my peace, and now I'm good—"

"Okay . . ."

"And more importantly, I learned the valuable lesson that the venue wasn't right for me. Everyone has their venue of self-expression, and that wasn't mine. Music is. This could be yours."

"I don't know . . ." The phone with all its comments suddenly felt hot on my lap.

"Just because it's the minor leagues doesn't mean you shouldn't do it, you know? It's prep for the majors. It's why I do Sound Impressions. To prep for my Grammy Award–winning recording career."

I looked over at Sophat from across the table. That after-school daylight was pouring in through the windows, and the yellow Brew'd awning outside created a sort of aura around him. He said those very words, and it was like he didn't even blink. There was zero affect or hyperbole. He was just telling you his truth. I wondered what it was like to be that confident. He might not be the next Jack Kerouac, but he never intended to be. The lit competition was just another go at building that . . . presence.

"Honestly, if I were to do it—and I'm not saying I'm going to do it—but if I were going to do it . . . being in front of all those people, how do you not want to like poop in your pants?"

"*Okay, thank you* for asking me for advice, because I've been waiting—"

"Okay—"

"And well, I think it's gotta be personal. You know that old trick where you're supposed to like, imagine people in their underwear to make you laugh or quiet your nerves? Well, for me, it's kind of the same. But when I'm singing with Sound Impressions, picturing audience members in their undies doesn't chill me, it like . . . excites me! It turns me on!"

"Okaaay." I briefly looked around to make sure people weren't listening in on this seriously perverse conversation.

"Come on, Soma! I'm being serious. Don't sex-shame me. I'm just saying it gives me power and language for what I'm doing. Performing music is like making people fall in love with you. You gotta figure out a trick that doesn't chill you out. You gotta figure out something that, like, thrills you in the moment and makes you want to keep your head high and feel what you're performing. And sure you gotta be relaxed a bit, but to me, it's more about finding the point of it all."

That was the funny thing about Sophat. He could say a bunch of things that were so completely outrageous, but at the center of it all was a jewel—a pristine, sparkling diamond that you could not deny.

What was the point of it all?

I'd been writing my own lines for some time. They were never for anything or anyone, per se. They were just for me. To get the thoughts out. To unburden myself from all that pressure. To have it not live inside of me, rattling around like it had nowhere to go. And once I got it out in that video, for better or for worse, there was some kind of conversation about it. It had moved from private to public. It was for other avatars to respond to. Maybe they liked it. Maybe they wanted more. Still, there was connection there.

But that was *that* venue. What would the point be for entering a lit competition and standing up in a dark theater and sharing my rhymes in a different kind of way? To me, there were too many possibilities for danger. You couldn't just do another take. You had people out there watching you, responding to you, judging you in their saggy Fruit of the Looms. And worst of all, you knew who they were . . . somewhat. And they knew you . . . somewhat. They weren't some faceless trolls. They had some point of reference or hearsay for my situation: sad girl whose father had been sent away. No, I wasn't a blank canvas. They were coming in with their own prejudices about who I was. How could I feel empowered like that? Unlike Sophat, the idea of sharing my rhymes in real time to these half-naked not-so-much strangers wasn't turning me on—it was turning me off. Completely. If I failed, there would be no connection.

And that would be only if I made the final round to begin with. Prospective contestants had to submit an initial poem first, and after, eight finalists would be chosen to perform live. Who knew if I'd even get that chance to connect with anyone at all?

"So, what would the point of doing this be for you?" Sophat looked at me intently, with that divine yellow glow all around me like he was some spirit sent from another world to prod me into enlightenment. I paused.

"I'm not sure. . . ."

"SOMA ON THE MIC!" A black blob of bob came through the front door, interrupting my existential crisis and providing me a completely new one. Evie Han always had such perfect timing. The previous question would go unanswered for the moment.

"Oh hey, Evie! Love this new haircut you're sporting this year. It's so fresh!" Sophat pronounced like he was the mayor of this coffee joint. He sheepishly looked at me to confirm my annoyance that our private convo had just been obliterated.

"Hey, Evie," I responded, trying my *very* best.

"OMG, thanks, Sophat! Coming from you, that means everything. I wasn't sure about the bangs too, but I needed something new for junior year."

"It frames your face perfectly!" Sometimes I hated how Sophat could just rise above to meet every social situation, regardless of how close he was to the person. He was a forever hype man to all.

"Soma, I'm sorry if I offended you the other day." What. The. Hey.

"What?" I pretended not to know what she was referring to.

"When we saw each other in class on Monday—"

"Not sure what you're talking about . . ." I was trying *real* hard.

"I was congratulating you on your amazing video, and you sort of retreated back into your hoodie like a turtle."

Why. Was. She. Doing. This? Evie always had a way of giving undesirable attention to the most uncomfy things. This was just her unnatural nature. Like when Ba was first deported, she and her dad were always at the house, trying to help out. Evie even brought over cookies that her ma made. It's like, are baked goods going to bring my dad back? No, they're not. Evie could get off her self-righteous oven, thank you very much.

I mean, I guess it was nice of Boo Soriya to help us out, particularly because he had some serious connections in Boston. I'd heard through the Lowell grapevine that it was him who got Greater Boston Legal Services to bring back Prak Lee when he was wrongly deported over a year ago. Okay fine, and the cookies were good too—honestly, I usually ate them all in one sitting—but there was something about Evie's need to help me that I found really grating. I didn't want to be taken care of or looked down on. Especially not by the Cambo family that had it all. Sometimes I wondered if that was why Evie rubbed me the wrong way. People like us were usually scraping by to get half as far as our white counterparts, but it was like the Hans were set apart. They'd clawed their way to the top of the food chain, and now they were looking down, throwing sad cookie crumbs to their people, feeling sorry that we hadn't gotten to their level yet.

Whoa, check the revelations, but maybe it was the Hans who were telling people around town about our business. They had the reach, and it'd make sense why everyone, in and outside of the Khmer community, suddenly knew about Ba. Maybe we were just some PR stunt for Boo Soriya's next election. We were the broken family they could help. No, it was good to keep Evie at an arm's length. I wasn't trying to be the subject of anyone's press conference.

"Yeah, sorry. I just wasn't feeling good that day," I replied quickly, trying not to sound too defensive and desperately hoping she wouldn't interrogate my former state any further.

"Well, your rhymes were so cool. I'm a big K-pop aficionado, actually, and your stuff is totally on par."

"I'm not really into that kind of stuff—"

"What are you talking about?! We are serious K-nerds," Sophat contributed unhelpfully to the conversation, knowingly adding agita to my state of distress.

I sternly whipped back to Sophat, who looked real pleased with himself, revealing our secret devotion. He was quickly moving from my Number One to my no-number-at-all.

"Like I said, I'm just goofing." I needed to shut. It. Down. Or we were never going to be done with this interaction. Not so luckily, Evie did not take the cue and sat smack down in the middle of us. The freaking gall.

"Your goofing is so good, though! You know, there's actually this singer named Laura Mam, who is like changing the game of pop music back in Cambodia. I think you'd be into it. I can send you a link to one of her music videos if you want—"

"Yeah, I've heard of her."

"Her stuff is so cool, right? Like very contemporary."

"Uh-huh."

"And like, it may inspire, you know?"

"I don't know."

"Oh. Yeah. Of course. I just thought you might be into it or something. . . ." Now it was Evie's voice that was recoiling. For the first time in the conversation, I could tell she was actually picking up what I was putting down, and it made me feel maybe, sort of, kind of, somewhat bad.

"Soma and I would love to hang out, Evie! I mean, we don't really do anything, but maybe you should come over to Soma's house one of these nights, and we can just do like a music share?" Sophat announced the invitation without even looking at me once. Et tu, Sophat?!

"S-Sophat—" I stammered, trying to not show too much obvious disdain.

"Yeah, Soma, wouldn't that be nice?" Now Sophat stared back at me to call my bluff. He knew he had me cornered. I wasn't just an unfriendly loner. I was a coward too.

I paused. There wasn't a way to get out of this one without outing myself as a big, mean, selfish baby.

"Yeahhhh . . . you should definitely come over one of these nights. I'd love to hear more about your music." I offered the fakest grin I could conjure in hopes that maybe Evie would see through my BS and just go ahead and hate me forever.

"Okay! Wow, that'd be cool. I have a ton of time next week, if you all are free." Evie looked like she was going to do a freaking backflip from the excitement of it all.

"That sounds great. Doesn't that sound *great*, Soma?" Sophat was going to die after this conversation was done. He had sealed his fate.

"We'll see you soon, Evie!" I responded gleefully on high, expecting that at least my confirmation would send her on her way and far away from this coffee shop.

"Awesome! Actually, I started working here this semester, so your next coffee is on the house! Speaking of, I should really get to my shift. Don't worry. I won't like hover around you while you're here. Just so excited we're really going to hang out for once!" And with that, the black blob of bob disappeared behind the counter, and I returned to aggressively staring at my archnemesis.

"Before you say anything, just listen, okay?" Sophat smiled innocently, as if he hadn't just put me out on the coals. I remained statuary, waiting for whatever unreasonable argument he was about to throw my way. "I know you have this thing about Evie, but she's not the enemy here, you know that, right? She's like us. Another Khmer kid in this town who's just trying to figure stuff out. And I know your families are like super intertwined with everything, but she obviously wants to be our friend, so, like, why the hell not? You know? It would help our social status a bit being with a future Harvardite, and she actually seems kind of cool. A little much, but she may surprise you. Maybe you might even connect. So what's your beef, my brilliant but sad, narcissistic sis?"

As Sophat handed that last question to me, Evie returned from the back area of the coffee shop and began to tend to her barista-y things around the front counter. I watched as she poured brown sugar into a dispenser without spilling a single grain. A customer stepped up to the counter, and Evie smiled and said she'd be with them in just a second. She then poured the customer a small drip, took their cash, gave them change, and sent the satisfied customer on their way. After, she screwed the lid of the brown sugar container back on and returned it to its original location. There was distance between us, but from my vantage point, I could observe that Evie Han was an absurdly proficient human being.

Okay, confessional: I didn't know what was wrong with me, but the minute she walked into the same space, I just got steamed up. We were both Cambodian girls in the same town, but we couldn't be more different.

I was the yin to her yang. While I was bringing that dark and melancholic energy, she was the bright light emanating from the sun. While I had a father who was just fighting to be with his family, her father was like the Khmer Obama, annoyingly charming and capable. While I had no idea where I was going or what would happen to me, everyone knew that her life would be Ivy-perfect. She'd be the one to get away.

Maybe my funk was uncalled-for, but so what? I was allowed
to keep my distance. After all, distance can sometimes protect
you from getting too close. When you get too close, bad things
happen. People can disappear altogether. It wasn't a wild leap.
I'd been taught my entire life to love Ba, and I did without even
thinking about it, what the consequences could be for doing
that with all your heart. Evie aside, I was reeling from the fact
that all that love could be for nothing. Why trust anyone then?

"Earth to Soma. I asked you a question. What's your beef
with her?"

I looked on at a smiling Evie giving another customer their
change and sending them on their way.

"I don't know, Sophat. Maybe I'm just jealous." I resigned
myself to the conclusion I think we'd both been aware of from
the start. That was what it was after all, right? Maybe with Evie
and the possibility of performing my poems, I was just scared of
connecting. Because not only is it intimate, sometimes you get
comfortable, and then the whole thing can go away altogether.
At some point, you can disconnect, and then you're drifting
solo.

"I get it. Look, I'm jealous of everyone who's not me. I know
that's like hard to believe because I'm so boss and steely, but
I get insecure too, you know? But you gotta just worry about
you. Particularly as you're about to reign supreme on this lit
competition—"

"I haven't made up my mind yet."

"Well, make it up soon, because I believe in you. I know you can do this." Sophat's intensity softened a bit. He grabbed my hand and squeezed it once. "Besides, you have until Monday to sign up, and I can't wait to see you make sweet, sweet love to that audience."

"You're a nightmare, you know?" I smiled back at my Number One, even if I wanted to drop-kick him for setting me up in every single way.

"Yeah, I know, but you'll wake up by yourself eventually." Sophat took a sip from his coffee.

I returned to mine and took a sip as well. Could I make sweet, sweet love to that audience? Did I even want to find out? I still wasn't sure.

I took another sip.

CHAPTER 11

Lovebirds

As frustrated voices drifted in from the back kitchen, I made the best choice I could: sit down on the ground and stay out of the way. The dance floor had been recently polished, but you could already see the Hennessy spilling and the Khmer people dancing around with their red faces all bloated and cheerful. The weekend had come, and with it, a trip to Pailin Restaurant, the site of Dahvy and Ruben's wedding reception, among the many, many, MANY Cambodian weddings that had come before.

To me, this place was like a scrapbook of bad decisions—where push-up bras were plenty, where alcohol gave boos delusions of dancing expertise, and where the electric guitar, drums, and piercingly high femme vocals would shriek out of the tower of mismatched speakers like they were legit trying to annihilate everyone's collective eardrums. Still, the place had some kind of charm.

I pulled out my phone, seeing if I could pretend to be anywhere else but here, thinking about anything else but this wedding.

BRITNEY (2:04 p.m.): Were we gonna hang . . . or what?

Ah crap. While I'd been trying to make an impossible decision about the lit competition, Britney had slipped my mind entirely. Not that she didn't have charismatic powers enough to sustain my attention, but the competition had been like Pandora's box. It brought out all these questions I hadn't even thought of. I was wrestling with myself, and the focus needed to address a goddess like Britney was all-in. I needed to go all-in.

SOMA (2:05 p.m.):   Um yeah. Wanna get married—

Yeah, no. Erase that text. Do not propose to your not-girlfriend.

I was daydreaming. I was a pathetic baby lesbian, and somewhere out there in the gay universe, the tiniest rainbow violin was heard playing out the saddest gay song. Subarus were screeching to a halt. Swatches of plaid were exploding into a million pieces at witnessing my total inexperience in gay-ass love.

Lesbian. Huh.

That was the first time I had really thought of myself in that way. Not that labels entirely matter (to me at least), but there was still something surprisingly powerful about thinking of myself as just that: lesbian.

When I initially told Ma and Ba I was gay freshman year, it was like they were *too* excited. Not that anyone can ever be "too excited" when parentals are supportive, but in this case . . . they were *too* excited. Before their response, I was nervous, unsure of how they would think of me after. Dahvy was so much older, but she was obviously everything they could ask for in a daughter (minus the burnt rice). I knew I could never step into her straight heels, and hell, I didn't want to. I felt comfy in my sneaks.

But when the truth came out, they wanted to throw me a celebration. I said that gender reveal parties and activities of the like start wildfires. They wanted to get me a whole new wardrobe. I told them I was not about to start wearing pants with extra pockets and hooks for hammers and shit. They wanted to get me a therapist just so I had someone to talk to who wasn't them. I confessed that a person might be good in the future, but right now I was okay. Or so I thought.

At first, they didn't ask me a ton of questions. I knew it was probably because they didn't want to get awkward, but there was something about the silence that made me unsure of what was really going on. Then, that night, I was brushing my teeth in the upstairs bathroom, and I could hear them talking in their bedroom. Ma was crying. I spit into the sink and crept toward their door, which had accidentally been left open a crack. Ba sat next to Ma with his arm around her shoulder. He was comforting her.

"I'm just scared for Soma," Ma said while wiping away tears.

"I know. Me too. But we can also be excited for her. We *have* to be excited for her," Ba replied in his always assured tone. Though you could still tell he was convincing himself too.

I returned into my room that night and lay in bed, thinking about it all. I knew they wanted to be happy for me, but even the best parents had to work for it. Why weren't all orientations, all sexualities, all genders, all expressions, all kinds of people just accepted right from the start? Why wasn't it automatic to have someone tell you who they were without fear of failure? Why did I even have to come out in the first place?

Sitting here now, looking out onto the empty dance floor, I wondered if I'd ever get married—if I'd ever have a wedding. Would Ma and Ba be "too excited"? Or would that be a step too far for them to understand? What would their limits be to my being out?

"Ma, why is Boo Nin telling me you ordered thirty-five tables when I said I could only do thirty?" Dahvy entered the dance floor from the kitchen. She was talking—no, yelling at her cell phone and our mother who still hadn't arrived yet. Ruben trailed behind with a clipboard in hand, looking like some sad wedding planner assistant. In fact, Dahvy had insisted on not having a wedding planner at all, because she thought that Ma would be around, but that plan was obviously backfiring. I didn't know why she was stressing at such altitude. Sure, the timeline was getting tighter with Ma's schedule changes, but she said she'd be back in time for the dreaded final fitting. That was the biggie. Even I understood that. But I guess I also understood that there were a lot more things to be checked off before that point. That to-do list was looking long.

In the meantime, Dahvy recruited an easily excitable but

inferior intern. After she aggressively shooed him away, Ruben joined me at the corner of the dance floor. It was safer closer to the ground.

"So, what do you think? The room looks bigger like this, no?" Ruben asked me, like I had any say in the matter.

"Kind of looks the same to me . . ." I didn't mean to sound so uninterested, but it was starting to feel like Dahvy was dragging me to every wedding prep activity for unknowable reasons. Did I have a say in the food? That was already set. Did I have a say in the musical selections? Probably not. Did I have a say in the number of tables? Yeah, clearly that wasn't going well, and there was no need for another Kear girl in the mix. So I was obviously just there to keep Ruben entertained while Dahvy and Ma fought, even nine thousand miles away. "Honestly, I like it like this. Without people. Without *any* sound."

"I hear you. Dahvy took me to one wedding before, and I think it took me a whole week to get my hearing back."

"Don't let Boo Nin mess with that soundboard. Game over."

"Noted," Ruben replied while making concentrated eye contact with Dahvy, who was now standing in the middle of the dance floor, flailing her arms. "Hey, your best buddy told me you're considering entering the lit competition."

My God. Sophat was sending me straight into the ground. I blinked once at Ruben and rolled back fully onto the floor, placing my arms across my chest like it was time to go. I was ready to be buried alive. I closed my eyes, hoping that when I did, all the pressure would just go away.

"Okay, so I guess it's a touchy subject. . . ." Ruben's voice sounded apologetic, even if it wasn't his fault for innocently asking. It was my former best friend's fault for grinding up the rumor mill.

"No, it's just . . . I haven't made up my mind yet, and Sophat keeps adding heat. Also, I didn't want to like offend you or whatever for not entering last year." I rolled up to my former sitting position, hoping he wouldn't hate me completely for disappointing him previously.

"Soma, please. You didn't offend me at all. I do think you should do it, but you can't do it for anyone but yourself." Ruben said it so simply, and still, I was having a hard time imagining why I would do it for myself.

"But who are the five other tables?! That's like fifty more people?" Dahvy shouted back into the phone, evolving into a full-on Bridezilla Pokémon. Even with only one loud side of the story, I knew the exact situation.

Khmer people weren't exactly the best at RSVP'ing, and sometimes people would just invite friends of friends to come on by. Regardless of whether they knew the bride or the groom, randos would literally roll up to the party for the free food and drinks, like some shameless wedding crashers. Still, we were Cambodian, and saving face was always the priority, so it wasn't like you could turn them away. And knowing Ma, I'm sure she was trying to avoid an awkward situation in not having enough tables.

Ma was always like that, looking for worst-case scenarios,

while Dahvy was always like *that*, looking to make sure things were exactly accounted for. Honestly, they were working from the same alpha language, but their goals were obviously different.

"I can't tell what would be worse right now, your mom and your sister having a fight in person or over the phone," Ruben hypothesized while looking at his helpless bride-to-be.

"Over the phone," I replied with absolutely certainty.

"How do you figure?"

"Because Ma's not here." I looked away to make sure Ruben knew I wasn't trying to blame him again for his line of questioning, but the answer was so obvious. It would always be worse with Ma not here.

"God, I could *kill* her!" Dahvy ended her call and immediately put both hands in front of her face like she was preparing to gather the chunks of flesh for when her head would eventually explode from all the stress.

I don't know why there aren't more horror films set at weddings. From all the ones I'd been to, this was clearly a chilling setup for a most gruesome mess. Bride murders bride's mother because of wrong table assignments! Bride then murders bride's younger sister for being an unhelpful bystander! Bride finally murders groom for being too much of a helpful bystander! Buckets of blood fall onto bride (à la *Carrie*), and she murders herself for just wanting loooooove . . .

Like a puppy, Ruben jumped up to meet her in the middle of the dance floor.

"What's up, babe?"

"Ma ordered thirty-five tables because Boo Nin said he'd throw in the Cambodian band for free, *after* I told her that our DJ was going to be my Spotify playlist."

"What?" I immediately jumped to my feet, hearing such sacrilege. "You were going to do the music by yourself?"

"We were going to have a couple of Cambo tracks, so we could appease the people, but I didn't want to get into all that, because it costs money and it's a lot of energy in general. Maybe I can still talk to Boo Nin. . . ." Dahvy reached back into her pocket for her phone.

"But you have to have a DJ for the Top 40 bangers! Like, have you ever been to a party before?" Dahvy looked back at me like she was so offended by my accurate assessment. "You need someone to get the party right. Like, someone who's feeling out what the people want to dance to."

"Are you paying for the DJ? Or better yet, are we premiering DJ Soma at the Diaz-Kear wedding?!" Dahvy shouted back, like she thought she was some kind of funny.

"DJ SOOOOOOOOOOMMMMMMMMMAAAAA!" Ruben chimed in like her embarrassing stooge.

"Well, it happened. I officially hate the both of you more than anyone else in the entire world, but I'm still going to offer my advice. You need a DJ. When the achaa gets drunk himself, when the mings push you around, when strangers show up to your wedding uninvited . . . the only thing you two will care about is some Hennessy and the music you want to move to." I rested my case. Annoyingly.

"She does have a point. I mean, our wedding is supposed to be fun for us too—" Ruben's affirmation was quickly met with a steely glare from Dahvy.

"Did you all not listen to anything I just said? Ma already made plans for the band, so we will not have space for that and a DJ. Period. So, thank you to the wedding planning committee for your counsel, but the decision has already been made without any of us in mind—"

"Baby—"

"Ma made the decision. What am I supposed to do about it?" Dahvy asked the question, but there was definitely a period at the end of it. I might not be getting married, but I also understood that when Ma made a decision, even from across the globe, the argument was closed.

For the first time in all the planning, imagining Dahvy and Ruben not dancing to the music they wanted really bummed me out. Sure, weddings were undoubtedly a kind of performance. A lot of attention was paid to the guests' experience. But wasn't a wedding about the couple getting married? The bride and groom? The stars of the event? Shouldn't they be entitled to have a good time?

It made me think of the experience of creating rhymes. I'd become so concerned with how they would be received, maybe I'd forgotten about how I felt doing them. The spark of creation. The moment when you have nothing and then you just go for it. You tap into an emotion, you name it with a word, and then you stick it with others. Sometimes it clicks automatically, and sometimes it sucks, so you try again. And then you try and try and try, and man, when you get it and it hits right . . . THAT FEELING! It's just fun. Because you're flowing, and that's a little like dancing. You lose sense of any kind of judgment. You yourself are having fun.

"Well, on the bright side, Boo Sokhom's been showing me some Cambo moves. . . ." Ruben took off his suit jacket and stood at the center of the dance floor, looking like he was about to commence something really embarrassing. The hairs on the back of my neck stood straight up. This *was* going to be a horror film.

"Uh-huh, and with things going the way they're going, you think I'll be in any kind of mood to Cambo dance?" Dahvy fired back, staring him down.

"It's our wedding, you remember that, right? *Our* wedding? And you and I are definitely going to dance, even if, especially if, it's Cambodian dancing!" Ruben dramatically placed both arms to his sides and then slowly but grandly lifted them up and down like he was preparing for takeoff. Then as he walked forward and backward, he began to bring his arms to the center, across his chest, forming an X, and then flapped his arms back to his sides just like before. "The birdie, baby!"

Yes, just like when you watch a horror film, even when it's scary and you have to place your hands over your eyes, you still leave space between your fingers to look at the bloody damage. You cannot look away. This scene was too scary to miss.

Ruben was of course talking about (and demonstrating) the Khmer dance saravan, probably the most recognizable social dance for weddings. In the movement of the arms that looked a bit like flying, it was easy to think of it as a dance between two birdies. Birdie #1 would flap toward the other, causing Birdie #2 to simultaneously retreat. Then it was Birdie #2's turn to advance, while Birdie #1 would fly backward. And on and on and on.

That was the dance. It was a monotonous one, but with all things, with the most basic patterns, you found ways to express your style. Ma would flap gracefully and look away like she couldn't be bothered. Ba flapped strongly like he was some bird of prey. Ruben's flapping was more like flailing, like a little baby bird flying out of the nest for the first time.

Now, with every floppy wing flap, Ruben chipped away at Dahvy's stone-cold exterior. It took a lot of energy to pretend not to be delighted by him, especially when he was in this state of extreme physical expression. Or maybe exertion. Regardless of what it was, the dude was sweating.

"Come on, Soma! Help me out here!" Ruben yelled out while still expressing, exerting, and sweating.

"Yeah, no, you got it, bro. Maybe try not to injure your bride with those arms, though!" I shouted back, hoping he would take the advice.

"Okay, but you're flapping like you got somewhere to go!" Dahvy finally intercepted, trying to place her hands on his arms in constant violent motion. There was now no way to help either of them.

"I got to get to my wedding, baby!" Birdie #1 advanced.

"Less arm action!" Birdie #2 advanced.

"I disagree: more arm action!" Birdie #1 advanced again.

Finally, the two birdies were moving forward and backward with their arms in growing synchronization with each other. Ruben was still thrashing about like his appendages were some kind of meat machines, but Dahvy's movements were soft and kind of sly. Dahvy let her guard down, and just for a second, she sort of looked like . . . Ma. Still angsty and powerful but moving with mad elegance. I envied the way she was able to transform—the way that when the armor was down, she seemed effortless. This was actually her style.

The two birdies were finding their rhythm. They didn't necessarily look identical moving back and forth, but more so opposite, complementary, like they each had something to offer the other. I wondered if I would ever find my birdie pair. I wondered if I had already found it. I looked back down to my cell phone at the text on read:

BRITNEY (2:04 p.m.): Were we gonna hang . . . or what?

I begin to type a reply:

SOMA (2:15 p.m.):   Maybe . . .

I immediately erased the text again. From afar, that tiniest rainbow violin played the saddest gay song again, declaring that I was, in fact, the baby bird with the wobbly-ass pegs for legs, looking for flight. What was I going to say? Was I going to invite her out on a date? Was I going to rally the courage to reply? And just as I was reaching the peak of my frantic questioning—

Ruben tripped and fell forward, taking Dahvy completely down with him. The flapping had turned into desperate attempts to find balance, and in the end, Ruben pancaked Dahvy. Splat. She was flat . . . tened. You could barely see her— only an arm here and a leg there. For a prolonged moment, they lay on the ground in silence from the shock of the fall.

"You guys dead?" I asked, pulling forward to see if I needed to check any pulses.

A groan and then silence.

Yeah, no. This wedding was definitely going to be a horror film. Cue the scary Cambo music now.

CHAPTER 12

Emails

I know you always wanted to be a Long Beach Cambodian because well . . . the beaches. Unfortunately, none of us choose what world we enter into. You can blame your Ma and Ba for that. Psych! We didn't choose either, so get over yourself. I guess you can think of every generation of Kears as a different karmic life, and we just keep trying to make it better each time. The things we can control.

I went out to Sihanoukville for the weekend. You jealous? I know I told you about that place before. It's funny. I used to think of it as just a sleepy beach town, but it's turned into a major developing area: lots of businesses and tourists. I think you'd be into it. It's got a Long Beach vibe, but a level up. The OG Cambo vibe.

I went with your ma, my brother, your boo Sovanna and his whole family, your ming and all your bongs. Every last one of them. Did you ever know you had so many cousins? Because you do. I'll send more pictures when I have the time. But the first day we got here, we went to the Phsar Leu Market, this stinky (wonderful) place with all kinds of wild things: fruits, veggies, dried foods, toys, electronics, and your ba's favorite, kuh-dam. You know how I love a messy crab feast! We got a bagful and headed to the water. We cooked it right there on the beach. Our bellies were full. The kids were running around in the sand. We watched the sun set on the water. It was like some kind of heaven. And still, a piece of me could not fully love it, without you and Dahvy. My girls.

Look: we're going to get you out here because the hotels are cheap! We're talking nice rooms for fifty dollars a pop. And I won't even make you pay for it. It's on your ba. We'll get you out here for a visit, get your fix, and then maybe for a moment, you'll feel less bad about being a Lowell Cambodian. Honestly, though, can you imagine being like a Tacoma Cambodian or an Oklahoma City Cambodian?! You're good, baby girl. At least you can thank Buddha every day for the Patriots, Dunkin' Donuts, and four actual seasons. Nope, Soma. You are a Lowell Cambodian. And it's a great thing to be. Don't forget that.

I want to relieve you of the pressure to respond to my emails. Ignore your dad being awkward and all, but I have noticed you've been a little on the quiet side. I also know these letters are sort of a funny space to chat in, but since I left, I've been thinking of how I want to communicate with you. These emails help me be a bit more thoughtful about my ideas. Not so hot and irrational as I'm sure you're used to. But seriously, don't feel like you need to reply. You're welcome to, but I understand if you'd rather not.

Or you need a little space. I'll still keep reaching out . . . just so
you know how much I love you.

—Your Ba

I reread the email again, and my eyes kept returning to the lines:
*We cooked it right there on the beach. Our bellies were full. The kids
were running around in the sand. We watched the sun set on the water.
It was like some kind of heaven.*

I mean, silly me, I guess, but it never occurred to me that Ba
would begin to create new memories. It never occurred to me
that he would eventually find comfort and actual beauty over
there. I was being willfully ignorant. Of course he would. It was
his home. It *is* his home. How could I expect him to hate every
part of it, in the way I hated every part of him being gone? He
was beginning to build a life out there.

And even more, he was reaffirming the fact that I was a
"Lowell Cambodian." I appreciated the sentiment. I got what
he was saying, but what'd that make him? Was he a Cambodia
Cambodian now? Before, the guy was trying to draw parallels,
and now he was making distinctions. Was he intentionally creating that difference, that space between us, so we could start
to understand our new realities? Was it time I started thinking
in that way?

I wasn't being altogether fair. I was creating that distance
too, and he was picking up on it. If in the first two emails he'd
been hinting at my tactic, in this one he was not only calling

me out, but he was giving up on me . . . well, the expectation that I'd write back, at least. I guess it was what I wanted, some silence and space to think things through without having to be any kind of way. I had desired a place that was mine, but now that I had it, in his confirmation of not wanting anything back, I suddenly felt even more alone.

Looking down at the phone now, I couldn't remember the last time we spoke in real time. It was sort of a slow fade-out. Did I have it in me to call him up and prevent it from going completely out? How much time did I have left before things became irreversible?

I put the monster box away and jumped over to my desk, which was covered in loose photos. I was buried in nostalgia. Without a doubt, there were plenty of candidates for the wedding slideshow. Arguably too many. I was starting to see double in my gathering of these moments. There was a picture of the four of us in front of the Excalibur Hotel in Vegas, that beyond-cheesy (to the point of *actually awesome*) medieval castle. The three of them looked wicked tired, but my eight-year-old self was sporting the rottenest grin while holding up a huge trash bag full of stuffed animals I'd won in the kids' area that night. I had crushed those kiddie carnival activities, and now I was happy to show off my loot.

There was one of Dahvy and Ruben from high school graduation that would definitely make it into the show for its high levels of cringe. It was like a tale of archetypal opposites. Dahvy was prepped down from her wedges up to her blond highlights, and Ruben looked like some confused skater goth who couldn't decide which mode allowed him to be more pouty. Even in their graduation robes, you could see how their personalities differed, but I guess opposites attract. Or maybe people change too.

As I was scavenging through the albums, I realized that besides the Vegas one, there were only a few pictures of all four of us together. There were full sections of me with our parents and just a couple of the three of them. I was only four when Dahvy went to college in Boston, so it made sense. But seeing it now and even stumbling upon the few pages with just Dahvy and Ba, it made me think about how different our experiences might have been.

We didn't talk about it much, but throughout most of Dahvy's childhood, Ba was in and out of jail and the immigration detention center. The irony was that most of his bad-boy behavior had occurred a decade before, when he was in high school, but the dude was loyal to a fault, and even when he shook that lifestyle off, he stayed connected to his friends. That loyalty would be the reason he got himself back into trouble.

Generally, we don't talk about what he did that day that set all this in motion . . . but the point was, Ba served some time, and after, ICE said he could stay if he was on good behavior. Ba abided, of course, but then earlier this year, out of the blue, he was called up and sent away. Just like that.

From the photos, the story goes that at least I got some uninterrupted time with him before he left, but Dahvy knew what it was like to lose him, and she knew what it was like to lose him again. Maybe that's why you could see her smile get smaller with every new photo in each passing year. Would mine do the same?

Turns out the Mimi *Rent* photo was just the tip of the iceberg. I remained shook. There were albums of her in various theater productions. My favorites included her as the second wife in *The King and I,* where she was obviously wearing yellow face on top of her already yellow face. I hadn't brought up her theatrical résumé with her yet, but I was sort of amazed by the whole discovery. She didn't just try it out once, but she had been the premier player of the drama program. How had I not known she was a such a rock-star thespian?

I was surprised to discover exactly how many extracurriculars Dahvy got into. Sure, I knew she had always been intense in her ambitions, but rifling through the photographic evidence, you could tell she was on a mission. Dahvy was the Evie Han of her generation, with one major difference. Evie had the time and space to be the most involved student at Lowell High. Dahvy had a father who was in and out of the house, and that baggage was not only serious, but it was purpose for her. From the albums, it was like Dahvy had made a choice: she'd channel all that hardship in staying busy, being accomplished, moving onto the next thing.

Aside from the obvious age difference, maybe that was a major reason why we struggled to understand one another. Dahvy wanted to fix everything. She'd done it my entire life.

Even if it wasn't my fault, in her way she made me feel partly responsible too.

I guess it wasn't always like that. I pulled out another album. I wanted to see if I could find a photo of the day when Dahvy inexplicably took me on a day trip to the beach. When the order initially came up for Ba to be deported, Dahvy came into town to seemingly assess the situation. Ma and Ba were fighting so hard, it was like you couldn't hear what was being said anymore. Everyone was just flailing. Eventually, Dahvy told me to come with her. We drove forty minutes to the coast, and we were on the beach. For once, she wasn't trying to pretend like nothing was going on, but maybe she wanted me to feel free from it for a second. She'd developed the ways for her to survive, and she wanted me to start that process myself.

Tucked between pages, not even appropriately mounted, was a selfie Polaroid of her and me walking down the beach. We looked happy. No, maybe just distracted. Actually, peaceful. I scanned the photo quickly and then pocketed the memory for myself. There was a moment in time when Dahvy didn't see me as another reminder of how bad things had gotten. Instead, I was something she wanted to take care of. And while I learned quickly how to look after myself, it was nice to feel like she wanted to protect me. Not fix everything. But just take me to the beach.

I looked over at the time, and it was already nine p.m. Balls. I had so much homework to do, but I hadn't been able to focus on a single thing. That wasn't really true. I was focusing on *many* things, but none of them had to do with passing my classes. With everything going on, how could anyone expect me to keep a schedule? Maybe my homework would be a good distraction, after all. Was I dead? Did I literally just say that?

I pushed the photos to one side of the desk and opened up my laptop, hoping it would encourage any kind of motivation. I logged onto my email, and the first one that popped up was from . . . Mr. Drakos. Dang it. The subject read, *Update? Meanwhile, do read this!* Yeah, no. Delete. I knew I needed to address the essay situation sooner or later, but something inside me just couldn't go there right now. Later it was!

I moved on, scrolled down, and there was an email from Sophat with the subject line *Enter the competition already! XOXO.* Double dang it. The competition. The deadline was tomorrow a.m. Why did everything seem so urgent these days? Or maybe it was just me. It was definitely me. I couldn't deny that I, well . . . denied things like . . . deadlines . . . or the truth. Avoidance was my game, and I was winning. How had a week already passed since I was first introduced to the idea of entering the competition?

I opened Sophat's email, and there was a link to a video entitled "Poet Monica Sok Reads 'I Am Rachana.'" Ma's name. I clicked on the thumbnail, and the opening credits displayed the words *AAWW: Asian American Writers' Workshop.* Huh. I didn't even know there was such a thing. I'd always been a little wary of school groups and things of the like that targeted only one group based on race, ethnicity, or whatever. It wasn't like

I didn't understand the power of an affinity group, but something always made me feel like I didn't quite match up. That maybe I wasn't Asian enough or Cambodian enough.

Evie Han, on the other hand, was not only a card-carrying member of those kinds of groups, but she was leading the charge. Maybe she knew they'd buff up her résumé, or maybe she really felt those things. But Evie didn't blink twice about claiming those identities. No edit, but sometimes I didn't always understand what it meant to be Asian. That was my own secret to keep. As far I as I knew, "Asian" was a way for the US government to lump us all together into stats, even if we didn't all eat the same grain of rice. "Cambodian" felt more right, but with Ba gone and thinking of Evie and me occupying that same space . . . "Cambodian" had to be much larger than I thought. Evie was on one side, and me on the other.

And then, just like that, *another* Cambodian girl (a little older, definitely prettier) appeared at a music stand, looking like she was about to perform. From the title card, I figured this was Monica Sok, and Monica Sok was going to recite her poem "I Am Rachana." Just a hunch.

She opened her mouth. Unlike me, she spoke quietly, firmly, with some music to her voice. She talked about a woman named Rachana, which means "fine arts" in Khmer. The woman was married to a man who, I thought, was history personified, or more basically, like an academic. I wasn't totally sure. (I guess that was the thing about poetry. It could be anything.) She talked about how this couple, Rachana and the man, were in a labor camp during the genocide, having to hide their work and who they were because they might be killed by the Khmer Rouge.

And then she turned a corner and talked about suh-law muh-jew yoon, the Cambodian soup dish made of boiled catfish, tomatoes, and pineapple for the muh-jew. Ma makes it all the time, and it's one of my favorite dishes, even if the pineapple sometimes gives me canker sores. I will sacrifice my mouth for that sweet-and-sour soup, which tastes like a party in my mouth. No, not a party, but a kind of warmth. Home. It was home to me. It was Ma to me.

I thought about how this professional poet, who I didn't even know, who was like a thousand leagues ahead of my fetus rhymes, performed her poetry with such . . . presence, it caught me completely off guard. I thought about how we both had probably eaten this dish a million times, and how likely some ingredients changed here and there (based on our Mas), but how it probably still had that perfect tangy pineapple taste that made our tongues tingle. I thought about how she was able to describe how a single bowl of rice in the camps replaced that steaming, delicious bowl of soup, and how that replacement told you everything you needed to know about what Cambodians had lost because of war.

I wondered if there was any way I could express this pain like her. Even if I didn't know her, this poet, Monica, had gotten so personal about her parents' history, and it shocked my system. Somehow, I thought I'd be annoyed by the sensitive, honest nature of it all, but I wasn't. I was just moved. She made me feel sorry both for what her parents went through and what mine had too. She drew that connection. She got personal so that she could get universal. Maybe that was the key: get into the icky personal stuff, draw it out in detail, and put it against rhythm to Frankenstein something that could maybe feel like a mirror to a stranger. Monica had done that for me. Maybe I knew I could do that for someone else.

With the video, I'd started something. I was scratching the surface with Ba's situation. This could be my opportunity to keep going. What was the point of all of it?

I exited out of the window and returned to Sophat's email. There was a line of text below the link: *She's one of us. Step into it. BecomeJK@gmail.com.*

I leapt back toward my bed and scavenged for the paper I'd been writing down my notes from sitting by the canal. I could start there. I'd write down that poem, and then if I moved on to the next round, I'd figure out a second one.

But first this email. I typed into the subject line: *Soma Kear Poetry Competition Submission*. In the body of the email, I began to transcribe my scribbles . . .

CHAPTER 13

A Khmer Scene

I've been thinking about calling myself . . .

Khmer Kerouac

Track that, Jack

All the way back

Yo, let me unpack

And get in this hack

Without any slack

Before you attack

This Lunchables snack

BE taken aback

By this rhythmic smack-

DOWN, down into Mill Town

Your girl's been around

She's not backing down

When she draws the renown

Industrial crown

Making the sound

Of immigrant ground
Don't sleep on this round
Don't get lost, GET found
'Cause it belongs to the brown

LOOK:
I'm trying to have a conversation
About my nation
She's got this reputation
Of declaration
And misinformation
And consternation
About legislation
Of immigration
In process of cessation
Breaking down the foundation
Encouraging ruination
Deteriorating liberation
At the regulation
Of our civilization
And leaving behind migration
For absolute separation

You see, my ba was deported
He was basically transported
Like a thing that's exported
And completely distorted
To something that's sordid

Even if he comported
For years, he was rewarded
Behaving like th'imported
But those dreams were thwarted
In being suddenly reported
So, WHO in this is being supported?

Because now he's there
And what I thought was fair
Seems more like a prayer
Or an act of despair
And I should just wear
Throw the load on and bear
This fucking nightmare
As if it was rare
For a person who was . . . Khmer
To fight for some air
In unending warfare
When you really could swear
That you just had been there
So, can somebody share
The location of nowhere?

BUT YO
This is getting too low
And I don't have the dough
To offer that flow
That's all about woe

The flow that I know
Is all about the glow—
UP in the show
Of lo and behold
That Kerouac biO-
Pic ON THE WHOA
Because I gotta go
Beyond what I know
Deep dive like Cousteau
In the depths of below

Khmer Kerouac on the scene
Caught in between
The gene and the teen
And trying to intervene
And sheen and clean
Or give some saline
Or find the vaccine
To understand sixteen

SOOO . . .
Get lean
Get keen
Get in that routine
Yo, it's already foreseen
Because
It's a—
KHMER SCENE.

CHAPTER 14
Crush Rut

"I said, 'Miss, are you ready?!'" With one hand holding a flailing wax paper and the other gesturing at the line behind me, the woman in the brown apron looked at me like she was ready to weaponize those donuts at any moment. I hadn't gotten my caffeine jump-start this morning yet (hence my presence at ye olde corporate donut shop), and the truth was, I was still daydreaming about the decision I'd made at the beginning of the week.

Had I really just submitted myself for the lit competition? And had I just done it by getting uncensored about our family's situation? Honestly, it felt pretty wicked to spill it—to put it out into the Universe—but there was still something that left me uneasy . . . off-balance. I'd finally gotten into my dad's story, but was it really mine to tell? Was this what it was like to be an actual artist? To be giddy and squeamish at the same time? I wasn't sure if I wanted to run through the streets or throw up through my face. Would either allow me the kind of release I was itching for in this adrenaline high? And what would it feel like if I actually made it to the final round? Was I even ready for that?

I pulled my headphones down. No, the woman with the frosty glare had zero interest in my pangs of buyer's remorse.

"Oh, sorry. Yeah." I tiptoed to look at the donut wall behind her. Sophat's previously proposed "rom-com makeover movie moment" had come, and this Saturday morning, we were going to go through all the boxes sent to our house to choose the kid's most perfect wedding attire. I knew this whole activity was going to require a full stomach, so I had to bring reinforcements. "I'll just take a dozen of whatever—"

"*Okay then.* Thank you for making me wait for you to decide on 'a dozen of whatever.'" This lady was not playing around. She swiftly turned her back to me and went to work, furiously drop-kicking donuts into the box like she was mad at these little bitch-pastries herself. Dang. Be mad at me, but those little sweeties. Save the sweeties! After I'd watched the heinous acts of donut terrorism, she tossed me the box and sent me on my way. I really considered apologizing, but I thought I'd better leave it alone.

As I turned to go, my back pocket buzzed. I waited till I was well out of the parking lot to check it. The distractions were getting me into enough trouble today as it was. When I got into the streets en route home, I checked to see who was still adding comments to my video . . .

BRITNEY (10:15 a.m.): I'm chalking it up to fear but like . . .

how long u gonna have me waiting for?

Face-plant.

Honestly, I had to give it to her. Even in Britney's private shaming, she was making me laugh . . . in that sad, self-deprecating, what-is-wrong-with-you kind of way. Something in her so effortlessly drawing attention to my fear made me feel like she knew what was up. It wasn't like she was immediately closing the door but rather trying to give me a boost of courage to get it together. Britney was sending me signals.

If it wasn't 100 percent clear, in the field of the romantics, I had zero ability. In fourth grade Eric Schaefer was so blond and blue-eyed I thought I should have a crush on him. You know, internalized colonization and stuff. Every time I saw him, I would slap him on his arm. It wasn't hard or anything, but I saw my ma do it my ba all the time. Apparently, that's something only Cambos do, show affection through "love pats." Then, later in middle school, when I had it hard for Rachel Chang, I bought her this Hong Kong egg custard tart at the market because I knew how much she liked sweets. How was I supposed to know they hadn't cooked the pastry all the way through and she *happened* to be allergic to raw egg? Was it really my fault she spent the rest of the night in the ER with an almost-fatal response to my innocent gesture? Was I just destined to almost bury people I was crushing on?

Like the love pats, I wish I could've blamed it all on heredi-tary reasons, but my parents had a disgustingly perfect origin story. They'd met as teenagers in the Angkor Dance Troupe way back when. It was near impossible to imagine Ba, a dude decked with tattoos, executing the same moves Sophat was now so gracefully performing. Ba told me Ma was the real dancer, though. She was the perfect Apsara, a dancing spirit that moved in service to the kings and the gods. Everyone followed her direction, including Ba, and that was how they sort of met. She helped him. He fell in love. The rest was history.

On the other side of it, I remember when Dahvy brought Ruben home to "officially" meet Ma and Ba two years ago. I mean, it was a joke, because the two had been on and off since high school. Even if they'd separated during most of Dahvy's time at grad school, Ruben had been a part of the family from the jump. Still, she wanted to have this one awkward dinner to reintroduce him to the family.

We were sitting through most of the night in this new-found mad silence, when finally Ba just shouted out, "Are you two getting married or what?!" We were relieved. Bless the dude for knowing how to break the tension. The lovebirds conceded that the whole setup was to announce their engagement, and from that point, the wedding planning had begun. I guess Dahvy proved that even if the love was easy, like ours for Ruben, people still find a way to complicate things more than they should.

I made my way back home from the donut shop with Blackpink's "Hard to Love" giving me a little energy in my questioning of the romantical arts. Through the kitchen window, I could see Dahvy reading something on her laptop, *always* on her laptop. That little machine captured her entire marital matrix, and it was obvious that despite whatever romantic shortcomings she herself possessed, Dahvy was going to master it all. If she could put work into where she lacked, maybe I could too. Maybe Dahvy would even have a suggestion for my writer's block. Maybe I could just ask her—

What was I saying? No thank you very much. I didn't need anyone to know I was in this crush rut, especially not her. I'd deal with it myself. Me and Blackpink.

Before stepping inside, I returned to Britney's message one last time. How much longer would she wait? Could I respond now and just move on with my day, my freaking life?

I knew . . .

I just . . .

had to . . .

text . . .

something . . .

The music changed to "Ready for Love."

Nope, I wasn't ready. Skip. (At least the Universe had a sense of humor.) No, there was too much going on in my life. I wanted to be right with my words, and I'd already exhausted all the good ones for the first round of the contest. I'd have to find more. My monster box would have to wait. I needed to get inside.

Through the window, I spotted a pile of boxes past the kitchen, near the base of the stairs to the second floor. They must have arrived just in time for Sophat's fashion show. Oh goody. If I could just slide through gracefully without being sucked into Dahvy's Wedding Company of Horrors or, at the very least, be asked any questions, I'd feel proud I'd accomplished anything today.

Solution: stay plugged in.

CHAPTER 15
Maid of Dishonor

"My *what*?" I shouted back while racing past Dahvy to the second floor and absolutely making zero eye contact whatsoever. I knew I had to keep moving. If I stopped for a second, she'd lasso me in. Get the packages and go.

In one swift move, Dahvy jumped ahead. I wasn't quick enough. At the base of the stairs, she turned back to me and stood her ground. I was caught. Sis looked annoyed as she tapped her ear aggressively.

"Your headphones!" Dahvy shouted loudly.

"Ohhh, my *headphones*! Are they bothering you or something?" I replied with an innocent expression stretched wide across my face. Of course they were bothering her, but maybe I could take her attention away from the boxes that were hanging out in my periphery. The last thing I needed right now was an inquisition about our loot.

"Why do all these boxes have your name on them? What've you been ordering?"

Ugh. Seriously caught. I looked toward my unblinking sister troll, who was ready for some answers. In emergency mode, I moved back into the kitchen to find any distraction that could help me out. If I was going to have to fess up about the boxes, I was going to have to fess up about sort of, kind of inviting Sophat to the wedding without her knowing. There was no way out of this one. I was going to have to find a way to gently drop the news.

My eyes suddenly caught sight of the glittery wrapped chocolates on the table. It appeared that Dahvy had pivoted from the computer to making gifts for the guests. Maybe I could soften the admission with a little help, and then she wouldn't go completely nuclear.

"You need an assist?" I pulled my headphones down and slowly meandered back toward the table. I still had a little time before Sophat was arriving, and I did not want the boob to reveal himself. It would be better coming from me. Maybe. "Want a donut?"

"These are for me?" Dahvy looked at the box of sweeties as if they were poisoned or something.

"Of course. I mean, don't get greedy. But for my sis, anything!"

"Okaaay." Dahvy remained skeptical. Maybe this wasn't my best performance. I could've used a little more subtlety here, but I needed to find a way to get the truth out before Sophat's arrival.

"So, how do I do this? Are there some sort of obsessive instructions on your trusty computer here?" I inquired while sliding Dahvy's laptop toward me. Apparently, that was the wrong move, because she quickly pulled the computer back with the furrowest of brows. I was getting the feeling she was hiding something too.

"Just put a couple of the chocolates in this cloth, wrap it, and then tie it with a ribbon. But don't make it look ugly." With those oh-so-pleasant instructions, Dahvy pushed the materials toward me. She watched closely while I attempted my first go. My hands moved quickly to show her my first result.

"Like this?"

"A little looser, but yeah, that's the idea." Dahvy was staring me down like a hawk. She knew something was up, and maybe my present cooperation was coming off as a little much.

"These gifts are really cute! I think your friends are gonna love them!"

"Soma, can you not be weird, please? I don't need that. What I do need is for you to not get wild on Ma's online shopping account with your orders. We're not exactly pulling in the dough right now." The irony of her telling me to chill out on Ma's account when we were surrounded by *all* her wedding purchases. "What's in all those boxes anyways?"

Ruh-ro. The jig was up. The moment of truth had come.

"Funny you should ask . . ."

"Is it funny?"

"Well, you see . . . those boxes are clothes."

"All of them?"

"Yes, but—"

"Spit it out."

"Some of them maybe belong to Sophat. . . ." Maybe if I got quieter, I could disappear altogether.

"Why?" Dahvy's hands stopped moving. You could already see the steam readying to exit her ears. Prepare for combustion.

"Because I sorta invited him to your wedding."

"SOMA!" Dahvy stood up from her chair. She looked like she was going to morph into that Bridezilla Pokémon I was becoming familiar with. I mean, I knew I invited Sophat without telling her, but did it really deserve this mythological reaction?

"Come on. I don't know why he wasn't on the list to begin with."

"Because we have to pay for everyone to eat."

"We'll bring our own food."

"You are *not* bringing in your own food."

"He's like the one thing I'm asking for in this whole thing." It was true! Through all this planning, it wasn't like Dahvy asked me once, not once, if I wanted to have some company at the party. Everyone got a say except me, so how was that fair? "Ma ordered those extra tables anyways. Why can't we just leave one seat for Sophat?"

"Even if Ma did that, I still had to not invite people that I wanted to be there too. Those tables are for Ma's friends or whoever is going to crash. And besides, I may need you to stay more focused to help me out on the day—"

"Why?"

"Because, damn it, you're my maid of honor, and I need you to pick up the slack!" Now I was in for it. This tone was hitting new heights. Up to this point, I knew Dahvy's two bridesmaids had been superbly unhelpful. Her snobby high school friend Botum Lim lived nearby in Andover but couldn't seem to get away from all her yoga classes or her kid's piano lessons to assist. Her college friend Rachael Ahmad was wanderlusting all over the world and barely got the news that Dahvy was getting married, let alone asking her to be a bridesmaid. She messaged Dahvy, letting her know she'd be in town only a day before. So, look: I got it.

"Ma's flight is delayed. She's not coming back tomorrow. She'll be back the Thursday before the wedding." Dahvy's voice was simple, cold, and a little bit sad. "I just found out a second ago."

Well, that news slowed me down.

"Why? Ba need her to be there longer for something?"

"I guess so, Soma, but she wouldn't get into the details about it."

"But she said she'd be here for the—"

"I don't know, Soma. If you're so interested, why don't you ask Ba? He's the reason, right? Seems like the two of you have been missing each other."

Dang it. Now Dahvy was triple-pissed. She was reeling from Sophat's unapproved invitation, Ma's update, and me ghosting Ba. This was not the direction in which I intended this morning to go.

I stared back at Dahvy. If you got past her pure seething, she looked a little vulnerable. Her forehead blood vessel was flexing and ready to pop. I knew what it felt like for me to hear the news that Ma would be out there longer: it sucked. So, of course it would suck a thousand times over for the bride who was in desperate need of keeping everything in control. I was her bridesmaid and her backup, and that was it. I knew I needed to step up. I had to get creative.

"I'm sorry, I'll help. Sophat can too. I mean, what about the DJ stuff? I know we were joking about it before, but the kid's got his own setup and everything. Sure, you have that band for the Khmer music, but who's going to announce the cutting of the cake, when the dancing starts, or even the wedding party speeches? You know Sophat's got presence—"

"Oh, he's got *presence*—"

"But he could be a great emcee for the reception, and he doesn't even need a seat at the table. Sophat can eat at his DJ booth."

"I don't know, Soma. That sounds a little weird."

"Don't you want to dance with Ruben? Not to some loud, high-pitched Khmer song about catching fish, but a song that you two actually like? I'm sorry I didn't ask you first, but we can help you. I can help you." I looked right into Dahvy's buggy eyes and pleaded my case in the simplest way possible: by begging. It was then I noticed that her eyes weren't so buggy after all, but . . . a little red. As if she had been crying. She looked tired. Something about her bloodshot pair sent a chill through me. I don't know why, but I could feel my eyes start to sting. I turned away, and the moment was over before it had even begun.

A silence hung in the air. I waited for the verdict.

"Yes, he can come," Dahvy whispered hoarsely. Her eyes and fingers returned to the laptop, as if it was back to wedding business as usual. "But we'll have to talk about the DJ thing."

"Thank you."

"And we're not paying for all these clothes."

"We're gonna try on stuff and return what we don't like." I checked my phone.

Sophat was on his way.

"And now, you *have* to promise me that you'll go to the boutique with me tomorrow to try on your outfit. I don't care if Ma was your protector against the evils of Ming Ani, but we cannot wait for her late arrival, okay? I'll do my best to make sure she doesn't make you feel like a horrible, ugly monster." The moment had seriously passed. Dahvy's eyes stayed glued to the laptop, as she returned to doling out orders like the queen of Cambodia.

For as bummed as I was that Ma wouldn't be there to play pass interference between the ladies, I knew the dear bride wasn't going to let me wait until two days before the wedding to make sure the thing fit. Whatever picture-perfect bridal moment of the Kear girls Dahvy was imagining wasn't possible now. We each had to compromise where we could.

"Yeah, okay." My hands moved quicker as I tried to finish

a few more presents before Sophat's arrival. While I honestly wanted to get more answers about what was delaying Ma, I had to drop it. We were on a roll of sucky updates, and it was probably best to show Dahvy I could be that backup.

I looked over the completed presents, perfectly wrapped and ready to be placed on each of the wedding tables. There were a lot, and Dahvy had done most of them by herself. Ma would be back eventually, but now it barely made a difference. The truth was, with each day she wasn't here, it mattered less and less. The wedding was moving along without her, and she'd get here when she got here. It was my job now. There were programs to make, trays of the groom's dowry to assemble, flower arrangements to handle, and then some. I glanced over at Dahvy scrolling through her laptop, her face becoming whiter every second.

"Hey, so, Mr. Drakos talked to me the other day—" Dahvy's voice was strained as her eyes stayed locked on her screen.

Straight from left field. I shouldn't have deleted that email from Mr. Drakos. I knew it would inevitably get back to her.

"I was only looking up a word on my phone," I deflected, hoping that we could reroute this conversation quickly.

"What?"

"I wanted to know what the difference was between 'irregardless' and 'regardless.' He uses them interchangeably all the time, and it drives me out of town. Use one, man!" Was she baited?

Dahvy looked back at me like she was in odd agreement, but that wasn't the topic at hand. Nope.

"*Regardless*, you should put your phone away, but no, that's not what I'm talking about."

"Then what is it?" I could feel that steam again, but this time building in my own ears.

"It was about an essay you wrote." Dahvy looked directly at me, like we were past the point of no return.

"Yeah, I got essays." I'd said this to Ruben earlier when he asked, and I liked the ring of it. I was seriously thinking of putting it on a T-shirt.

"About immigration reform, right?"

I nodded. Dahvy's eyes returned to the computer. She scrolled up.

"'Clinton doesn't know shit. Bush doesn't know shit. Obama doesn't know shit. What's His Ugly Orange Face doesn't know shit. The new old one doesn't know shit. The Chinese Exclusion Act, the Palmer Raids, the Mexican Repatriation, Operation Wetback, Illegal Immigration Reform and Immigrant Responsibility Act, Homeland Security Act, Cambodian Repatriation Act. Why do we have to be surprised by the legacy of deporting some brown people in this country? Why do we have to be surprised by keeping kids in cages? Why do we have to be surprised by kids being separated from their parents? Why do we have to be surprised by kids dying in custody? It's all legalized shit. And I'm tired of having to write polite essays explaining why white people do awful things. I'm tired of writing essays about how those awful things become laws. I'm tired AF of writing essays that make it seem like everything is long-ago history, as if people aren't history. I don't want to write any more of your white people essays.'"

Dahvy returned her gaze to me, to see if I had any reaction. I just stared back, trying to gauge where she was at. It was funny. Hearing it back now sort of made me feel proud. Maybe it was kind of a lot, but my thesis was clear, it had a freaking pulse, and it was getting a rise out of people. Wasn't that what good writing was supposed to do?

"Drakos sent it to you?" I asked, breaking the silence.

"Ruben via Drakos—"

What? Okay, now I was pissed. Ruben was supposed to be my mole, my accomplice in all my mad dealings with Dahvy. How could he betray me like that?

"Why's Ruben sending it to you?"

"Because he cares about you."

"So, what is this? You, Ruben, and Drakos all conspiring against me?" There was something about people talking behind my back that was starting to get me hot and humming. Like they were building consensus about whatever emotions I was expressing. As if the emotions were the problem—that I was a problem. I could feel my face start to flush and my hands ball up. My muscles began to tighten. My body was telling me it was time to go. I got up from the table and began to move toward the stairs.

"No, Soma. It's just, I wanna talk to you about this."

"What's there to talk about? My thoughts were pretty clear."

"They are, but it's also an essay you turned in, so there's a way to write your feelings within a form, you know?"

"I was pissed off."

"Yeah, but you can't just tell your teacher to 'Fuck off, I'm not writing any more of your essays.' Drakos gave you an F for this. He thought you were being insubordinate."

"It's one essay."

"Okay, but just because Ma and Ba aren't here doesn't mean you can start going off."

It was beginning to feel like that was her last-resort ammo: bring up Ma and Ba when she wanted to guilt me for not behaving like a perfect student, a perfect sister, a perfect anything.

I gripped the donut box and began to make my way up the stairs.

"You can't just leave whenever I bring them up. Seriously, what is going on with you? If you want to talk about Ba, let's talk!"

"With you? Hell no."

"I know you've been avoiding him, and I can understand the impulse, but we have to figure this out as a family. You can't do this by yourself."

"I'm going to my room!"

"I'm trying to have a conversation with you, Soma!"

"Why don't you talk to yourself about your crazy sister! You already been doing it—"

Leaving Dahvy in the debris of her wedding nightmare and her unresolved bull, I ran upstairs, my feet feeling like they were on fire. I couldn't get up there quick enough. When I got past the door, I turned to slam it as hard as I could. The sound reverberated throughout the house. I wanted her to know how angry I was, how much her unfounded accusations left me wrecked. The door couldn't be heavy or strong enough.

I threw myself on the bed, and I closed my eyes. Darkness again.

Dahvy made me feel like my words in my essay were violent, inappropriate, too hot. Crazy. I felt confused, like how was I supposed to know how far I could go in my writing? Everyone else seemed to understand how to modify their thoughts to the right situation, but me . . . every expression I put out there was catching fire. I didn't know the results of my submission quite yet, but maybe it was best if I didn't move on to the next round, after all. Maybe it was best if I never spoke again. Maybe I should just shut the hell up.

We have to figure this out as a family.

What family? One where the dad wasn't even here, where the mom was disappearing more every day, where a sister was stomping around like a dictator, making the other one feel too crazy to handle? No, maybe there wasn't anything to figure out. This family was broken.

CHAPTER 16
A Rom-Com Mome

From head to toe, Sophat was decked out in full tie-dye: suit, shirt, and beanie. He walked down our makeshift runway, pivoted like *anyone* was watching, and then returned to the bathroom door to make his case.

"I'm getting a lot of tie-dye," Sophat pronounced while locked in his over-the-shoulder pouty smolder. I looked up briefly from my phone.

"Yeah, man." I was happy to confirm his fashion delusion.

"Is there such a thing as *too much* tie-dye?"

"Yeah, man."

"But what if—"

"Yeah . . . no, man." We had already been at it for forty-five minutes, and Sophat had dismissed the *fourteen* outfits before this one. I was feeling some serious fashion fatigue, and more importantly, I was preoccupied by what I was going to message Britney. I knew that after her message this morning, time was ticking. My window of opportunity was quickly closing, and after the all-out brawl I had with Dahvy, I was determined to do something for me. Something that would make me feel like I was in control of the situation that was my life.

I was drafting the message when I realized it'd been a minute since I had heard the swishing of fabrics and plastic bags. I looked up again, and Sophat was there—a foot away from my face, looking all twisted in knots.

"I'm sorry—"

"You're no help, Soma! You're all up in your phone like it's telling you the answers to life. I need your fashion instincts—"

"I don't have any fashion instincts!"

"Well, develop them! With me!"

"I'm sorry. My fight with my sister left me vibrating."

"But that still doesn't answer why you're all up in your phone. Are you texting her? Because you could just pull up your big-girl pants, roll downstairs, and handle it so we can return to the matter at hand: *me*."

"No, but . . ." I paused, wondering if I could really get into it with Sophat. I knew if he was privy to what was transpiring between Britney and me, he would run—no, *fly* away with it.

Sophat batted his gorgeous little lashes at me. The kid was my Number One. I had to share.

"Britney and I might be going on a date—"

"What the WHAT—"

"But it isn't set up yet, and I have to message her soon—"

"What the *freaking* what?" In a matter of seconds, Sophat's supreme annoyance did a 360 wheelie like he hadn't even been pissed to begin with.

"So, like . . . what do I say?" I asked earnestly, looking for any kind of intel on the romantic front.

"First of all, totally offended you didn't tell me sooner. Secondly, I've been waiting for this moment my entire life, to see you jump out of the nest to find love. I'm so turned on by this conversation! And third, just say: 'Boo, let's boop.'" Sophat rested his list like that was it. Like that was the way to secure love. Like that was the way to Britney's unattainable heart. I remained unsure.

"I don't know what you say to your boys—"

"I would never—"

"But Britney is like classy."

"So, be like: 'Hey, classy lady. I know some Cambodian spots . . . being that I am Cambodian.'"

"Like she doesn't know a Cambodian in this town?"

"Take her to Mill No. 5. I mean, you got everything there—"

It was true. Not only did Mill No. 5 have a coffee shop, a record shop, a thrift shop, and whatever shop, it was also where Britney and I had first formally met. Maybe we could cement it as our place.

But no, it didn't feel right. And having people all around us while I was sweating was not something I wanted to pursue.

"I don't know, though. . . ."

"Soma, I can't do all the work for you, sis. I got my own stuff to think about—"

"OKAY. I'm sorry." I knew that I had been dragging him through my emotional mess. I was being indecisive and all over the place. It wasn't his fault. I needed to pet the pup. "By the way, you look perfect in your matching tie-dye. . . ."

One compliment activated his glow.

"Thank you. Now take a pic." Sophat had reengaged.

I obliged. He smized.

"And show me, please."

I was happy to relinquish the clutch on my monster box. Sophat, on the other hand, seemed downright displeased.

"Nope." And with that he marched over to the bathroom to change. On to the next one. How was there even a next one?!

"You know, my ba has some vintage stuff from the nineties still in his closet. We could go through that." Maybe that would relax Sophat's need to send a bunch more boxes over to the house. I didn't need Dahvy getting pissed all over again. "Bro? You think you can go retro?"

"Sorry, yeah. Just completely distracted by this ensemble. You're gonna bug! But yeah, totally down to go to retro town." Sophat's voice boomed through the closed bathroom door. From his reaction on the other side, it seemed this outfit might be more pleasing than the last. Maybe the search was over. I threw myself back onto the bed and returned to my digital courtship.

"Look, I think the important thing about your first date is that you feel comfortable. That you feel in your feet, in your body. In my limited expertise with love, there is so much you can't control. What the person thinks of you. How you'll feel in the situation. Whether or not you two will connect in that way. I mean, I'm sure you got that electric shock, from what I've seen—"

"Dude—"

"The point is, you can't control many things, but you can control where you're at. Where you feel most comfortable. Choose a place where you can really be yourself."

The door flung open, and there in the frame, my dear friend was on fire. Literally. Sophat stood there in a black suit entirely bedazzled in flames. What in the fresh hell was this look?

"You look . . . hot," I tried.

"I was hoping that flames would be more artistic."

"Oh, they are."

The model did a couple of turns. I looked at my revolving rotisserie of a friend and felt grateful he had once again offered me a bit of advice that made total sense. I had an idea of where we would go, but I'd never really been there with another person before. I guess I would have to try out my luck.

"Do you need to stop, drop, and roll?!"

"SOMA! Tell me the truth. What does it look like?!"

"I think you're really hot in your flaming-hot suit, you hot flamer, you." Honestly, the look grew on me.

With his sound advice, I figured it might be good to offer back some good news to the kid.

"By the way . . . I signed up for the lit competition—"

"Yes, yes, yes you did!" Sophat jumped onto the bed and

landed in the most obnoxious pose—right up in my face, like he was waiting to hear more.

"See, this is why I shouldn't have told you, because you're acting all foolish now."

"That is exactly why you should have told me, you best friend, you. Because now, I'm your marketing, media, branding team all in one. We about to blow you up."

"Please don't blow me up. And besides, I may not even make it to the finals, and then none of it will have mattered to begin with."

"Soma. You will make finals. But in some alternative universe in which you don't, then it will still have meant something. *So*, what's with the change of heart?"

"I'm on a roll, bro. Let's see where the dice land." I offered some cool reasoning, but inside I knew I was all tangled up. Electricity shot through the wires. I'd said it aloud, so I guessed there was no turning back. Sophat's face lit up like it was freaking Christmas.

"And all you need to do is write a poem, right?"

"I already submitted a poem for prelims. If I make finals, I'll perform another."

"And you've been working on that one already *because* you're gonna make it?"

Sometimes I really wish I had Sophat's confidence about these things. Maybe I was going to make it or maybe I wasn't, but something about writing out a finals poem felt like I was tempting fate. Like when actors write out acceptance speeches for awards. You know there are plenty of people going home without a Grammy but with a sad index card of people they'll never get to thank. I mean, the competition was in only two weeks, so I had begun to write it out, but I was definitely moving slowly and slyly, hoping to be unseen by the fates.

"I've started . . . ," I assured him tentatively.

"Well, share what you got!" I knew Sophat would be like this. He'd been the one to present the idea to me, to follow up with my anxieties, and now, it was clear that he was going to be a passenger on the road trip. There would be no pee breaks. The destination was set to the Jack Kerouac Lit Competition Finals.

"W-we're actually doing this?" I stammered.

"Pull out that phone, Kween!" Sophat didn't give me a chance to get precious.

Kween. There was something about the way Sophat said it that stopped me in my sneaks.

Kween. It was history. It was born from Black and brown gay icons of the ballroom scene, like Crystal LaBeija, who was brave enough to shout, "I have a right to show my color, darling!" I wondered if a yellow-brown girl with some love jumping through her veins could inherit this kind of legacy.

Kween. It'd been tossed around enough in gay pop culture without reverence for its rituals. Could I take on the moniker if it still made me somewhat uncomfortable?

Kween. But then there was the first. Queen Soma. Imagined to be the first monarch of Cambodia. Bare-chested, this warrior goddess who put Xena the Warrior Princess to shame. Though I seriously praised Xena and all those lesbian antics . . . Queen Soma was *my* first ancestor.

Kween. Was it my cross to bear, my crown to wear?

I pulled up my phone and tapped my notes, where I kept most of my rhymes. The competition would be held in front of a live audience. If I wanted to throw it down, I couldn't do it by myself. I needed to start somewhere.

"Okay, it's obviously just a start, but I'm working on it. . . ."

"Oh, shut it. And drop it, please." Sophat was still wearing that ridic suit bedecked in flames. He continued to look like a chicken rolling around on a stake. It was hard to take him seriously, but the whole sight of him actually quieted my nerves. For a second, I'd forgotten all about the extreme highs and lows of the day. I wasn't thinking about my sister battle with Dahvy. I wasn't thinking about my ma or ba. My inner thoughts were focused on something for me. And only me. My words.

I cleared my throat and began:

> Khmer Kween in ya lane
> Trying to investigate this brain
> Not trying to complain
> But master the reign
> Of this godawful pain
> That won't wane
> But continues to strain

Makin' me insane
By leavin' a stain
That's hard to explain
And oh so arcane—

You see
This godawful pain
Is not what I gained
It's what I've maintained
And I can't even feign
That it's simply ingrained
In my brain
And my veins
Like a ball and a chain
Constraining
Containing
Migraining
Maintaining . . .

The sadness that you've inherited and you cannot get rid of because it's so deep in your DNA that sometimes you wonder if your current family situation is broken because of that karmic and scientific luck and your parents are just going to move to Cambodia forever and you'll be forced to stay with your sister who hates you and then your broken family will turn you yourself into a broken person and then literally all will be broken so like . . . why does anyone even try?

A silence sat in the room, as the roasted chicken looked back at me with a pair of confused eyes.

"I was into most of it, but the ending . . ."

"Yeah, I gotta work on that."

Maybe I needed a little more work before my coronation.

CHAPTER 17

One Sneak In, One Sneak Out

SOMA (11:11 a.m.):	Sup.
BRITNEY (11:14 a.m.):	Wowww. I was beginning to think you were never going to message me, but . . . strong opening. Sup.
SOMA (11:14 a.m.):	Yeah . . . I know . . . but I did!
BRITNEY (11:15 a.m.):	You did, and so . . .
SOMA (11:16 a.m.):	And so . . .
BRITNEY (11:16 a.m.):	. . .
SOMA (11:16 a.m.):	. . .
BRITNEY (11:16 a.m.):	. . .
SOMA (11:17 a.m.):	So . . . sup? You free tonight? Maybs 8?
BRITNEY (11:17 a.m.):	Ha. Got a place in mind?
SOMA (11:18 a.m.):	Thinking Kerouac Park . . .
BRITNEY (11:19 a.m.):	That old junkyard?

SOMA (11:22 a.m.):	I mean . . . we can go anywhere! It doesn't have to be there if that's weird! Seriously, I'm like good for anything and everything! Whatever you want to do, that's what I'm about! I'm flexi! FLEXI FOR REAL!
BRITNEY (11:23 a.m.):	OMG. I kid. I'll see you there at 8.
SOMA (11:25 a.m.):	Cool cool! See you!
BRITNEY (11:25 a.m.):	!!!
SOMA (11:26 a.m.):	EXCLAMATION POINTS!
BRITNEY (11:26 a.m.):	. . .

I began to breathe again. Blood was beginning to rush back to my body, and my head felt suddenly hot. Like for this tectonic plate-shifting convo, my body just dropped dead as some survival stunt, and upon completion of asking my dream girl out, I was resurrected again to check the results.

Dang. It worked.

I'd finally messaged Britney like she asked me to do, and she responded. Like within seconds. We had an *entire* text message conversation with a little bit of volley, a little bit of game, dare I say . . . a little bit of flirting?

Dang. It really worked.

Sophat recommended that I take her to a place that meant something to me, and there was only one real answer: my spot, Jack Kerouac Park. What we would do there I had zero idea about, but I'd figure that out later. One step at a time.

Dang. It freaking worked!

I went to examine the conversation again when my monster box slipped from my fat fingers onto the ground. It didn't matter much. Nothing could bring me down from this high I was feeling. I was about to go on my first date. Tonight. Maybe things weren't going so bad after all.

"Chagh. Chagh. Mm-hmm. Chagh. Chagh. Chagh. Chagh—" Maybe . . .

Dahvy's voice trailed in from the hallway connecting the dressing room to the front area of the bridal boutique. Even if we were pissed at each other, this weekend, I couldn't escape my fate of playing fashion runway. There was a door to the hallway, and Dahvy could've easily knocked on it, but it seemed like her phone call was keeping her distracted. We hadn't talked the entire ride here, and it seemed like we weren't going to get much further now. As she swept into the back dressing room, it became apparent she was fielding some kind of situation. I mean, with weeks leading up to the wedding, they were all "situations," but this one seemed to drone on and on. It was best not to interfere.

I attempted to retrieve my phone, when I quickly realized that Cambodian outfits were not meant to bend in. Or move in. Or breathe in at all. It was tight and itchy, and if you moved too quickly in one direction, one tucked end would come undone and unravel the whole wedding uniform. I thought I'd better get used to staying as still as possible if I didn't want to accidentally moon anyone on the day of the ceremony. Yeah, that would be another kind of situation.

I abandoned the phone on the ground and looked up at the

reason why we were here to begin with. There, reflected across the way in the floor-length trifold dressing room mirror, was Yours Truly decked out in a bedazzled blouse and a sampot jong gk'bun that rivaled the pants of MC Hammer. Thanks be to Ma and Ba for more of my early musical education and, honestly, fashion. For as spacious as the pant legs were, the whole thing was held up together by some tucked-in fabric, safety pins, and a wish. When MC Hammer said, "You can't touch this," he meant it literally. You can't touch these pants . . . or they'll fall down.

The clothing pieces were the same as Dahvy's, but that was about where the similarities ended. For one, I refused to wear that bubble-gum pink. I suggested black, but apparently funerary vibes were not welcome at a wedding. We settled on yellow. And secondly, while Dahvy looked like a perfect Disney princess, I looked like her quirky, short sidekick.

Generally speaking, I didn't give much energy to appearances, but there was something about being forced into this wedding uniform that made me realize how different Dahvy and I looked. Rift or not, I had to admit she wasn't just the ideal Cambodian bride, but the ideal sister and daughter who took care of everything. The one who my parents entrusted to look after me. I was the one people were always worried about, who didn't fit the outfit exactly right. The top was too tight.

"Chagh. Chagh. Chagh. Chagh . . ." From the reflection, I could see behind me Dahvy's head bobbing up and down with every "yes." The chorus of "chaghs" meant she was talking to some older man with zero awareness that a conversation was between two people, not one. Unfortunately, in female Khmer tradition (regardless of how problematic it was), you ultimately just had to *chagh it out* until the old man got tired. They would eventually. They always did.

"Chagh. Chagh. Chagh. Chagh Mm-hmm. Okay, then. Agkhun." Dahvy looked down at her phone as she ended the call. "Motherf—"

"Did that go well—"

"*Oh my God, you're there!*" Dahvy jumped back like she'd never talked to a person before, launching her phone straight onto the ground too. It'd become obvious that Dahvy's bridezilla energy was morphing into raw panic. The girl needed to lay off those double lattes she'd been chugging for the last week. "You scared me. I didn't see you. . . ."

"Well, I'm trying this on like you asked me to."

"Yeah, sorry. It's just the achaa."

"So, it's still all good?"

"With the achaa, yes. Lots of instructions and things I didn't understand. Wish I had someone to help me translate some of the seriously ancient ideas he's trying to convey."

If Ma had been here, she would have been able to decipher what the achaa was saying. Hell, if Ma had been here, Ming Ani wouldn't be sharpening her pins in the front, waiting to return with her scrutiny. If Ma had been here like she said she would, neither Dahvy nor I would be searching so desperately for what to say next.

"How's the fit?" Dahvy asked, while kneeling down to grab her phone.

"Ooh, can you get mine too?"

As she returned the phone to my grasp, I suddenly felt her grip remain. I pulled away, but she held on, staring me down with her expanding eyes like they were dilated or something. Was my look wrecking her? Maybe Medusa had no game compared to whatever scary vibes I was putting out in this yellow MC Hammer getup.

"Oh my God," Dahvy whispered.

"What?" Was I too monstrous to look at?

"My goodness, Soma. You look gorgeous."

All at once, I felt even more agitated. The dressing room lights were burning against my skin. I could feel the scratchy fabric claw at my body. I don't know what it was about Dahvy's words—I guess I should have been flattered—but in the moment, it felt . . . wrong. No, Dahvy was the one I trusted to tell me the truth, no matter how brutal it was. Once I tried to bleach my own hair, and while everyone else was trying not to knock down my already low self-confidence by telling me sweet lies, Dahvy took one look and said, "That's the ugliest thing I've ever seen." I honestly loved it! Now the worst had happened. Dahvy was feeling sorry for me, just like the others.

"*Okay*, time to take this off," I pronounced.

"Wait a second, Soma. I need to pin some things for Ming Ani to adjust." Before I could even protest, Dahvy grabbed the box of pins sitting on the chair next to the mirror and began pulling at the fabric of the pants. "The more I do, the less she will. I promise I'll be stern with Ming. I'll make sure she does what we ask her."

While I was still feeling heated from her initial reaction, Dahvy was working. Her focus had shifted as quickly as it had previously turned to me. Apparently the Kear girls didn't do well with this kind of intimacy. We were just some awkward girls trying on some awkward dresses.

"Don't stab me, though. . . ."

"She's got jokes."

"Seriously. Don't."

"The pants look good, but how about the top? How does it feel?"

"It's a little tight."

"It's kind of supposed to be that way."

"Am I supposed to not be able to move my arms?" I barely lifted my limbs before the whole shirt rose with the rest of my upper body, making it look like my bobblehead was drowning in the lacy blouse.

"We can loosen it up around the arms a bit."

"Thank you."

"Ooh, I forgot about this. . . ." Hanging from Dahvy's neck was a gold plastic beaded belt that was supposed to give the illusion of holding the pants together. She pulled the belt around my waist and clipped it into place. It might have been purely ornamental, but there was something about it that gave it a nice final touch. "Oh, and these!"

Dahvy pulled a pair of chunky gold bracelets off her wrists and transferred them onto mine. To be clear, on the regular I wouldn't be caught dead in all the formal bling, but for the wedding of my controlling only sister, I figured it wasn't worth the fight. Much to my surprise, the loud-ass bangles fit perfectly with the vibe. I returned to face the mirror to survey the damage. I was sure I would look like some scary, coming-of-age lesbian nightmare in a Halloween costume, but honestly . . . I looked all right.

From behind, Dahvy looked on in the mirror too. A pause fell between us. We caught eyes for a second, and then broke away. Dahvy returned to adjusting the belt, pulling it left and then right, and then . . . left, and then . . . right . . . it was pretty clear she was just fussing, but neither of us knew how to break the ice.

"Where's Ruben?" I asked, knowing he couldn't have been too far getting into some kind of trouble.

"Out front, yapping to Ming Ani about what bling he wants." Dahvy sounded both annoyed and unbothered by Ruben's antics.

"Does he know it's not like a choose-your-own-adventure kind of thing?"

"Do you think that would stop him from trying?" A smile broke out on Dahvy's face. Ruben always seemed to have that effect on her. He was the only one who did.

A silence fell again, as Dahvy returned to adjusting the pants. It was clear that only I could save us from this awkward cold war, and who knew what other surprises were in store for these intended nuptials? Maybe it was worth it to yield a bit.

"I'm sorry about walking out on you." Our eyes locked. I meant it. It wasn't my fault I got that temper from Ba, but maybe it was my fault for not trying harder.

Dahvy looked back at me, almost startled at my admission.

"I should've come in less hot. Ruben shouldn't have gotten involved. Drakos should've come right to you," Dahvy replied, finally affirming that the annoying game of telephone was uncalled-for. That being said, what she was saying wasn't altogether true. If we were really doing this, I knew I needed to fess up too. No edit.

"Yeah, well . . . Drakos sort of did come to me. He wanted me to talk to you. I just didn't know how."

"He seemed concerned. I mean, even more than he usually is."

"I'm not crazy. I just . . . needed to express it." I finally resigned myself to telling Dahvy how I actually felt.

"I get that, Soma. I really do. I personally wish I had some kind of assignment or essay where I could get some stuff out too. Ba leaving, Ma being gone, changing her flight, this wedding . . . it's a lot, right? I know how stressed I am. I can only imagine how you feel."

"Yeah. It's a lot." I was thankful Dahvy was, maybe for the first time, just acknowledging it instead of always whizzing past it or bringing it up in a passive-aggressive way because she was frustrated or whatever. She was recognizing this whole thing had been A LOT, and it wasn't just mine to bear.

And there was something else. She was even imagining that my stress might be worse than hers. Not that I'd ever intend to compare grief—I knew we each had our own unique grab bag of, well, shit—but now we were both sharing a diagnosis: total heartbreak.

"I saw you signed up for the lit contest." I knew she was going to find out one way or the other.

"Ruben tell you?"

"I promise that'll be the last snooping we do. I think it'll be good for you."

The clothes started to itch again. It seemed like the right time to change back into my own threads. I stepped into the curtained area and pulled the fabric between us. Even if Dahvy was being understanding about the competition, I was kind of embarrassed. I wasn't exactly shouting my entry from the rooftops. I was nervous.

"You need help in there?" Dahvy asked.

"I'm good." I needed a little privacy to process.

It was possible I could not advance to the finals. And if I did, would I get my second poem written in time? I had thought about just pulling out some old rhymes, but something inside was telling me it needed to be new. To capture this moment. Of where I was exactly. But was I spooking myself? Was I staring down the fates before I even knew if I would get the chance to speak my truth?

"Please don't get weird about it like Sophat," I instructed Dahvy sternly. I wasn't about to have everyone adding heat to the situation.

"He bugging you?" Her voice sounded honest and curious. Even through the curtain, I could tell she was trying to be helpful.

"He's just hell-bent on making me a celebrity or something."

"I mean, you got that kind of energy."

"What?"

"I know I give you a hard time, but . . . you have a way about you. Like a power. Do what you did in your video, and you'll be fine."

"You saw that?" Barely back in my clothes, I yanked the curtain to one side to address sis, who apparently knew more about my activities than I had anticipated.

"I'm on the socials! I got my eyes on everything and everyone." Dahvy looked proud of her admission, even if I felt dazed about the discovery. I could feel the blood rushing to my face again. It was becoming obvious that my body wasn't made to accept feedback. Like a gnarly allergic reaction, I could feel a hum move across my body. This was really embarrassing.

"And you weren't wrong in your essay," Dahvy said, looking directly in my eyes. "Do *not* tell Drakos this, but after I thought about it for a bit . . . I realized I was kind of proud of you. For your honesty."

I couldn't believe it. The Bridezilla Pokémon had devolved into just . . . my sister. She was taking my side. I don't know what it was about her affirmation, but suddenly it opened up a channel in me that finally made me feel seen.

"*Thank you*. It's like all semester Drakos has been saying it's not theoretical. It's living. It's about human dignity. And I'm

like, what? You don't want me to get a little personal? And I
know you're gonna say I was being insubordinate, but I really
did follow the directions. I did the assignment! I thought I was
being subversive in my conclusion! *God*, that feels good to say!"

Dahvy just stood there stunned, taking in my verbal diarrhea.
After a moment, she blinked and offered a thought.

"It's good that you went there. I mean, when I was your age,
I never believed I could speak that way to a teacher or any adult.
I admire it. Your personalization is what makes your writing
special. One bit of advice that I would offer . . . if you're willing
to hear it . . ."

"I'm willing if it's good."

"When you're up at that podium—"

"I don't even know if I'll get that chance—"

"*When you're up at that podium*, find confidence in your audience. It's one thing to go personal; it's another to have enough
humility to know there might be someone out there who knows
what you're going through. Feel the connection. You're not
alone in this."

I didn't want anyone to think I was some self-serving nar-
cissist who had no perspective, but up to this point, honestly,
yeah . . . I felt kind of alone. And maybe because I was dealing
with it inside myself, it became easier to feel like no one else
understood. But I was learning that with any kind of writing,
with any kind of art . . . a major part of the experience was the
sharing of it. Sharing it so neither the author nor the audience
had to feel so singular. That was what I'd felt when I watched

Monica Sok's poem online. There was an immediate understanding. And I didn't feel like she was being self-serving. No,
it actually felt like the opposite. It was a gift. Dahvy was now
asking me to look out in the audience for connection, and if I
got the opportunity, maybe I could offer a gift too.

It was funny. When Sophat first told me to find the point
of it all, I had thought about connection. And now Dahvy was
saying the same. Maybe we continue to return to the answers
that have always been there . . . if we look hard enough.

"So, if you make finals, you want me to film the contest or
what?"

"Roll over and die." I was trying to be subtle.

"Sorry, I just don't know how you feel. Could you be clearer
about what you want?" Dahvy reached for the clothes draped
over my arms and smiled back. "Thank you for trying these on.
And thank you for hanging in there with me."

"You're welcome." I dropped my gaze, unsure of how to
take this all in. Before today, we weren't talking, and now she
was thanking me for things? I don't know what it was, but
anytime something felt good, it was followed by something
bad. I couldn't stay locked into this moment for too long. One
sneak in, one sneak out.

"Knock, knock." Saved by the Ruben again. "Am I
allowed in?"

"She's already changed," Dahvy shouted back.

"I wouldn't want to see the spirits again." Ruben shielded
his eyes as he'd done before, but it didn't matter. *He* was

the thing to look at. While the groom wasn't exactly in his complete royal ensemble, Ruben was showcasing some essential Khmer wedding bling paraphernalia: a massive gold chain around his neck, a pair of bangles similar to the ones I had tried on before, and probably the most important element to finish the look: a golden sword.

"What's happening here?" Dahvy looked at her soon-to-be with a little bit of disgust and a little bit of love.

"Men's clothes in Cambodian weddings are so much more interesting than the penguin suits God-fearing people wear." Ruben looked proud. That was for sure.

"Honestly, the look crushes." I figured it didn't cost me anything to pay a compliment once in a while.

"Did you hear that, Dahvy?! I crushed someone."

"That doesn't sound like a good thing." Dahvy remained unimpressed.

"So, what's the sword all about, anyways?" Ruben proceeded to awkwardly wave it around like he was ready to take someone's eye out with it.

"Careful!" Dahvy's teacher tone was on.

"You mean, *the golden sword*?" I echoed back, recalling what I'd learned about the ceremonial instrument. Not only had Ma's instructive album captions fully detailed the ritual, I did remember Ba telling me about this one when he showed us his wedding video. I listened like I was learning a new language. It felt both familiar and so foreign, like something out of a fairy tale. I couldn't believe that something as domestic as getting married required such medieval preparation. Ba used to tell us all the time that we were descended from queens and kings. Looking at Ma's wedding photos was the only time I felt it to be actually true. Maybe Dahvy's wedding would remind us both of our royal blood.

"Sompeas Ptem. The bride and the groom hold the golden sword, while people tie red strings around their hands. After, they walk around the room, led by the bride, who holds some kind of receptacle. Go ahead," I instructed, trying to see if they'd actually get into it.

"Now? Oh no. We are not doing this before the wedding. It's bad luck," Dahvy declared without even knowing if that was true. I mean, I guess with weddings, there was always that concern of doing one thing wrong that would drop-kick all the dominoes. But I was starting to feel like, in my life, in everything that was going on these days, bad things happened regardless of what you did or didn't do. So why did it even matter? I figured Khmer people were versed in spooks, so why not just lean in? Why not take that power back into our own hands?

"Oh, come on. No one ever practices for Cambodian weddings. White people have a rehearsal to walk down an aisle. Cambodian people can afford to practice processing with *the golden sword.*" My logic was on point. I could tell Ruben wanted to partake in the cultural cosplay, but Dahvy looked tense. You could tell she was calculating the fallout of violating some phony wedding superstition versus the fallout of not rehearsing for an already chaotic day. We'd seen it so many times before at other weddings we'd been dragged to. The bride and groom being mercilessly dragged around like some rag dolls at the whim of the achaa or the parents or whatever overeager ming or boo had nothing else to do.

"Come on, babe. You love being prepared. Some might even say overprepared—"

"Watch it, you."

"Soma's just suggesting that we be as prepared as possible." Ruben winked at me, confirming that he was hitting the right notes with Dahvy. We both knew that there was only thing that could make Dahvy more scared than Cambodian superstition: not being ready. It was working.

"Fine, but we tell no one. You got me?" Dahvy stared back at the both of us with a glare you would remember only in your nightmares. Ruben made a quick gesture of zipping up his lips, and I repeated in similar fashion. "So, what do we do?"

"First of all, you have to stand next to each other, and Ruben, you have to hold this in your right hand." Maybe I wasn't currently talking to the guy, but I could still hear Ba's voice narrate every glossy photo in the album. In these moments, I remembered everything he said. His voice was warm, but direct. With perfect, concise instruction, he wanted to make sure that the second he closed the album, you knew exactly what to do— what to do without him. I missed him so much . . . but I had a job to do. "So, then you walk behind her. Sword's in the right hand, and in the left is the bride's tail."

"What tail are you talking about?" Dahvy looked puzzled and a little perturbed.

"The flappy thing on your dress. What kind of Cambo bride are you? Just pretend like it's there." It would have probably helped to practice with the full wedding outfit, but any additions to my instructions would've only stressed the bride out more.

On one side of the room, Dahvy stood one step ahead of Ruben as he trailed behind, pretending to hold her bridal tail in one hand and the sword in the other.

"And then you walk clockwise around the room."

As I stood in the center of the small changing room, Dahvy walked the perimeter slowly as Ruben followed honorably behind. At first, they looked mad awkward because their tempos were sometimes off. Ruben kept running into Dahvy, and she'd turn back like she was going to pummel him. But gradually you could see them finding their steps together. For a moment, it felt like time stopped. There was only the sound of their steps against the old, ragged carpet. From my axis at the center, I followed them with my eyes, only slightly turning my whole body to watch them complete the circle. When they returned to their original spot, they froze like statues. All the nervous energy had disappeared from the room. A calm came over all of us.

"And then you're married. Kind of. Partially." The couple smiled back at me like I was the magical achaa or something. Dang. Maybe I should go into the wedding officiating business. Was there money to be made in marriages? Hand me that dowry!

Dahvy and Ruben shared a look, and for the first time, I didn't want to throw up chunks. It was simple: they were meant to be. Even if life had been upside down for the last couple of months, their love was solid. I believed that.

I wondered . . . would I ever find someone like that too? Did I even want someone like that? Maybe a person to help me feel a little less alone in the world. Someone who could make me laugh when things got real weird. Another being that I could walk circles with.

Ma had Ba.

Dahvy had Ruben.

Who would I have?

CHAPTER 18

What's God to You?

My bony butt was growing numb as I sat on the cold, hard marble bench waiting and watching that red Elmo jacket weave in and out of the matching standing pillars. Britney would go up to one, read the inscription, give a *meh* look, and move on to the next.

MA (8:12 p.m.):	Have you eaten yet?
SOMA (8:12 p.m.):	Yes, Ma. I'm always eating.
MA (8:12 p.m.):	Ok good.
MA (8:13 p.m.):	Well . . . you need to talk to your ba.
SOMA (8:13 p.m.):	Wow, what a transition . . .
MA (8:13 p.m.):	Soma, I'm serious. I know things are hard, but he's still your father.
SOMA (8:14 p.m.):	I know, I know. I'll talk to him later. I'm busy right now.
MA (8:15 p.m.):	Does this have to do with the fact that I'm coming home later? Because I'm sorry, gkoun. There's just a lot to get done . . .

Wow, Ma was coming in hot. Airing all that dirty laundry, as if I could even comprehend any of it, given this current moment. I needed to respond quickly, before Britney caught wind of my distraction.

SOMA (8:16 p.m.):	No, I get it, Ma.
MA (8:18 p.m.):	I really am sorry, Soma. It'll just be a second longer.
SOMA (8:18 p.m.):	I know, I know . . .
MA (8:19 p.m.):	I love you. You know that, right?
SOMA (8:20 p.m.):	I know . . . I'll text you soon.
MA (8:21 p.m.):	Call your ba.

I immediately lodged the monster box back into my pocket. What was Ma getting into? Honestly, she was stunning me with her guilt bombs, unabashed talk of what was actually going on, and subsequent requests to do my daughter duty. It was a lot to take on, especially after this being her first mention of her delayed arrival. She hadn't even told me herself—she'd relayed it via Dahvy! What'd she expect of me? And now, in this current context, where I was trying to figure out what was going on between Britney and me, she wanted to talk about it all? No, ma'am. I was going to have to get into it with Ma at a later time. Or never. Whichever came first.

Truth be told, neither Britney nor I had said a thing in the last ten minutes, so on the down-low, it was a welcome distraction. But still, I was content with just being in her orbit.

Red particles were floating away from her shaggy jacket, and it smelled like she had put on some kind of floral scent. Lilac? Or maybe it was lavender? I'd never been very good at figuring out flowery smells, but whatever was emanating from Britney was welcome.

It was definitely lavender. God bless lavender.

With her back to me, Britney turned over her shoulder to give a last evaluation.

"Anything?" I hollered while holding out for at least one not-horrible verdict.

"Meh." Britney shrugged like she was apologizing, and then sat directly at the center of the circle of pillars. Dang. She wasn't buying it. I could feel a tug inside. If she didn't understand my affinity to Jack, would she understand me at all?

I stared at her, framed perfectly at the center of the circle. For a second, I was struck by the image. If you didn't look too hard, it was almost like watching myself in a private moment. But it wasn't me. It was Britney. I wondered if passing randos sometimes eavesdropped on my intimate moments in the park too. When I'd been alone previously, moving through my thoughts, what had strangers thought of this yellow-brown teenage Cambo girl being totally enamored of this very dead, white French-Canadian writer dude who was six feet under? Had they been confused/surprised/totally weirded out by my obvious, not-so-subtle reverence? Or had they thought I was just another teen passing by, using the locale as a safe spot to smoke a joint?

"Nothing?" I asked innocently, while making my way over to join Britney on the bricked ground of Jack Kerouac Park. The spot usually elicited two reactions, depending on who you were, of course. Tourists usually floated around, taking endless pictures and barely reading the passages marked on the pillars while saying, "Mmmm, yes, mmm." Townies didn't pay it much mind, unless you needed a spot for your dog to poop. Most of Lowell was a National Historical Park, so the park rangers didn't look too kindly if your dog needed relief in the surrounding areas. By default, this sacred area became the canine pooping spot. Maybe Jack was rolling around in his grave. Or maybe he thought that was some serious poetic justice. Or maybe he didn't think anything of it because . . . well, dude was dead.

"It's just . . . look, I know you've got this Kerouac thing going on, but besides the obvious reason: Why him?" Britney asked point-blank, no sidestepping, just the direct question.

I was taken aback. She was so blunt with her inquiry. Personally, I knew for myself why I kept coming back, but would it sound silly now? Would I learn I'd been a fool this entire time?

"If the obvious reason is that he's from here, the less obvious one is that . . . well, he's from here," I replied tentatively, knowing that sharing the same hometown wasn't quite enough to idolize a troubled writer.

"Yeah?" Britney seemed disappointed there wasn't more to my argument. I took a beat and began to think through what existed in the overlap between him and me.

"Well . . . he's an immigrant, French-Canadian kid who felt like an outsider. It's like he started out so soft (I guess, like everyone), and then life made him hard. But still, the soft parts are maybe the truth? And so maybe the truth is being young? Maybe he just got lost along the way to getting old? There's something sad about it too. It's like, in my poetry, I carry the desire for him not to get lost." I was just going out on a riff, but it was feeling more like a ledge.

"So, you're like . . . caught in a dream of Kerouac."

I paused. God, Britney was a poet herself. What did it mean to be caught in a dream of someone?

"If the moment before being told the truth about life is a dream . . . yeah," I replied, half understanding what I was spouting out.

"I guess I'm just annoyed because all his books are like men being tortured by what they want as society tells them what men should be. It's like wah, wah, heard that one before."

"That's real." I knew Britney was right. White dudes had always been the neutral narrator, and even if they were raging and churning out reasonable, solid points about humanity—inspirational even—the stories were still about them. Cats like Kerouac may have felt on the fringe of society, but were they actually? And did I have to denounce a connection that felt more emotional than logical? Could I hang with Kerouac still? I felt my devotion being challenged, and for the first time, it made perfect sense.

"And like, even if I do feel badly for him as a person because of his past and stuff, I can't be trying to fixate on authors who don't give me solutions. I need ones who are looking forward. Not backward." Britney signed, sealed, and delivered that argument, and I was right there, humming along.

"So what do you think Octavia Butler's books are about?" I asked earnestly, just trying to get a feel of the booky world she was working from. What made Octavia Butler's stories so different from old Jack's?

"Black women saving the world."

"Yeah, you win."

"And looking forward, obviously! And to your point about sharing like a geographic home . . . that's real, but as a writer, don't you want to follow the ones who, in a totally fucked dystopian place, are trying to move forward and away?"

Britney was right. Kerouac was always pulled back to the past. If you read his lesser-known book *The Haunted Life: And Other Writings*, you could see how his early life—his little brother dying, his angry father's influence, his own feelings of being a perpetual outsider—stayed with him forever. I had to think about this one. Was I so connected to his words because I was in pain too? Too stuck in the past? Was I giving myself an out from looking to the future?

"In *Parable of the Sower*, the protagonist, Lauren, she's our age, and she's got this thing called 'hyperempathy syndrome,' where she can feel the pain of others. Not in some theoretical way, but like actual pain." Britney was launching into the book I'd seen her holding a couple of weeks ago. We were talking sci-fi now, no doubt, and this syndrome—this one-of-a-kind disease—sounded almost unbearable. How could you do anything if you were constantly taking on the suffering of others, let alone dealing with your own?

"At first, she's encouraged to hide it because the world is so awful, and evil people could take advantage of her vulnerability. But throughout the story, you can see how hyperempathy and her smarts lead her to develop her own religion, which might just save the world. Or at least the group of survivors she's with."

"What is the religion based on?"

"God is change."

"Dang."

"I know, right?"

"Dang."

"*I know, right?!* Like she's saying the only fixed thing is change, and so God must be it." In the dark of night, Britney's eyes lit up like they hadn't before this moment. You could tell she was really feeling this book, not just because it was a thing to read, but because it was working on a whole other level of understanding.

"Okay, but doesn't it seem unfair that someone that young is like cursed—"

"Or blessed . . ."

"—blessed with this thing that makes her feel like she has to solve the world's problems?" I was starting to feel like it was kind of unfair for someone so young to take on a whole organized religion.

"Okay, but spoiler, you good?"

"Yeah."

"She goes on this epic journey northward from Los Angeles, fending off drug-induced pyromaniacs, cannibals, and rapists—"

"What the heck is this book?" Were we talking *The Walking Dead* here?

"—survives all that, ends up on some abandoned farm, and starts like a new colony with her religion as the foundation. She might not have saved the world, but she's saved some."

"But even still. It's like . . . leave the child alone. She should be smoking out and running around parking lots, not creating a whole other religion."

"But that's not her world. She's got to survive. And the adults are the ones who have led them into this mess. How can we expect them to save us?"

"That's real real."

"If Kerouac was alive, I don't think he'd be the one. I'd trust a supernaturally hyperempathetic kid." Britney had made her case, and it was a convincing one at that. "Also, by the end of the book, she's eighteen. She grows up. We'll grow up too."

We'll grow up too. There was something about how Britney said the words so matter-of-factly that really got me in my gut. Maybe it was because she already understood this truth so well, and I was still holding on to what held me to the past. More and more, it seemed like everyone understood it. Britney was already looking at colleges. Dahvy was getting married in two weeks. Even my Number One, Sophat, was talking about auditions in New York like he could see the end in sight. Why couldn't I see that far ahead?

When I'd run into Ruben by the church and he tried to allude to our future family situation. When on a task for the bride, I'd gotten stuck on the album pages of former photos for just a minute too long. When I'd avoided/was avoiding Ba because he was working so hard to transition us into our new situation. Yep, I was clawing into the past because any other alternative was just too much. I didn't have emotional capacity for the future; I was saturated in my longing for before.

"Maybe I have that hyperempathy too." The suggestion popped out of my mouth, and I didn't entirely know where I was going with it.

"Oh yeah?"

"Well, it's like, I'm not like my sister Dahvy, who does take on people's problems and is always trying to fix them. But for me, I do feel people's emotions. Like it sets up space inside of me. I feel it all the time. It makes me heavy. How do I even move forward with all that stuff?"

"You ever let other people take on yours?" Britney scooched in a little closer. I could feel the change in proximity.

"Everyone's got plenty to deal with." I tried to toss it off, but I could feel Britney's lock on me.

"Sure, but isn't that just like relationships? You give. You take. Sometimes it's equal. Sometimes it's not. And maybe we can *all* aspire to be superhero hyperempathetic, so it's like: we got you. Everyone."

"Ha. Yeah."

"That was ignorant, right?"

"No, it wasn't." Maybe Britney was right after all. I had to believe that the mess we'd gotten into was because there was so little empathy left in this country. I can't say I've ever been really political, but it's like the minute I turn on the news, all I see are these people in suits in glossy studios or big marble hallways talking about immigrants like they're just statistics. Not human beings with blood running through their veins. Not neighbors who live right next door to you. Not human beings who are waiting for answers about how their lives are going to turn out. Just statistics.

"What's the situation with your dad, if you don't mind me asking?" Britney posed the question with that unafraid tone that got me shaking in my boots.

"You really wanna hear about it?"

"Yeah, if you feel comfortable."

I paused for a second. Did I feel comfortable downloading my ba's story on Britney? I hadn't even really shared the finer details with Sophat—I hadn't shared them with anyone—but now, in this moment, Britney's words were giving me some support. She had previously asked if I let anyone take on my problems. Maybe I needed to share them a bit to just make a little more space inside. I looked forward, as I began to tell Britney about Ba.

"Well, like . . . way before I was born, my dad was into all kinds of stuff. Not trying to excuse it, but as a kid during the war, he saw some stuff, and that doesn't go away if you don't deal with it. He had a group of troublemaker friends in high school, and after college and stuff, he was honestly fine. Just working and being a family guy. Years later, one of his friends who had moved away came back into town, but this guy was like still getting into trouble. He asked my dad to drive him to this person's house. Apparently, the friend was shaking down someone for money, and they got into a fight on the front lawn of this guy's house. My dad didn't know what was happening, but when the guy started beating up on his friend, my dad ran out of the car and he got involved. My dad and his friend were arrested."

"That's shit. It wasn't even his fault."

"I know! I think my older sister, Dahvy, was like five years old or something when it happened, and it's been funny to hear all those details, because I wasn't around. It always seemed like a story that happened to some other family, because all I ever knew of Ba was that he was a kind, gentle man. Anyways, he served some time, even went to a detention center, and afterward, he was on it completely. They were going to deport him, because he was still a permanent resident, but they saw he had done really well for himself. So they let him stay if he kept reporting back. Then my parents had me, and Ba told me I was his new start. He was gonna be better for me. But then this summer, out of nowhere, he was called into the office, and they deported him."

It was funny. Previously, no one in our family had talked

about the events that led Ba down this road, that led us all down this road. But in the presence of Britney, it just poured out of me. It was so easy. Like a story that didn't even make me emotional when I shared it. It was sad, of course, but it was more like sharing facts as they were, as if they'd happened to someone else. Not me. Britney had this effect on me.

"That's awful." Britney looked back at me with a pair of sympathetic eyes. It wasn't her fault, but I hated when people pitied me like that. I didn't need pity. I just needed things to be different. "You worried about him not coming back?"

I was shook. Like a stun gun froze my entire system. With one direct question, Britney had broken down all the carefulness that most people would sidestep through. Everyone else was trying so hard not to hurt my feelings, while Britney wanted to know the truth.

Of course I was. I hadn't admitted it to another soul. I wouldn't dare breathe out that possibility. Everyone was working hard to get his case looked at, and between governments, it seemed like there was a shot that he could return. But what if he couldn't? And it wasn't just that. Ma was pushing back her arrival. I could feel her disappearing more and more with each moment. What if she made the decision to stay in Cambodia to be with Ba? What if they both were gone? One domino set off a whole maze, and soon enough, I wondered who I would have left. Was I worried about Ba not coming back?

"Yeah. I am."

The sky wasn't clear tonight. You could barely see the stars through the wisps of clouds, which looked more like eerie tendrils of an octopus. The night wind was picking up a bit, and dead leaves swirled about. Once again, I had not brought a heavy enough jacket for the situation, so I pulled my hands into the sleeves of my hoodie as a desperate attempt to keep myself warm.

Suddenly my back stiffened, as I could feel a firm warmth against it. Britney had found a way to match my sitting position, and now we were back-to-back, spine to spine, staring out into our own worlds but connected.

"This okay?" Britney's question trailed into my ear, as I tried my very best to allow my back to sink into hers.

"Yeah, of course." I could feel the tension melting from my back and down from the rest of my body, as we began to support each other.

"If you came up with your own religion, what would God be to you?" I threw a question back into Britney's space, honestly curious about where she stood with all this philosophical, spiritual debate.

"Nothing," Britney replied like a mic drop.

Dang. She was a stone-cold atheist, and I was kind of into it.

"Ooh, she's in the crypt, y'all! With no heaven or hell or reincarnation to save you."

"I just wish people believed more in their own power. Like the lit competition next week. You're about to tap into that power!"

Sophat. Was. Dead. Meatballs. I knew that little rat had

been going around telling everyone about my business. Too bad he wasn't here for his inevitable execution.

"Oh. You heard?" I feigned casual surprise.

"Yeah, your boy Sophat said something about it. You nervous?"

"A little bit. I mean, I may not even get to perform, but I'm working on stuff, just in case."

"It's huge, what you're doing. Saying your truth to all those people."

"Don't say 'all' those people." I was starting to feel a little nauseous from the idea of so many people turning out in person to judge my words. And honestly, I was feeling a lotta queasy from Britney claiming that it was "my truth." Sure it was, but in my poems, I'd also been sharing my struggles with my ba's situation. Was it more accurate to say "our truth"? And what did it mean for me to speak about someone else's situation and go no edit in my emotions? I knew that what I was doing was important, but was I going a step too far? Should I have just stuck with speaking for my singular self?

"Sorry: some people who don't matter but support you and are gonna witness your truth." Britney laughed, cutting through the tension I was feeling just imagining myself being up there at the podium.

"Are you gonna be one of them?" Her jokes made me brave.

"You want me to be?"

What I wanted to say was, *Doy. Of course. I don't give a funk about any of the pedestrians out there. I'm into you. So let's be done with this silly charade and be a power couple. Okay? Okay. We out.*

But what I actually said was, "Maybe."

"Cool." In her way, she said she'd be there, and it was giving me a little more confidence in preparing for the moment. She wasn't done interrogating me, though. "Can I ask you the same question? What's 'God' to you?"

"Mmm . . ." I could feel Britney's question buzzing in my body. I could feel her back attentive and wanting to know what my answer would be. I could feel my heart jumping out of my body and watching me to see if I would just tell the truth.

"Honestly, I don't really know. I'm trying to figure it out."

A silence followed, and then out of the blue, I felt her hand on top of mine. I looked down at it and then quickly craned my neck back in search of some confirmation from her. Britney's gaze was locked into the stars. I followed suit, mirroring her focus, but all I could feel was how her palm radiated warmth and understanding. For once, I felt totally lost but . . . totally okay. I was caught in a dream of us.

"Maybe try to answer that question for the contest."

I closed my eyes and imagined the question before me: What's God to you?

CHAPTER 19
A Dragon's Story

It was a good thing Britney and I didn't share any classes together, because I would have been buried seeing her. Even the very thought of her walking around this building, sitting in a classroom next to mine, breathing the same air, made me vibe all sorts of ways. Honestly, I'd felt some regret plowing through TOO MUCH INFORMATION LAND at last night's park hang, but if I were to be real with myself, no edit, no self-sabotage: it was perfect. Even when Britney challenged my link to Kerouac, I felt like it wasn't just to be argumentative but to really question how narrowly I'd been thinking about our hometown Sad Boi. It was like she made more space for my impulse, and I was starting to view myself not just as an inheritor of some lit legacy because of geography, but because I had something wild inside of me, too, that I had to get out.

But that was last night, and no one ever talks about what happens after: the dreaded follow-up. If I ran into her in the hallway now, what would I even say? Would I throw myself at her feet and confess that my sorry-excuse-for-a-heart was hers? Yeah, no. That wasn't in the range.

Would she even remember what it had been like for us to connect hours ago, when it felt like we were the only two people in the world? What would Britney even have to say about what had gone down? Who knew? I had zero premonition of a future interaction, but once again, there was something nice in staying in the "before." No one could touch what happened before—

"Ms. Kear, did you need something?" A familiar voice entered my orbit of private questioning.

"Huh?" I stared back at the front of the classroom, and there was Mr. Drakos across the way, leaning back against his desk, like this was his forever neutral stance. For decades past, he'd judged students from this position, and for decades in the future, he'd do the same.

In this particular moment, he looked intently back at me, as if I was the only person in the room. I looked around briefly. I *was* the only person in the room. Yeah, I'd been in a fog of my romantical thoughts and immediately snapped back.

"The bell rang. I don't know if you heard that or not."

"Oh yeah . . ." Weeks ago, I couldn't have gotten out of there quicker, but today my daydreaming had left me out at sea. I grabbed my bag and books and began to make an embarrassing exit out.

As I walked down the row of desks, I briefly looked up at Drakos, who you could just tell was ready to relaunch into it. I had two options. I could stop and reveal to him that Dahvy and

I had actually talked about the essay, preventing him from further pressing for a sit-down meeting. Or I could leave the sucker in the dust like Flo-Jo, speed and style and nails to boot. (Don't ever say a kid doesn't do research after being compared to one of the world's greatest athletes to do it . . . those nails, tho!) As my limbs moved me in the general direction, I realized that either scenario would not circumvent chaos. I had to face the music.

I got to the front of the classroom and stood eye to eye with the dinosaur.

"Hey, Mr. Drakos."

"Yes, Ms. Kear."

"I really wish you'd call me Soma. Ms. Kear makes me think of my mom. And not because of the tragical reasons you're thinking of, but because I don't want to be interchanged with a middle-aged woman. I'm Soma."

"Point taken, Ms. Soma." It'd gone well so far. Drakos had accepted my request without going into full beast mode. Not that I had any sense what full beast mode for Drakos would be like, but I was glad to see I wouldn't find out . . . yet.

"My sister read the essay." I almost felt relieved to just get it all out there.

"Yes, she did. I admit I sent it to Ms. Kear, only because I didn't get a response to my initial email to you." It wasn't even archived; it had been trashed and sent out into the internet space to be lost forever. It was definitely my bad.

"I know, and I'm sorry for that. Anyways, we did talk, my sister and me, about the essay and . . ." I trailed off, trying to decide how much to get into it. I didn't want to have to write the essay all over again, but maybe there was another way to show up for all parties involved. Maybe I could apologize partially for some of my language. Partially. "We both agreed I was still in my right to feel how I felt."

"I agree with that." I was surprised to see Drakos join ranks.

"But I didn't mean to come off like I didn't care about the subject or your teaching. I've just been, I don't know . . . angry." The minute the word popped out of my mouth it was like I could see it for the first time. For the past year, it had felt like rocks were piling up inside of my stomach—just building up a wall and weighing me down. Now I brought one out to look at, and I could see so clearly it was exactly what I felt: angry.

"I understand, Soma—"

"But you don't. That's the thing. Your father wasn't deported."

Maybe I should have feared *me* going into full beast mode instead. I hadn't intended on coming in so hot, but it was Drakos's comfort with relating to me as if he even had any clue. I mean, what could we share that was similar?

"You're right. I don't understand what it's like to have a family member deported, but I do know what it's like to be angry, and you should know anger is not off-limits in your writing. Maybe the cursing is pushing it, but I told your class that history isn't theoretical. I mean that. It's about people. You are a person. You are history."

Something about Drakos's phrasing weirded me out. It wasn't like I had done or would likely do anything epic enough to have it printed in a textbook. I wasn't some ruler who brought democracy to a country. I wasn't some activist with a sign who fought for the freedoms of people. I couldn't even claim to be some incredibly generous person at all. In fact, I was a historically selfish teenager who, yes, had some things happen to her but was really struggling to get past it. So what did Drakos mean by me being history?

I impulsively blurted out, "But how?"

"Soma, when we read from our textbooks, you must be aware that someone wrote this, right? And while we hope there's been a process of vetting facts and historical events, we know that up to this point, American history has been told primarily by geriatric white geezers like me." I looked back at Drakos, startled. Maybe he was more self-aware than I'd thought. "That has been by virtue of who's always had the pen and the power. Up to this point, they have told American history. But anyone can ultimately hold a pen. Anyone can have power."

Drakos was getting philosophical, and I was really struggling to stay leaned in. I mean, I knew Thanksgiving was some kind of ploy to make Americans feel okay about killing Indigenous people and taking their lands. And, of course, over three hundred years ago, someone had to tell a story that made people believe Black people could be made into slaves, as if that was just a normal idea one could sleep at night with . . . and not a nightmare we live with today, every day. Then I also remembered when Drakos told us in class that during the Vietnam War and after, the US dropped more bombs on Cambodia than the Allies dropped during World War II. That made Cambodia vulnerable for the Khmer Rouge to take over and began the four-year genocide that killed so many. What always got under my skin about the way that history was told (if it's even told) was that the Khmer Rouge were monsters while the US government were some kind of white saviors who took all our families in without any bit of guilt. Until, that is, they didn't want us anymore. I was beginning to see what Drakos meant by the power of holding that pen and writing down the story of American history. And leaving out so very much.

"You know, a couple of years ago, I helped put together an exhibit at the university called 'Acropolis of America.' We told the history of the Greek community right here in Lowell from 1874 to 2020. In 1880, there were fewer than ten Greeks, and by 1925, there were about thirty-five thousand. Now we're the third-largest Greek population in America." Drakos was bragging, but I had it one better.

"Yeah, and we're the second-biggest Cambodian population in the country." I was proud of that fact, and at the same time, I didn't even mean to give off superior vibes. It had just occurred to me that maybe this place, our little town, was home to more people that were so different in culture, but perhaps undeniably alike in journeys.

"That's true, Soma. I know most people in town just think of food when they think of Greek culture, like the Athenian Corner—"

"Yeah, that spanakopita is for serious!" I immediately got red, realizing I'd confirmed his point of being completely culturally illiterate.

"Yeah, it is! But the Greeks worked in the mills too, started their own businesses, became political forces in town, and created social organizations to gather our community and to write down the history. We detailed all that work in our exhibit."

"Our community?" I was surprised. I didn't know that Drakos was Greek himself.

"I am indeed! Drakos means dragon."

"Ha. And Soma was like a snake princess."

"So I guess we've both got scales and tails!" Drakos immediately leaned back on his desk abruptly and promptly fell off the edge in laughter. The guy looked like an awkward little kid getting a kick out of his own joke, and for once, his presence didn't rattle me. It just made me smile. Finally, the dinosaur—er, the dragon—regained his composure and wiped tears from his eyes.

"Look, we worked on that exhibit because we wanted to be a part of telling our history."

"But Mr. Drakos, can I ask you a question?"

"Of course."

"When you see your history displayed like that, just out and about, do you ever feel like you're doing something wrong? Like, how can you be the single person telling that story? What if you get facts wrong? What if your intentions are perceived incorrectly? Like what if you're considered to be an illegitimate storyteller?"

"I think I understand a little of what you're communicating. It's one thing to write your story, and then it's another to go public. It becomes no longer just yours. Other people judge it, identify themselves in it, or sometimes, yes, reject it altogether. But hopefully, we tell our stories responsibly, and after that, we hope there are more. That should be the objective. History is made better or even corrected by the multiplicity of stories. So tell your story, and develop hard scales. Maybe your sharing can encourage the next 'Soma.'"

For the first time since I'd been in his class this semester, I felt like Drakos was talking straight to me. Not past me. Not around me. Not in a general gaze to the rest of the class. But straight into my eyes. Honestly, there was no better feeling in the world. I felt important.

"So we don't have to have a formal meeting, since everyone's pretty much talked it out?"

"No, I suppose there's no reason for that anymore."

"And I guess that also means I don't need to rewrite my essay either?"

"I'm happy to have you turn it in next week."

"But the competition's next week, and I might be . . ."

"A finalist? That's the kind of confidence you need for it! I bet you will be, so get to work, huh?" Drakos looked back at me, smiling, as if he hadn't just made my timeline even more difficult than I was expecting. Just as I was thinking we were sharing a moment, the dragon had returned to his own ways and breathed fire. I was straight scorched.

CHAPTER 20
After

Dear Ms. Soma Kear,

Thank you for your submission to this year's Jack Kerouac Literary Competition for students. Every year, we get countless entries, and it is our thankless job to whittle down those preliminary numbers to eight finalists. Foremost, we cannot stress enough that to express oneself through writing is a feat unto itself. You have already won, and we appreciate your courage to submit.

That being said, we're thrilled to announce that you have been chosen as one of eight students to perform at next week's finals competition. Congratulations! As a reminder: you must perform an additional original piece that was not previously submitted.

We will send more information soon, but in the meantime, do relish this moment. Your voice is important, and it carries the legacy of Lowell's greatest poets forward. Be a Beat!

—Mr. Lozano

I exited out of the email and immediately put the phone facedown against the tabletop. I grabbed the basil, mint, and bean sprouts and dropped them into the big bowl, followed by a squeeze of lime. I liked my soup hot, sour, and filled with veggies so when the noodles were gone, I wasn't just slurping beef bone broth. There would be sustenance till the last drop. Finally, I took the sriracha and went to town. Hot two ways. As my fat fingers forced the rice noodles into, onto, and around the chopsticks, my other hand, equipped with the plastic soup spoon, went into the bowl for a hearty dunk. The two met in my mouth, and once again, I remembered why it was so good to be Cambodian: gkuh theeuw.

"Um, Earth to Soma." Across the table, Sophat looked back at me with doe eyes, foolishly not yet jumping into his lunch. "What'd the email say?"

"Oh, they said I advanced to the finals," I replied while shoveling another blissful soupy bite into my mouth.

"Sorry, what?"

"I said I made it to the finals. . . ." The words and even more so, the ellipses that followed began to suspend time. Suddenly, in cinematic slo-mo, the spoon dropped from my hand, and I watched it sail down toward the table at gravity's request. Sophat's frozen eye contact slowly shifted into more of a disgusted glare, responding to the fact that I had not yet registered what I'd just announced twice. Apparently, the news was too much for my brain to compute, so all I could do was watch the plastic utensil descend onto the reality of the situation. And when it finally made contact with the table, more severe than a whiplash caused by seeing that girl walk past that you couldn't stop crushing on, the thought finally occurred to me: *I made it to the finals.*

Our collective brains exploded! We jumped up from the table and started shouting and dancing like we had never learned about shame before! As if joy was our only language! And no matter how rowdy we looked to the common passerby, we were going to keep looking wild! The volume ratcheted up to max, and no one could quiet us down! Not even the unbothered Khmer people slurping their noodles at the Red Rose! I'D MADE IT TO THE FREAKING FINALS!

"Okay, okay, we're wasting our lunch here," I shouted back to Sophat as I began to notice the unbothered people quickly becoming, well, bothered. I returned to my seat and began to wipe down the film of broth that had made its way onto the table. I gathered my utensils to return to the task at hand.

"My friend is *finalist status.* What what?"

"Okay, we had a moment. Thank you for that. But now let's eat."

"But bish, you're on your way. One performance, and you're, like, the winner, right?"

"Sure, but I'm not even trying to do that. I just want to perform. I think."

"Don't undersell it. You could win this whole dang thing."

"But win what? Like some cheesy plastic medal."

"Sis, are you even paying attention? Like they give you a scholarship to college. I, mean it's not a ton, but it's more than you probably have right now (no offense). And like, if you win, it's a line on that CV. Another thing to set you up for your future." Sophat devoured a piece of tripe, while looking at me like, *You should know better*. But the truth was, unfortunately, I didn't. Entering the competition was enough. Imagining winning was a whole other thing.

If I won, I'd have some pocket change to put toward . . . me. Would I actually put it toward college? Where would I even apply? Or would I abandon the suggestion altogether and bank on some bedroom sound recording equipment so that Sophat and I could go platinum? Maybe my narrow lens on the future was about to blow up. Maybe anything was possible.

I began to feel that stress again from Britney's and my initial conversation by the canal. She was already on college tours, and I was seriously in the dark about what direction to take. I looked back across the table at Sophat, who was busy slurping on his noodles. It occurred to me that even though we'd always joked about becoming a pop duo sensation someday, I'd never really asked him how serious he was about the whole thing. Was he just vibing with confidence and dreams of grandeur? Or was it worth interrogating him about what he was actually planning for the future?

"Well, what about you? What would you do with that money?" I threw the question back at my Number One.

"Why are you even trying to bring me back to last year's disaster? I told you I would never again—" Sophat raised his utensils defensively.

"No, I'm not trying to make you feel a certain way! I'm just asking, like, for you, what are you trying to do after school?"

Sophat paused and dropped his utensils almost ceremonious-like. He went inside himself for a moment, seemingly trying to gather the most appropriate response. Ironically, I knew he had the whole thing plotted out, but truth be told, I didn't really know his answer fully myself. From his deep breath in, I knew I was in for it now.

"Well, since you asked, I'm getting my audition cuts ready, so that I can go to the University of Michigan, University of Cincinnati College-Conservatory of Music, Carnegie Mellon University, Baldwin Wallace University, New York University, or one of the other top elite musical theater programs in the country. I'm going to get a full scholarship, because you know I keep my grades right, and how could anyone ever pass up some sad Cambodian genocide/immigrant story? You know those essays are going to be *full* of drama, mama. I'm picking that scab and making someone else pay for the healing. And when I get in, I'm not going to be passive about my strategy. During the semesters, I'll learn what I need to learn, improve my craft, while auditioning for stuff in the summer, because I gotta get my Equity union card ASAP. I'm not trying to do summer stock for the rest of my life. By the time I graduate, I'm going to have a top-tier agent, book a Broadway show or tour, and then put in that time in the chorus so that I can show the industry what I got. They'll see me on the side of that stage and think, 'Who's that golden-brown kid doing all that work glowing while the others are just phoning it in? How can we make him famous?' I'll move from chorus to principal to Tony to television show to Emmy to movie to Academy to sipping green juices with Lupita Nyong'o in Brooklyn, because we'll be friends at that point. And when I finally write my memoir about how this Cambodian kid went from the Mill Town to Tinseltown, I'll think back and reflect on how important it was for us to imagine exactly the future that we want and that we deserve. Unlike our parents, who were victims of circumstances beyond their powers. The sad truth is, they suffered so that we could thrive. And while they deserve absolute peace and happiness, our success is a part of that equation. Our win is a win for them. Period. That's what I'm going to do after college."

Silence entered the chat. I was straight-up stunned. Sophat returned to devouring the remnants of his soup. I remained fixated on my dear friend, whose vision of the future electroshocked me in my sneaks. He wasn't just speaking on his behalf like some self-interested hack, but on behalf of all of us Khmer kids trying to figure it out. In a single prophetic monologue, the kid made it seem like to know exactly what you want and to plan out every step along the way was *the way*. It was our responsibility. It was his responsibility. It was my responsibility.

Suddenly, getting into the finals and doing well wasn't just about me, it was about what I stood for.

"So get your shit together, Soma, because I'm about to campaign for you on the socials." Sophat barely looked up as he concluded his epic rant.

"Your plans are . . ."

"Baller? I know. And it is going to happen."

I had zero doubt in my mind that what Sophat set out to do was going to happen.

"And while you're praising me and all, I confirmed with Evie that we're going to meet at your place tomorrow night at eight p.m.—"

"Sophat—" The love was over. The kid wasn't a visionary. He was a villain. A thorn in my side. A Brutus to my Caesar.

"Don't be mad at me, okay?! We said we would hang out, and now we have to follow through. Besides, I ran into her after chem, and she asked me about it again. It's not like we can keep avoiding her."

"Yeah, see, I don't know why we can't."

"Because it's inhumane. We're just like listening and trading music. Like what could be so horrible about that? So, get over it, Finalist." Sophat brought the big-ass bowl to his mouth and sucked in the last bits. It was like he was trying to disappear behind the bowl, but to fully do so, he'd have to bring it to full tilt. His eyes still hovered over the bowl's edge, staring back at me for a reaction. At some point, he was clearly done with the broth, like some starved child, but he was still holding it up for protection.

"Would you just . . ." I brought my hand across to his bowl and lowered it so I could look back at my cowardly friend's face again. "It's fine."

Sure, I was supremely annoyed by Sophat's agenda to make nice. Deep down I knew he wanted Evie and me to be friends, but I couldn't fully process that bump in the road right now. I'd made it to the final round, and I was going to get the chance to perform in front of actual, real-life people. None of them would have profile pics or cutesy usernames that were just too embarrassing to say aloud. No, when I got up there to the mic, I was going to get to speak to real humans, and for the first time, it sort of, kind of, maybe, felt exciting. From the preliminary poem I submitted, the judges thought I had the talent to get up there and throw it down, so they passed me onto the finals. No, nothing was going to get me down right now. Not even Evie Han.

Just as the wave of anticipation hit, another wave came compulsively crashing down: fear. The judges could've thought I was talented enough to make the finals or . . . they were feeling pity about my story. It was a good narrative: Cambodian girl bemoans her father being unfairly deported and uses trauma porn to feel important or like her life has some purpose. Maybe the words weren't enough, maybe they needed the 3D effect . . . the YouTube video for the socials . . . the remembrance of the tragic, left-behind girl—

Stop, Soma. Stop. At the peak of my happiness, the insecurities were waging a full-on war. They wanted me back at my sad, scared neutral. No, for the first time, I was beginning to plot out my future, and that felt good. Not Evie, not my insecurities, not even myself, could stop me from trying to move forward. I was looking ahead, and I needed to stay focused. I had a finals round to slay. Or attempt. Or dream about a bit.

I told myself again: *I made the finals.*

CHAPTER 21
Searching for Signs

I'll be honest with you. There are some days that are better than others. Sometimes I wake up early in the morning and forget I'm lying in a bed that isn't mine. I forget I can't walk down the hallway and check to see if you're sleeping in your room or if you're still up on your cell phone doing whatever it is you're doing. Probably texting Sophat, even though you're going to see him the next day and the next day and the next day after. (Did I mention I like that the two of you are such good friends? I didn't see it at first, but now it's obvious. You need each other. It's important to need people.) And now with Ma here, it's like I really forget I'm not back there with you girls. It's disorienting. To be so close, but so far away.

When the morning finally creeps in, I walk over to Wat Phnom, this big temple at the center of town, and walk around to think. I try to sneak out quietly, so I don't wake up your ma. You know she's a light sleeper. Anyways, the temple has A LOT of steps, so I have plenty of distance to cover most of my thoughts. Most of them. Like many temples in Cambodia, the whole setup gravitates around a statue of the Buddha. In this one, though, listen . . . the Buddha be blinging. I'm serious. If you've never seen an eighty-eight-foot gold (actually bronze) statue in your life . . . I mean, what are you even doing? And if you've never prayed at the altar of one of these mega-karmic statues, are you even doing samsara right?

According to the legend, a rich old woman named Doun Penh lived on a small hill where the rivers connected in the city. One day when it was raining hard, she went down to bathe by the water and saw a Koki tree either by the bank or floating down the river (you know how these stories change from person to person), and so she solicited the help of some villagers to investigate the tree. They broke through the surface and found a treasure trove inside the trunk of it: four statues of the Buddha! The woman believed this was a sign from the Buddha that he was requesting a new home, so she immediately suggested that the villagers build a hill, where a new wooden temple would sit. There the statues would live, and monks would pray to these gifts from the Buddha. Ta-da! Wat Phnom!

I share this story with you because I want you to know I'm also looking for signs. It may be raining all the time (it is monsoon season, after all), but I'm looking for the hidden treasure that will give me a vision of the future. A direction. It isn't easy always, but I'm searching. Always know that.

—Your Ba

The emails weren't getting any easier. Nope. They were getting harder and, quite honestly, leaving me wrecked. Now the old man was being vulnerable. It was the first time he had. Before, he'd seemed rock solid in his confidence about the situation, but now he was breaking a bit. He was looking for signs. He was searching for Buddha statues in trees that would offer him karmic direction. He was grasping for anything.

At first, I'd resented his initial certainty. It was impossible, and it made me feel like my fears were weak and selfish. But now it was like, I wished it back. I didn't like knowing he couldn't sleep, that he was feeling lonely. Was the guy emailing me as a lifeline? He had Ma now, but maybe he needed someone who really thought in the same way as him. A reflection. Everyone always said that Dahvy was more like Ma, and me like Ba. Perhaps the guy was looking for some confirmation that what he was experiencing was valid.

Yup. My guilt was mounting. How could I even share with him the simple (not so simple) truth that I just needed time? Was there even time to get? In his last email, Ba had confronted my avoidance, and now in this one, he hadn't even mentioned it. What if I waited too long to respond to him and the emotional cracks became bigger until the whole thing fell apart? What if Ba fell apart because of me?

Slow it down. Slow it down. Slow . . . it . . . down.

I was catastrophizing again, and while I could feel my anxiety bubbling, I needed to put some context around it. I needed to search for a little perspective.

Ba was walking around Phnom Penh in the mornings now. Next to seasons, weather, and time, it was just another thing we were on opposite ends of. While he was getting up early to sort through his thoughts, I was currently rehearsing my rhymes in the dim darkness of Jack Kerouac Park, looking for a bit of inspiration myself. But then again, maybe that was a reassuring reality. For as far away as we were, we were searching together. I could imagine that. The finals were next week, and if I didn't give it everything I had, none of this avoidance would've mattered to begin with. No, I knew I had to put the phone away and keep going. On the other side of it all, there had to be a sign that would save us all. Whatever that meant.

I turned the monster box off completely and put it in my back pocket. I closed my eyes, breathed in and out, and remembered why I was here to begin with: to find out what I wanted to say. I had to believe Ba wanted that for me.

Now . . . when I first entered the competition, I understood that this was the basic setup: submit a poem and be prepared to share another at finals. I told myself to get the first one out, and the next would come. Before I read Ba's email, I had been searching through my old journal scribblings, my voice memos, but nothing was hitting right. They were half-baked thoughts from someone who'd never thought she'd share them with anyone. So, now what? Did chick have to start from scratch? Chick probably had to start from scratch.

This was the trouble, though. The video came from impulse. The submission poem came with a bit of inspiration and a deadline. Now, the finalist poem was looking out at the precipice of not just competition, but consequence. People were going to see this, so what did I have to say for myself?

I'd already written about my dad and his deportation, and

the subject was beginning to feel embarrassing altogether. I
didn't want people to think I was milking a sorry situation and
pretending like I deserved those tears. And honestly, I'd even
gotten into my own personal experience of what it felt like to be
a young person in this town. The video wore that subject out.
So, now what?

Maybe love? Lust? No way. High levels of cringe. What's
between the two? Attraction? The hots? Magnetism? Or
something similar? I'd been on my first date, and I didn't
spiral into the surface of the earth in flames, so maybe it was
worth getting into those thoughts. But the poem was going
to be public, and Britney might see it. To present some lines
about her or even some semblance of my romantical quanda-
ries in front of her would be a death sentence. Yeah, nail me
in a coffin now.

No, it couldn't be directly about her. Maybe it could be
about something we'd talked about on our night together.

I was reminded of the question Britney had asked me: *What's
God to you?* I hadn't turned up an answer, because I honestly
didn't know. The character in Britney's book, Lauren, had made
up an entire religion based on the idea that God was change,
and when I asked Britney what she thought, she said that *God
is nothing.* I think she meant to say God is actually people, that
maybe we put too much stake into the spiritual world, as if
people weren't full of power themselves. Or maybe I was making meaning out of the space between. Maybe her initial answer
was exactly what Britney meant after all.

Then it hit me . . . what does the word "God" even mean? I hadn't even thought about its intended roots. I pulled out my phone to check. I could use the monster box for one speedy reference. Madame Merriam-Webster stated that God was "the supreme or ultimate reality." I thought the first answer would be coded in a religious context, but what Ms. Webster was saying was that it was the supreme or ultimate reality for whomever . . . for said beholder. So, what did *I* perceive to be "the supreme or ultimate reality"?

A humming fell on my lips, my tongue began to tense, and then . . . words began to form in my mouth. I gave it a go:

> "What's God to you?" she said
> Like she was leaving me on read
> Asking for the room
> As if even to assume
>
> That I had a notion
> About the potion
> To the question
> Of my obsession—

All right. I was working out something. Things were rhyming, and honestly, I liked starting out with the question itself. It felt like a nice spark to get the fire going. It would allow me to hunt for the answer in poetical terms, without having to decide on a definitive answer. Keep going—

That I had a notion
About the potion
To the question
Of my obsession

That God was a man
With some ultimate plan
That only he knew
How to really break through

"What's God to you?" she said
Like she wasn't trying to tread
The intensity
Of this perplexity

As I try to understand
Even push to expand
What I think I know
As I grow, as I flow, as I break it down like whoa

Break it down like whoa. It needed some work, but it was flowing in a direction I could follow. Ironically, I used to think the pursuit of a poem was the pursuit to answer a question. But as I moved through these impromptu lines, I was beginning to wonder if it had anything to do with the answers after all. I mean, maybe it was a cop-out, but for some reason, in this very moment, all I could do was ask the question. Ask the question over and over and *over* again. Maybe it has never been about the answer. Maybe it has always been about just asking the question.

Just ask the questions.

What was Ba feeling when he walked up the steps of Wat Phnom? What pulled Doun Penh over to the tree containing those statues? What did I really feel about God? When Ba was sitting before the blinged-out Buddha, what did he pray for? What actually made Doun Penh decide to build a massive temple? What did I want to say to a group of strangers in a dark room? What sign was Ba looking for? What sign was Doun Penh looking for? What sign was I looking for?

Just ask the questions.

> "What's God to you?" she said
> Like some hundred-pound lead
> Understanding what it means
> To break the routines
>
> Of thinking that he's there
> When it was only a prayer
> And behind the curtain
> Is absolutely uncertain
> "What's God to you?" she said.

CHAPTER 22

Evie Has Entered the Chat

I had just come home from rehearsing in the park, when I heard her through the door: a high-pitched tone bubbling on about whatever senseless, unmeaningful topic I already knew I couldn't care less about. It was paired with another high-pitched tone that seemed to make a perfect match. The two cooed, laughed, and seemed to just enjoy the crap out of each other. Did I need to confirm my suspicions or walk away in the opposite direction to avoid this disaster at all costs?

I peered through the kitchen window next to the door, and there she freaking was: Evie Han sitting at the kitchen table, cozying up to Dahvy like it was so simple, like she'd been doing it all this time. Like Dahvy had put out a job request for "Younger Sister/Wedding Assistant Who Doesn't Complain but Smiles Incessantly and Does Not Think Twice About the Unpaid Servitude."

Oh, Evie had been waiting for a listing like this, and it was clear the position had been filled. The two looked easeful together, huddled around Dahvy's laptop, every so often looking and pointing at the screen like it was just about the funniest thing that ever was. The sight was nauseating.

I paused before entering. Obviously, I was mad hot by the sight of the two lovebirds perching at the table. It was clear that Evie had annoyingly arrived early to suck up to Dahvy. It wasn't enough for her to be the most perfect Cambodian girl in town, but she also had to be the most perfect Cambodian sister too.

What got me precisely heated was that, as of recently, things had somewhat settled into a groove with Dahvy and me. Since I'd tried on my wedding attire as she had requested, I felt like we'd had our stuff out at the bridal boutique. She'd ask me to do a couple of things since, but I didn't feel that same tension as before. We were just trying to get along. But now, seeing her and Evie together so naturally got me twisted.

I should've just jumped over to the front entrance to avoid them altogether. Then maybe Evie would have forgotten about why she was there to begin with. We could forfeit this bogus night after all. But just as I was about to pivot to the front, I realized the simple truth. The quicker I walked through the door, the quicker I could be done with this forced courtship.

I turned the knob with purpose and put my full weight into the door. Apparently, it was lighter than I remembered, because in a split second, I'd launched myself into the center of the kitchen, my feet completely losing balance and shooting me right into the table where they were seated. Water glasses wobbled and the pair of guilty-looking suckers jumped right to their feet. Dahvy grabbed her laptop quickly. Evie stood there, scared and stunned.

"Soma, careful!" Dahvy shouted out, as if I had intentionally meant to be a mess. As soon as I regained my composure, I looked at the two and said absolutely nothing. I immediately marched my clumsy (embarrassed) ass toward the stairs.

"Nice recovery there!" Evie jumped toward me. I whipped back around and looked blankly at her.

"What are you guys doing anyways?" I asked, trying to decide how much of a grudge I should commit to.

"Evie and I were just messing around with the table arrangements and thinking of the worst combinations. What do you think? Should we put the drunk, gambling Lees with the MAGA-loving Lims? Or maybe replace the Lims with Rithy Vong, the guy who just can't get a real girlfriend because 'all women are crazy'? That should be a fun conversation . . . ," Dahvy mused, followed by an outbreak of laughter from the giddy wedding planners.

I stood there frozen, unsure of how to respond. The pairs of bug eyes stayed locked into me, like I was a captive animal. I was feeling like it too. Any moment, I could either pounce or escape very quickly.

"You okay, Soma? We saved you some pizza." Evie was so helpful in her offering.

We. They were using the plural pronoun *we* now. I had to redirect the conversation from myself and move it right along.

"Ma said that you need to practice making bigh," I blurted out. It was all that could escape my mouth hole. At this point, I was moving from impulse to impulse.

"Okay, well, I make bigh plenty."

"But you always burn it."

Dahvy looked real annoyed by the reprisal of this culinary allegation.

"Okay, well, I'll practice then. In the meantime, take the rest of the pizza box up with you for your hangout. What were you doing anyways?"

I'd been working on my poem in the park, but I didn't want to let people into my process, let alone these two. I was going to keep my finalist status under wraps until the very last minute. I knew I wouldn't be able to control the news breaking—it was going to come out soon—but I wasn't so sure how people were going to react. The imagined range went from pity applause in recognizing how good it was for the sad girl to be doing something to heal herself to abject shock at my finalist status, because in what world could this know-nothing have the talent to do such a thing? In some perfect society where people were just rewarded for their ability and no other factors were considered, would people be actually stumped that I had that inside of me? And if they thought it was false, would they revolt? I wasn't ready for that feedback yet, that measuring if I really deserved this. No, I wanted to keep my head low and do the work. I'd see my haters at the mic.

Maybe I could fend off the unnecessary attention for a while.

"Sophat's not here yet, is he?" I redirected the conversation as I stumbled farther toward the stairs.

"No, he texted me earlier that he was running late," Evie replied, sharing the grisly fact: that my Number One was texting his new Number One. Why hadn't the dude texted me? It was my house.

I had to put my game face on. There was no point in getting into this betrayal right now. I flashed a big, fake-ass smile and kept moving to the pace of getting this over with.

"Okay, well, let's get up to my room, right? Evie, grab the box." As expected, Evie obliged and looked totally unfazed by the request. How very Evie of her.

"Oh, and take those cookies too!" Dahvy shouted, adding insult to injury. Of course Evie had brought her mother's cookies to remind us all that only she had a normal-functioning, cookie-baking family that had so much love they just had to share it with others. Barf.

I stomped up the stairs for maximum effect and, at the top, from my bedroom doorway I catapulted myself onto the mattress. I landed facedown on the springs. Maybe she wouldn't see me, and she'd just go away. No luck. From my buried vantage point, I listened as some gentler steps followed. Evie was on her way to my room, and as I lay there, face pressed against my jersey sheets, I understood that I had to find a way to make the next not-more-than-an-hour bearable. She was already here. I couldn't do anything else but bear. Grrr.

"Should I close the door?" Evie's tentative voice entered my room.

"Oh, just leave it, will you?!"

Let the not-more-than-an-hour bearing begin. Grrr.

CHAPTER 23

The Competition

"For me, and I know this is probably an unpopular decision because it's like *way* before our time, but the ultimate K-pop girl group has to be Girls' Generation!" Evie threw down her opinion with a kind of confidence I was honestly in awe of, partly because she was so certain and partly because she was so wrong.

"Does it . . . ?" I whispered under my breath, looking over at Sophat, who knew exactly what I was thinking. Evie continued in her explanation.

"They set up the premise for what K-pop girl groups could be. I mean, yes, their overall energy is that cutesy aegyo vibe, but because they had nine members—"

"Eight. RIP Jessica Jung." Sophat threw a kiss into the air like the singer had died or something, not in fact created a multinational brand that had already outlasted the girl group.

"But because they had eight members, each one was then able to have their own individual persona. On the other end of the aegyo spectrum, you had Hyoyeon, who was giving harder, edgier vibes, which essentially created the dancer/rapper slot in groups. That made it possible for other queens like Blackpink's Lisa." I scoffed at the thought. I don't know why she had to clarify "Blackpink's Lisa" as if she wasn't conversing with some Blinks. I understood that Evie was trying to make a case for Girls' Generation, but she would never convince me that Blackpink's power belonged to that sticky-sweet group of grandmas. Blackpink's power was unto themselves.

"Interesting choice, Evie!" Sophat pronounced, trying his very best not to tell her that she was totally wrong. "I'm more of a Sunny fan myself—"

I cut in. "Okay, but don't you think that if you're going to bring it back, you should go like *all the way back*? I mean, if you're talking about K-pop lineage, you should take it back to the nineties with S.E.S., the first girl group repped by SM Entertainment, which sold 650,000 copies of their debut album. Or if you want to talk 'hard' and 'edgy,' maybe we should look at Blackpink's legit ancestors and label mates, 2NE1. I mean, those girls were hitting hard. Spiky bras, baseball bats, and like, literal guns? I understand that Girls' Generation had one member who sort of, kind of, rapped every so often, but maybe you should dig a little deeper for that connection."

Sophat studied me as I finished my diatribe. He was already on my hit list for previously texting Evie over me, but I knew that he knew I was feeling off. He stared me down like a hawk.

"Nice flex, Soma, but I'd have to agree that at least with eight members, Girls' Generation made it possible for a K-pop star to be any kind of person." Et tu, Sophat? "Why don't we watch my fave of GG: 'The Boys'?"

"OMG, yes!" Evie exclaimed, like she was fixing to bust a vein in her forehead.

Sophat began to type away at *my* laptop, and there on the screen of the music video, the members of GG, decked out in full-on fashion prom dresses, began to dramatically walk around a floor filled with rose petals. Every so often, they'd look into the camera while mouthing the words. Finally, the beat dropped and the girls began to move through their choreography. I'll admit, it was a fierce era in Girls' Generation's evolution, but it still paled in comparison to Blackpink. And if I were to be a little fair, perhaps somewhat objective, maybe more kind . . . I guessed I could see how Girls' Generation wasn't shy about the drama, mama. They were the blueprint for many current girl-group vibes.

"What do you think, Soma?" Sophat pushed his face right into mine, trying to trigger me in some kind of way.

"Yeah, yeah, it's cool." I offered my honest reaction.

I sat back, trying to determine if Sophat was checking me or if he was beginning to really see eye to eye with Evie Han. I knew the kid had good intentions, but he was bugging me. He was trying so hard to make us friends, but things like that couldn't be forced. Not with all the elements at play. If he wanted us to get chummy, he needed to lay off.

God, why was I even here to begin with? Pretending to make nice with Evie Han when I had work to do? Sure, I kicked it with K-pop plenty, but that wasn't going to help me in the finals of the lit competition. Time was ticking, and I couldn't just hang tight and play nice. I had to get out of here. I reached for my hoodie, hoping someone would get a clue.

"*Actually*, Evie, didn't you want to show us some Cambodian pop stars? I know the market's way different in Cambodia than Korea, but I've seen some stuff on YouTube too." Sophat popped the question back at Evie, while side-eyeing at me for approval. I looked away, knowing he'd caught my impulse to jump ship.

"YES, I thought you'd never ask." With a goofy grin stretched across her face, Evie grabbed the laptop and began typing in whatever she was trying to search for. We were in for it now. "So, like I mentioned before, there's a singer named Laura Mam who is Khmer, and she was actually born in the US, but after college and working a bit, she moved to Cambodia to try her hand at being a full-on pop star. She even created a label and made opportunities for other Khmer people to join the ranks. And the thing is, I love old Khmer music"—*liar, what a liar, no one likes old Khmer music*—"but she's making, like, legit pop-star music. Over the last decade, you can like see her change with the times."

Okay, admittedly, my curiosity was piqued. I'd heard of Laura Mam before, but I hadn't listened to her stuff or really knew her biography. I was surprised, not by the fact that she was singing pop music, but that she was doing it in Cambodia. She was an American girl like us, who'd moved back to the motherland to make it. My bad. *Moved* to the motherland. She'd never been there before, and then she was.

It dawned on me: a person could make a decision to relocate to Cambodia. Whereas Ba had no choice in his move—he was forced against his will—a single person in the world could make a new start there. I could. I'd spent so much time worrying that Ba wouldn't come back, but maybe I was thinking about the whole thing wrong. After I graduated, who knew? I could go to Cambodia.

Now I was listening.

"So, we're gonna watch this Laura Mam video?" Sophat asked.

"No, something even more amazing. That was just setup for how pop music in Cambodia is changing. What I wanted to show you was this." Evie hit the return key, and there on the screen appeared a video of an old-school record player sitting in front of a screen with a man's face.

It was Sinn Sisamouth. I knew it immediately. Ba used to call him the Elvis of Cambodia, but I thought that was kind of a stretch, in appearance at least. As the record played what I assumed was his voice, I guessed I could begin to sort of hear it. They both had a sweetness to their tones. It definitely felt like a love song.

The screen remained static as the song continued to play. I was really all about it, but the rhythm was slow. I was starting to wonder what the point was.

"I know you like old Khmer music and all, but—" I tried to move things along.

"No, but wait. You'll see," Evie protested.

Eventually, the music was replaced by guitar chords, and the video panned out from the record player to a young woman who could have honestly been Sisamouth's clone. A guy sat next to her, playing guitar and offering some light acoustic vibes. The girl then began to sing what I assumed was the song on the record. My heart jumped. The transition was so gradual but kind of shocking.

"That's his granddaughter, Sin Setsochhata. She used to say she would never follow in the footsteps of her grandfather, but now she's her own recording artist in Cambodia. In the video, she's doing a cover of his song." Evie shared her intel with both of us, but I could feel her eyes fall on me to see what sort of reaction I was having. I didn't let on. I stayed locked into the screen, taking the experience in.

"Evie, this is so dope! Her voice is gorg. I bet if she messed with her brand a bit, maybe bring the whole Apsara silhouette forward (like seriously BLOW IT UP), add some mixed patterns, rapped a little, did a more upbeat dance version . . . she'd put Cambo artists on the global charts. What do you think, Soma?"

I thought Sophat was being ridiculous. K-pop stars had only been getting on those charts in the last couple of years, and they'd been at the hustle forever. Cambodian singers would have a long way to go, but honestly, it didn't matter. Because what Setsochhata was doing was different and something I recognized. She had this righteous legacy. Her grandfather was the most famous Cambodian singer of all time. The dude was an icon, and he'd been murdered like the rest of the artists during the genocide. In one dark moment in time, the country had

been set back decades in music-making because a whole generation died. But after, people put together the pieces from the
recordings that survived. It wasn't altogether gone.

That was what we were watching: the Elvis of Cambodia
passing the baton to his granddaughter and the new generation.
Her rendition was beautiful. It was close enough to the original
that I could recognize it, but far enough that it was undeniably
hers.

"Yeah," I responded while trying desperately to fight back
the tears I could feel on the brink of popping out of my emo
face. This was not the content or reaction I'd been expecting.
That was an entirely different thing. I wasn't prepared. I quickly
retreated from the bed, where the three of us were lying, and
flung myself onto my rolling chair, which sent me crashing into
the desk. I reached inside the pizza box and shoved a cold slice
into my mouth. The two of them looked at me from the bed
tentatively.

"What?" I asked with cheese hanging out of my mouth.

"You hated it, didn't you?" Evie asked like she, too, was
about to burst into tears.

"No, Soma didn't hate it. She's just feeling . . . stuff. Isn't
that right?" Sophat lobbed the question my way, trying to do
dual political service.

"Sure," I responded, as matter-of-factly as I could. I wasn't
intentionally trying to be rude; I just became overwhelmed.
Cambodian people, my people, had been through so much.
And even though I hadn't experienced war or genocide like my
parents had, sometimes it just felt like that stuff was still always

present. The fear of being punished or erased for no reason whatsoever. The sadness of not being considered human but a casualty. The feeling that the dead follow us everywhere. I felt that inside me, but it wasn't until I saw Setsochhata singing her grandfather's song that I realized I wasn't just writing rhymes for myself. I was writing them for all the Cambodian people who made it possible for me to do so . . . especially the artists who died because of who they were. The artists who were murdered because of the potential for good they possessed. I had to carry on their legacy, which had been unfairly cut short. That responsibility felt heavy.

"Soma's overwhelmed, because she just got news. . . ."

I threw a death look at Sophat, explicitly telling him to stop in his tracks, do not pass go, do not collect two hundred dollars, do not share news that wasn't his to share.

Sophat cowered from my message and thankfully did not proceed. Unfortunately, though, it was still too late. Evie had already picked up what Sophat had almost thrown down.

"News about the lit competition?!" Suddenly, Evie's eyes got big, as I prepared for the worst. Let the patronizing, pitying salutations begin. "I asked Mr. Lozano who the other seven finalists were, and he showed me the names. Congratulations, Soma!"

"Other seven?" Even if my brain was beginning to stall, my mouth insisted on moving toward a suspicion.

"Yeah, I'm a finalist, too!" Evie pronounced emphatically, not even knowing what sort of effect it was going to have on me.

Immediately, my heart dropped into my butt. I looked briefly at Sophat for some kind of confirmation that he was hearing what I was hearing. He returned the glance but then fully pivoted back to Evie for the inquisition I was doing inside of my own brain.

"You're a finalist for the Jack Kerouac Literary Competition too, Evie?" Sophat asked gently but directly.

"Yeah. I've been thinking about entering for years, but I just never found the courage until now. I was actually inspired by what you did last year, Sophat. I thought you were robbed!"

Sophat sheepishly looked at me, as if he was navigating both pride in finally finding an ally and the shameful discovery that he was the inspiration for this shocking revelation. Evie was a finalist and now my competitor. Whatever had felt theoretical before was now a reality. Just like in life, in this contest Evie and I were going to be compared, and eventually, one of us would be chosen as the victor. KO. Knockout.

"How are *you* feeling about everything, Soma?" Evie asked without knowing how complex the answer could potentially be. Sure, if I had some sense of perspective, maybe I could be proud for her, maybe even happy. But I wasn't. I was mad. Angry. Upset. Fuming.

I was finally starting to feel like I was finding my own voice. Sure, there were speed bumps in the process. I was still wrestling with what it meant to share a piece of my parents' story. I didn't want anyone to think I was taking advantage of something epically tragic just for my own gain, and so I kept on going. In these fresh lines I was about to share in the finals, I was already repping even more of myself. I was putting my obsessive thoughts onto the page. I was asking epic, existential questions so maybe I could get some answers. On that stage, I was preparing to put my voice in the spotlight.

And to be perfectly clear, crystal clear—look-through-me-and-see-through-my-guts clear—it had zero to do with winning some phony award. But maybe doing well would make me feel like I was right on track. Like all the bull I'd been through was meant for something. For me to rise above.

But now, the writing was on the wall. Evie would conquer this like she conquered any test, any extracurricular, any college essay she committed to. While I was trying to make purpose for being a mess in the world, Evie just needed another line on her résumé, another credit to get into an Ivy. She couldn't, wouldn't, understand how that could make me feel.

How was I feeling? Well . . .

"Like shit, Evie. Like poo. Like, why are you even doing this? Why did you enter the competition in the first place?"

Evie looked stunned at the question I threw back.

"Well, because I felt like it might be an interesting adventure—"

"That specific, huh?"

"Soma." Sophat looked at me like he was wary of what I was about to say next. And that intuition was correct. He should be worried.

"Well, I've just seen people do it for years, and I've always admired their ability to be so honest. I write in my journal sometimes, and I thought maybe there would be something to share."

Not good enough, Evie. The reason was weak sauce. While other people were trying to spill their guts, I wanted her to confess that for her, this was just another ploy to get into college.

"You know, in poetry, you have to have some kind of dramatic tension, right? And to have dramatic tension, you have to have a problem? So, like, what problem do you have?"

"Not any major ones I think are bigger than anyone else's."

"Then why do it at all, if your problem isn't that big?"

I wanted to confirm that this was just another award to win and nothing else. She had no real problems to contend with. She was standing on shallow ground.

"It is . . . I just . . . I know everyone has problems. I don't want anyone to feel like I think mine are more important or whatever." Evie was floundering under the questioning, and at this point, I didn't care. I thought it was counterfeit to do something if you didn't feel like you *had* to do it. Otherwise, it was just a writing exercise.

"Well, I don't know if this is what you're talking about, Soma, but for my finals performance, I'm sharing a piece about my parents' time in the refugee camps in Thailand and the Philippines. I mean, that was a pretty big deal. And there are so many smaller stories of the wild stuff my parents had to do to get by, even if they were safe. My dad told me once . . ."

Bingo. Evie hadn't changed a single bit from freshman year.

From sob slideshow to sob poetry contest, she was going to milk this event until it was bone-dry. Until everyone knew she had a monopoly over the genocide of our people. It was an easy way to get people to cry a little, feel sorry for you, and manipulate them into giving you first place. I should've known as soon as she showed us the video of Sinn Sisamouth and his grand-daughter. She was already on that track. While I was feeling uneasy about claiming my people's story—Cambodian people's story—Evie had commodified it into something she could use to get what she wanted. In the moment, I couldn't let it go.

"Never mind that you and I never experienced that ourselves, but you're going to leech off your people's history to make the adjudicators sorry for you. Is that right? So that you can win again at all costs—"

"*Soma—*" Sophat tried to intervene, but the tiger was well out of its cage.

"What? Am I wrong? It's a tactic, no?" I asked the room looking for some confirmation.

"I think I'm going to go now." Evie's eyes began to well just as she turned away and moved quickly toward the door. With her back to me, it suddenly felt like a snap of a drum. I could feel the bass shaking me back into reality.

Damn it. What had I just said? What had I just done?

"Evie, you don't have to." Sophat tried his best to bring her back, but the damage had been done. I'd gone full beast mode, and Evie was my prey.

At the door, she immediately turned back around to look

me straight in the face, and with the same courage she was doling out for Girls' Generation, Evie said the following without
blinking or wavering: "Soma, I know you feel some kind of way
about me. I'm not naive. But I want you to know, you and I are
more the same than you think. That also doesn't mean I want
to replace you. It means we can coexist. I know you think we
can't. And to be clear, I'm not using my parents' history as a
tactic to win. I'm trying to figure out how I feel about it."

With that last word, Evie walked out the door.

A silence fell on the room. Sophat looked at me, but I didn't
know what to say. I knew I had crossed the line. Worse, I'd obliterated it.

Evie wasn't wrong. She was exactly right. I couldn't shake
the feeling that as long as she was around, I couldn't be. Why
hadn't I found out that truth sooner and faced it?

Finally, I asked the question I already knew the answer to: "I
screwed up, didn't I?"

Sophat wouldn't hold my hand on this one. I was beyond
deserving of any sympathy. No, all that was appropriate was for
me to feel very, very bad.

"Sorry to say, but . . . yeah, you really did."

KO. Knockout.

CHAPTER 24
After

For the next week, I was feeling soft. Real soft. I'd done an awful thing, and all signs were telling me I needed to be more aware of what I was putting out, what I was expressing. It didn't take a rocket scientist to see I was on the burner and overflowing. All the things I'd been wrestling with had made their way to my mouth, but it was the wrong audience. No one deserved my heinous acts of displaced junk, especially not Evie. I knew I needed to find her and make up for what I had done, but my sneaks were dragging.

In the meantime, I needed to *also* make sure I didn't accuse anyone else of using the Cambodian genocide to win an award. Yeah, that was something I could strive *not* to do.

I got up early, took a shower, and made sure I was punctual for when Dahvy would eventually ask me at breakfast if I needed a ride to school. When I got downstairs, though, there was no usual commotion or morning shuffle. Dahvy wasn't anywhere in sight. There was some coffee brewing, but no expected hum. No sporadic shouting about being late. Every-thing was so still, you could see the heat from the coffee swirl in the light.

"You're up early." I immediately jumped at the sound of Dahvy's voice. Sis was trying to sneak up behind me like a sulky ninja. I turned around to face her, and much to my sur-prise found her fully in her bathrobe, as if this wasn't a weekday. She was suited up like she had nowhere to go.

I paused, unsure of how to take in what was going on. It couldn't be the weekend. No, it was the day before the competi-tion finals. Why was she playing hooky?

"What's going on?" I asked.

"I'm taking the day off. You can walk to school, right?"

"Yeah, sure. But why?"

"I just needed a long weekend."

"It's Thursday."

"A longer weekend. More wedding stuff to do." Dahvy looked away a little, like there was more to the situation than she was letting on. She didn't look sick. She appeared a little distracted, but there were no noticeable ailments that offered more information.

"Are you feeling okay?"

"Yeah, just lots of stuff to do."

Though her sudden calm was surprising, I was honestly relieved she was taking a chill pill for once. With everything coming up, I'd had a front row seat to watching the stress rise, and I knew Dahvy needed a break. Though the timing felt peculiar, maybe it was actually genius. She needed to slow down to get everything done before the big day.

"Hey, I'm still coming to your performance tomorrow night, by the way. Drakos told me about the finals. Congratulations. I'm really proud of you."

It had slipped my mind. Or rather, I hadn't found the right time to tell Dahvy yet. It was bound to get to her anyways.

"Oh, thanks."

"You cool if I'm there?"

I swallowed down my pride. While I would have earnestly desired not knowing anyone out in the audience, I knew better. People were going to be there. I was going to have to face that fact. I would build my armor in doing what I intended to do: represent myself at the mic. For the moment, that was all I could control.

"Of course," I said, and moved past her toward the door. If I lingered any longer, I'd change my mind.

With one hand on the knob, I suddenly remembered I had a question for Dahvy that had been on my mind since rifling through Ma's albums. "Hey, why did you do plays in high school?"

A pause passed between us as Dahvy seemed thunderstruck by my sharp left turn.

"What?"

"I found old photos of you in the albums. It seems like you were really into it back in high school. Those blue tights—"

"OMG, those blue tights!"

"Yeah, I was just surprised. I didn't know you were such an

actor. And don't get weird about it, but I'm just curious . . . for you, why did you do it?"

I was really rolling the dice on this one, asking her such a random question at such a vulnerable time. But perhaps the randomness of it was perfect for the moment.

"Okay, wasn't expecting that question, but . . . you know, I think at first I did it because people told me I was good at it, and so I went through the motions. But there were these moments when I'd get a role, like one in a musical—"

"*Rent?*"

"Well, there were these moments when I thought it was all a little cheesy. I had to pretend to have a drug problem, but instead of dealing with it like humans do, I had to sing about it. And it didn't work if you were being half-assed. You had to really get into the emotions of it. So sometimes it felt corny, and then other times . . . I *really* got into it. I would start out faking all these huge emotions, singing the lyrics and riding the score, and then all of a sudden, I'd be seriously snot-faced and crying. I would have a real emotional reaction, and it felt amazing. Like cathartic. Maybe things had been bottled up for a while, but these moments felt like unexpected gifts to me. I had an excuse to cry, and it was glorious. It was like a reminder I was still alive."

Dahvy looked a little perplexed, but in entertaining my question, maybe she knew what I'd been searching for all along.

"You going to do that in your finals performance?"

I wasn't sure, but a good cry couldn't hurt.

"Who knows? Maybe."

CHAPTER 25
Set Sail

"I do not enjoy proceeding in the following manner, but you leave me with no choice. Since you did not rewrite your essay, I will have to maintain your F and refer you to the school counselor for an evaluation. I know that may seem severe, but it's standard protocol in cases like this. It's just an opportunity to talk to someone. I've already emailed your parents and sister about the matter. You will no longer have a chance to redo your paper, but I would encourage you to reengage and try your best on the next one."

I could feel Drakos's eyes stay on me, even if I couldn't match them with my own. I was too embarrassed. I was too tired. I was too everything. Of course, I knew that Drakos was waiting on me to jump on his second chance, but with everything going on—Dahvy's wedding, the contest, my most irresponsible, epic shutdown of Evie—there was no way I was rewriting that essay.

Standing before him in his classroom now, I didn't have it in me to protest or come up with some snide remark. I was fully resigned to my fate. I kept my head down, waiting to be dismissed.

"Oh, and I saw you made the finals of the lit competition. Congratulations, Soma! Are you ready for tomorrow tonight?"

My head must've popped right off my neck from the subject change. The man was a master of the non sequitur. What the what. A second ago, Drakos was sentencing me, and the next, he was telling me to break a leg. Zero response dropped out of my mouth. I just stared back, looking a little defeated and definitely dumbfounded.

"Something wrong?" Drakos asked.

"Sorry, I just, I thought you were mad at me or something."

"Well, I haven't been mad at you. I've certainly been frustrated by your avoidance, but it would be inappropriate for me to be mad at you. I want you to succeed, that's all."

I was surprised to hear him say that. I knew he had encouraged me with a flyer before, but I guess I just figured he'd handed them out to everyone. Or pitied me. I didn't think he had any real skin in the game.

"Are you feeling ready for the finals?"

At this point, the question was almost irrelevant. Sure, I was low-key panicking still, putting the last couple of lines together and trying my best to get off book so I wouldn't be glued to the paper. But yeah, the prevailing feeling that rose above all others was just . . . lousy. I felt utterly lousy.

Honestly, way before when I started thinking of myself as a writer, it was like I needed to give myself permission to fully lean into what I was feeling, to be unapologetic about myself, to speak my truth and nothing but the truth. But now, it was seemingly backfiring. With Evie the other night, I'd been communicating raw instinct, pure emotions. But other people feel things too. Evie certainly felt plenty. So how are you supposed to keep people safe from your truth?

"I'm a little stressed out right now. Not just about the competition, but everything. I may not have it in me. . . ." I trailed off, searching for a way out of this conversation and honestly, a way out of the competition at hand.

"How come?"

"Because . . . because . . ." Here we go. The gates were coming down. The emotions were in control now. I certainly couldn't protect Drakos from what I was about to unleash. Whatever it was. "Because sometimes I feel like I was born into something, and I can't escape it! Like bad luck. Or maybe it's bigger than that. Karma. It's like I can't escape my own karmic destiny. Maybe some people are just meant for a mess, and there's nothing to be done. I can't believe I ever thought that I could change that."

While I'd literally just warned myself against over-expressing to the wrong audience, I'd done it again. Too late. I was too embarrassed, too tired to care. It was what I was feeling.

I dared not look back at Drakos. I'd already said too much. And now I felt my eyes welling at everything I was realizing. I could never change my fate.

"You know, Laskarina Bouboulina was actually born in a prison, and that didn't stop her from elevating her situation."

Laska-what? Boubou-who? I'd definitely not heard those words before they came out of Drakos's mouth.

"I'm guessing from that confused look on your face you don't know who that is?" I nodded in agreement.

"Well, my mother used to have this framed print of this Greek woman named Laskarina Bouboulina, standing at the edge of a ship. She has a wrap around her face, and her scowl is very severe, like she's in charge of some business. That business being war. If you end up taking my AP European History class next year, we'll talk a lot about how the Ottoman Empire ruled much of Europe, Asia, and Africa between the fourteenth and early twentieth centuries. One of the countries they ruled was Greece, until they achieved its independence in 1829. Bouboulina was a part of that fight. From the money she inherited from her two passed husbands, she built several ships used in the Greek War of Independence. In addition to that, she made arms and recruited men to fight, and on March 13, 1821, she flew the Greek flag on the mast of her largest ship, the *Agamemnon*. She was a real naval warrior. Zito Hellas!"

"And this woman was born in prison?"

"Oh, yes! I buried the lede there, didn't I? Her father was also a captain, who had been imprisoned in Constantinople for being a revolutionary too. On one of the visits by the mother, Bouboulina was born. You see, she could've looked at her life and said, 'I'm destined to repeat my father's fate,' but she didn't. She grew up to have an incredible legacy that was full of fight. And to be contrary too, she didn't escape some things her father gave her.

She became a captain like him. She became a revolutionary just like him too. She became those things, but unto herself. *She* was her own captain, and *she* was her own revolutionary, and arguably *she* left an even more important mark than her father did. I'd say, sometimes it's not entirely about breaking from what you've been given. It's about knowing how to use those gifts to chart your own path. What do you say, Soma?"

Soma. Hearing my name, I was suddenly reminded of the other badass woman in history who was my actual legacy. These women—Soma and Laskarina—were fighting battles with consequences that were life and death. If they could start a culture, win independence, be role models for girls to come, what was I doing licking my wounds at the first sign of trouble? Not that my family's situation wasn't tough. It was. And still people had gone through similar hardships, sometimes even worse.

And then something hit me. I knew Ba had prepared me.

You are a queen. This is your inheritance. And with that is your ability to say, to do, to be whomever you want to be. Don't be afraid. Step into your legacy.

In his initial email, he'd been setting me up to move forward. I needed to break out of jail. I needed to make our legacy my own. I needed to set sail.

For the first time since Ba had begun sending me emails, I finally felt the impulse to call him back. For real this time. I couldn't exactly articulate why, but I knew it had something to do with his messages, which were coded with purpose. It wasn't

just in the first one, it was in the ones that followed. It was in
his will and imagination to dream a new reality. It was in his
vulnerability to share that he'd been shaky himself in searching
for signs. It was in his fearlessness in staring straight into the
eyes of the problem, even when I wanted to look away. It was in
his grace in giving me time to find my way. Without evening
knowing it, Ba had been setting me up at the mic this whole
entire time.

I'd call him after the final competition.

"I should probably get going. I have some work to do," I
replied simply, feeling like it was entirely true. If I was going to
show up to the competition with my senses straight, I needed
to stay focused.

"Well, good. I personally can't wait to see you perform."

"Hey, thank you, Mr. Drakos. I really appreciate it."

"You're welcome."

"And . . . zito hellas."

"Zito hellas."

After seeing Drakos, I walked down the path along the canal
to the bench across from St. Anne's. I needed the lunch break
to gather my thoughts. Drakos had offered me some words of
encouragement, and I was trying my best to translate them into
what I understood them to mean. For me. That was the thing
about advice. People could give it, but only you could make
meaning out of it for yourself.

Seated on the bench, I felt this unexpected urge to revisit

the video that had started it all. The last viewing was honestly shocking. My self-doubts of my self-view had gotten the best of me. But now I felt purposed. Like I wanted to know. I wanted to search what in that girl motivated her to share her truth without really thinking about the repercussions. How could she know? She was going out on a limb with the basic premise that she had something to say. How could I bring that girl back?

> Set on self-view . . .
> Like she's even got a clue . . .
> 'Bout that red light . . .
> Flashing hot, bright . . .
> Counting up the time
> As she's waiting for that rhyme
> To find its other pair
> Like palms kissing for a prayer

She was nervous, but she was handling metaphors like Shakespeare. "And palm to palm is holy palmers' kiss." Okay, so chick was drawing from reading *Romeo and Juliet* in Ruben's class previously. But this time, the palms were solo and the intention wasn't romantic. The words just evoked the intensity of a hopeful prayer.

> But she's out on a limb
> While things are looking dim
> And she needs something to do
> When her life is feeling new

See, even when things were dim, there was the impulse to *do something*. Like when the body senses danger, we run. Our brains, our hearts, our bodies are wired to do something, and maybe that was what this was all about.

> What's she gonna say?
> When she's some kind of way?
> What's she gonna do?
> After what she's been through?

The questions were already there. What's she gonna say? What's she gonna do? The inquiry was the point. Never was the answer.

> Ooh, she's touched on a nerve
> And now she's looking to swerve
> Because she's trying to work through
> What she knows she cannot undo

She wanted to swerve to avoid tapping that nerve. That girl felt like there was much she could not undo, but now what did she think? Maybe there wasn't much to undo, but there was possibility *to do*. The finals were tomorrow.

> Dear self-view . . .
> Who's even got a clue . . .
> 'Bout that red light . . .
> Flashing hot, bright . . .

She might not be performing for the red light, but she was performing for the self-view. So what did she have to say for herself? What did she have to face? Who was the speaker at the podium?

Just as I was about to put the monster box away for good, there across the way with her most impeccable timing was Britney Roe walking directly toward me. I hadn't seen her in person since our first outing to the park last week. It wasn't like I was avoiding her (we had texted some), but there was a lot going on. Still, our intimate conversation had a direct impact on what I was going to represent at the competition. She'd helped me, even if she didn't know it.

"There she is!" Britney exclaimed, as if she'd been looking for me this whole time.

"What's up? How are you?" We awkwardly went in for a point of contact that more resembled a handshake than an actual hug. The weirdness was undoubtedly clocked, and then we retracted, trying to pretend like it was all good.

"You excited for tomorrow?" It was the question on every-one's tongue, including Britney's, but I was in the mix of what I was feeling. I didn't quite know how to accurately share that.

"Yeah, I think it'll be good."

"That doesn't sound too convincing." Britney's BS meter was unfailing. She knew there was so much more than that canned response.

"It's just, I'm feeling nervous but motivated. I'm honestly not horrible, which is great, but I got work to do before tomorrow."

Under her bucket hat, her eyes got big, and her brain got to thinking. I could tell that she was devising.

"It's not the solution, but here." Before I knew it, Britney took off her red shag jacket and thrusted it toward me. "A little bit of armor."

"Huh?" I was sincerely confused and a little shocked that she was just giving me her most iconic piece of clothing. In years to come, when Britney would be imagined in lore by future storytellers, she would be illustrated in this jacket. Why was she offering it to me now?

"It's on loan through your performance, okay?"

"I couldn't—"

"You can. Let it be a boost to you."

"But it's yours."

"You wanna know the truth? I'm not all that confident as you might think I am. Honestly, I'm kind of a coward. I can't watch scary movies, I freaking hate spiders, and heights give me hives. No joke. But when I wear certain clothes, they give me a little bit of presence. To make myself feel strong, even though sometimes I don't feel that way. I can put all my fears into my style. It's not only an expression, but protection. It's a good-luck charm, Soma."

I was outright startled/shook/stunned by her generosity. If I had a jacket like this, nobody's grubby hands were getting on it. It would stay on my person until I was buried in it.

"Are you sure? It feels like sacrilege to try on your most historical uniform."

"Oh, whatever. Sacrifice the preciousness. Get into it. Let it be iconic for you." Britney seemed so assured. If only I could strive for a percent of that confidence.

Nervously, I slipped one arm and then the other into the jacket, and immediately, I felt its warmth wrapping around me. I didn't think it'd look the same on me as it did on Britney, but no edit: the fit was right.

"How do I look?" I asked, but already somewhat knowing it didn't matter. I felt good.

"It looks like . . . you." Britney smiled back at me, her eyes looking confident in what I was about to do. If she believed in me, maybe it was worth it to believe the same.

"I have to get back to class, but break legs, Soma. You got this."

Just as she'd arrived, Britney walked away in a blur, probably unaware of the significance of her gift. She was good about that. And truthfully, she wasn't the only one. Reeling it back, probably without any of them knowing, in the middle of all the mayhem, many people had given me gifts. Dahvy had offered me a little bit of calm and catharsis. Drakos had offered me some historical perspective and futurism. Britney had offered me some armor. The question was, what was I going to do with it all?

Set sail.

CHAPTER 26
My Confusion

The latch clicked again. Another audience member disappeared behind the auditorium door. I peeked into the window slot just to check out the capacity, and . . . dang. There were people here. For some reason, I thought a lit competition possessed a kind of repellent, if not irrelevant, nerdy aura about the whole thing, but maybe I was wrong. Maybe poetry was the new rock and roll.

My eyes scanned the auditorium, and right there, perched at the front, just feet away from the stage, were Sophat, Dahvy, and Ruben. Wow, they were struggling to read the room. My room. I figured given some of the most recent events, they might consider lying low and not adding heat to an already tense situation. They knew I was nervous. Why were they making their presence known?

I looked around to see if I could locate Britney too. I hadn't seen her in the hallway after I arrived, but maybe she got to her seat before? No, it was good I couldn't find her. If I saw her while I was performing, I'd be wrecked. There were plenty of recognizable eyes to inspire terror. Being sly and intuitive as usual, Britney probably understood that.

I needed to focus. I couldn't let anyone's attendance distract me. If I was going to steer the warship out of prison and toward my intended future, like the Greek woman Drakos had told me about, I had to keep my eye on the goal.

Stay cool.

Stay focused.

Stay Soma.

"Excuse me, can I get through?"

I knew that voice, and I knew I had to face it. I turned to find Evie staring right back at me. It was the first time I'd seen her since that awful takedown last week. I'd wanted to apologize to her before, but when I dropped into Brew'd, her manager told me she didn't have shifts for the rest of the week. I had hoped I'd just run into her, but I guessed this was as good a time as any to grovel.

"Yeah, of course," I meekly replied while stepping out of the doorway. Still, I knew I couldn't just let her walk past. This was my one and only opportunity to set things straight. "Hey, actually, Evie, can I talk to you for a second?"

"We're almost at time, aren't we?"

It was true. The countdown was on, so I'd better start talking quick.

"I'm sure I'm the last person you want to see right now, but . . . I just wanted to say how sorry I am about what I said.

No edit: it was all propaganda. It was total shit. I know each of us Khmer kids have our own relationship with our history, and I was spouting some bull. Cambos have it hard enough, and there was no reason for me to go off like that. You deserve to be in the finals like everyone else and to express yourself the way you want to. I'm a jealous piece of turd who can't think straight when I feel like someone's better than me. I've never done therapy before, but I imagine they'd tell me it's because I'm wounded. All these feelings are coming from other parts of my life, and I made a real mess of it conflating all my issues. And boy, do I have a lot of issues. Anyways, I'm talking too much, and you probably think I'm super extra now, but the point of this all was to tell you . . . I'm sorry. I'm so sorry. I'm the most sorry person that ever was."

I really didn't think my apology would come out like verbal vomit, but I couldn't help it. It was everything I wanted to say to her. Poor Evie looked a little stunned but also a little different. Unlike her usual cheery self. She looked serious and kind of grown-up. Like something had changed inside of her, and maybe I was the guilty cause of that.

"You know, Soma, I've always thought you didn't like me—"

"I do, though."

"You don't. At least own it, right? But I always thought maybe it would change. Like maybe it was our age or this time in our lives. It's like you're supposed to be kind of irrational while trying to figure things out. But you hurt me. What you said. It really made me sad, because I thought I would never use my history for my own advantage like that."

At this point in the conversation, I could feel my stomach churning. If I'd felt guilty before, that was just the layup. The shame was hitting its stride. I wanted to throw up.

Evie looked resolutely at me, but then something appeared to catch her attention. She took a beat before speaking again.

"The truth is . . . maybe I was going to. Maybe you were right. Maybe I was going to take advantage of the war, the genocide, the assimilation, all the horrible things our parents went through. Maybe I honestly don't know what to do with that history. Maybe sometimes that history feels like my own, and sometimes it doesn't. Maybe sometimes I do exploit it because I'm trying to figure it out. Maybe, in some fucked-up way, I don't even know how to be without tragedy." She paused her "maybes," and maybe I'd found someone else who thought in "maybes" more than I did. Maybe we were the same. Finally, Evie started again. "Maybe I keep talking about tragedy in everything I do, because I want it out."

I was off my sneaks. It wasn't like I expected Evie to fold in on my accusation or to validate it. I certainly didn't deserve an apology. But to hear Evie actually embrace what I was saying made me feel a kind of way. We were both revealing our truths, and there was nothing neat about it.

"Well, Evie, it wasn't my right to tell you that. And the truth is, I accused you of it only because I was feeling it myself. It's easy to project when you're so jealous of someone."

"OMG, what are you talking about? Jealous of me?" Evie seemed in utter disbelief.

"Yeah, your grades are, like, perfect." I led with one of the most obvious reasons, knowing there were a bajillion more.

"Because my parents force me to get As."

"You're in so many extracurriculars."

"Because I'm nervous about college. I need to get a full scholarship."

"And you have such a positive attitude about everything."

"I'M FAKING! I'm a liar! I'm negative about everything! Most of the time, I feel like throwing cute animals against a wall. I know that's effed up, but I want to *destroy* things sometimes. That's why I like doing poetry to begin with. Because I can get it all out, and no one will have to know that I'm actually horrible in real life."

Okay . . . well . . . I didn't know if I could be surprised again, but that took the cake. Aside from the animal cruelty bit, everything I thought was perfect about Evie was coming out of some sort of perceived deficiency. The girl had her own problems. Go figure.

Evie continued. "I've always been so jealous of you. You seem so confident, like nothing bothers you. You don't try like me. You're just effortlessly cool. I wish I had an ounce of that."

What Evie didn't know was that I did try, and I was low-key—actually *high-key*—obsessed with what people thought of me. Even the "effortlessly cool" was, well . . . efforted.

It was so obvious: Evie wanted to be me, and I wanted to be

her. Before, we'd been functioning from so many assumptions, we barely could see each other. But now, those judgments were shed. Maybe we actually had a shot at being friends.

"Crap! What time is it? We're going to miss our performance!" Evie pronounced, shaking me back into consciousness. This conversation had been long overdue, but on the other side of the door, our contest was moving in that direction too. If we didn't get in there, neither Cambo girl would prevail.

"Six fifty-five p.m. Yeah, we gotta go, but thank you, Evie. For all of this. For understanding."

"We have to support each other, right?" Evie asked simply, but making sure I knew she meant it. I felt charged with the ask too. I would support Evie, in whatever way I could. Things were different now.

Evie slipped behind the auditorium door, and I could have just followed, but I needed to review my rhymes one last time. I shot down the hallway and pulled out my folded piece of paper. I had rewritten the poem and memorized it a thousand times over. Before today, the words had flowed out of me like I wasn't even thinking about it. They lived in my throat; they just needed a little push, breath, and resonance.

But today, I went back to the paper and that muscle memory felt slack. In the last hour or so, the words had felt like they were running away from me. In the narrow hallway, I tried to close my eyes to keep my focus, but all I could see were my thoughts receding into the darkness. My palms were slick and sweaty. My stomach started to grumble again. My heart was thumping out of my chest. My body was in full self-preservation beast mode.

"Soma?" I opened my eyes to find Ruben staring straight at me. "You got your poem?"

"Yeah, I got poems," I answered, trying desperately to identify what this man was asking of me.

"So, you want to come in now? Mr. Lozano is asking for you. I think it's past time." Ruben's eyes got bigger. I knew that he knew that I was beginning to lose my chill. He treaded carefully in my orbit. "How're you . . . feeling?"

"Okay. Kind of. Sort of. Not really, actually. Not great. Horrible. Stunted. Like I hate it here. Like I just want to run out the door and jump into the canal and be the subject of some criminal investigative television show, except there would be no crime to solve, because it would be clear. The victim couldn't do the lit competition, so she jumped into the canal."

"Wow, so strong feelings."

"I'm just . . . what am I doing here? I'm sweating. I don't know why I let Sophat talk me into doing this. The kid is the worst. And it's like he gave me all this pressure to level up, but why do I need to? Can't I just be at sea level? I don't need to be standing on mountains. Or hills even. Let me stand in prairies, where there is no elevation whatsoever, you know what I mean? Or like a cornfield! I know climate change is real, and we're going to have to climb some shit, but I know my fate. I'm going to fall off that ledge and be a bloody carcass in some cavernous pit. Like why do I have to be a bloody carcass, for what? To prove that I have some thoughts. *What am I even talking about?!*"

Ruben calmly intertwined his fingers and moved his hands toward his mouth. He blinked, and then returned his hands to his side. While I apparently couldn't stop monologuing about chaos today, Ruben knew the only remedy was to counter with a little bit of legato and a little bit of silence.

"*Okay.* Let's just take a deep breath. You're obviously stressed—"

"You think?!" I looked down at my hands, and they were full-on vibrating like they were swatting away flies. I clasped them together to prevent them from falling off my arms, but their union just made it look like I was doing a kind of violent vocal exercise. I mean, my jaw was tight. I should be preparing my body, but the second I tried to control one limb, it sent a ripple through the rest of my shaking bones. I was straight rattling.

Ruben's hands fell onto my shoulders. The vibrations began to slow down. The muscles began to melt.

"Close your eyes." His centered but forceful voice felt like a wave over me.

"And find your feet." My angsty toes were wriggling around in my flats like they needed to break free, but Ruben's instruction, and particularly the word "find," felt like a direction I could take. I found my feet, and my toes began to calm.

"And breathe deep." I placed my hands on my belly. I

inhaled, feeling the oxygen move in through my nose and mouth, travel down the length of my body, and back up again. I exhaled.

"And hear me out: 'I had nothing to offer anybody except my own confusion.'" Ruben's words felt familiar. Where had I heard that before?

"That's *On the Road*, right?"

"Yes. Offer us that, and it's more than enough."

If Ruben was suggesting I go up to the podium and share my confusion, well, maybe there wouldn't be enough time to get into it all, because I had plenty. I was confused by why my ba was thousands of miles away with no solution or end in sight. I was confused by my relationship with Dahvy. Sometimes she was like a sergeant barking orders, and sometimes I could see her sadness, up close and personal. Would I have to take care of her too? I was confused by Britney—was she into me or not? Was all my emotional baggage just a little too much to travel with? I was confused by Ma's prolonged absence. Was this the new normal? Was I losing a mother too? I was utterly confused by the future.

It was more than enough.

It wasn't Kerouac's words that were staying with me. It was Ruben's.

If my confusion was me, then I was enough.

I was enough.

Stay cool. Stay focused. Stay Soma.

I opened my eyes again, and there Ruben remained.

"Even if they can't be here for the next couple of weeks, I know your parents are proud of you." Ruben gave me one last sympathetic smile and began to walk toward the door, completely unaware of the epic truth bomb he'd just dropped.

"They? What do you mean?"

The ground seemed to disappear from under me. My entire body began to hum. I looked to the messenger, forgetting what it was that they say about them. Don't kill them, right?

Aha. Ruben's eyes got real deep, and he began to clear his throat. He looked at me harder, as if to keep staring at me in silence would bring some clarity to the situation.

"Your parents. Dahvy didn't tell you? She said she was going to. . . ."

That was why she'd been so weird yesterday morning. That was why she was staying home for an extended weekend. That was why she looked so calm. The calm before the storm. Now was the storm.

I blinked once.

I blinked twice.

I blinked three times.

Then I finally asked: "Ma isn't coming to the wedding, is she?"

Now Ruben understood, and so did I.

"No, Soma. I'm so sorry. She's not."

And just like that, the sound went out, and time slowed down. It was like the moment in the movie when a character finds out the truth that will change them forever. Afterward, you'll never be the same. Ruben was mouthing words I could not comprehend. He squeezed my shoulder, opened the auditorium door, and ushered me in.

The lights went out, and all I could hear behind me was the clicking of the door finally closing. I stepped into darkness.

CHAPTER 27
The Performance

Ma wasn't coming to the wedding.

Aside from the rope lights lining the aisles, the room was dark. From my chair onstage, all I could focus on was the aggressive stream of spotlight floating from the balcony toward the podium downstage of our row of seated finalists. With dust particles dancing around, the spotlight looked kind of mystical, like some UFO beam coming down to retrieve the poor poet at the mic. I imagined myself stepping up to it, feeling the light hit my face, and being zapped right up into an alien spaceship. Extraterrestrials might wreck my brain for research, but at least they would have saved me from myself. I offer myself as tribute.

Apparently, the aliens were a little behind on their schedule, because Evie Han was still up there, waving around and yelling at the mic. Not *in* the mic. But *at* the mic. When she had previously revealed her finalist status, I thought her lyricism would fall on the lighter side of things. Boy, was I wrong. She'd changed her finals poem (thanks to me) and was not happy about it. Evie was shouting about the time she got a B, and how broken academia was. It had failed her, and she was getting revenge by way of *screaming couplets*. Maybe the aliens were too scared to take her.

Ma wasn't coming to the wedding.

My focus was entirely a blur. Just half an hour ago, when I was out in the hallway, I was mad frenetic, talking nonsense to Ruben about jumping into canals, off mountains, and being a bloody carcass mess. But now the competition was almost over. I was in a cloud. Free-floating. Seeing that things were happening and understanding the general vibe, but not being able to quite make out what exactly was going on. I was moving slowly in sepia tones. There was panic, no doubt, but it took the form of a low hum. Like a drone signaling the end to something.

I looked down at my paper. No hope there. It was folded so many times it was beginning to disintegrate. The words looked like some lost language faded and worn away, like they'd been around since biblical times. Longer than that. Buddha times.

Ma wasn't coming to the wedding.

My eyes went left. Evie's empty chair stared back at me like a sinkhole. Across from it, the six other finalists sat attentively in their chairs. They looked relieved. I envied them. They'd done the deed, and now they could embrace the chill. On the other side of it, though, was me. I'd drawn the last spot and would follow Evie shortly after. I was on an island all by my lonesome. I did actively nod to pretend like I was listening to what she had to say, but the real real was that I was on a little piece of land floating out at sea. I was adrift, among natural disasters, and soon enough, alien abduction would be my only salvation. This state was called calm chaos. Or was it chaotic calm?

Ma wasn't coming to the wedding.

"PSSSSSST!"

Sophat's big-ass head entered the frame from the front row. Though we were mere feet away, the divide from the stage and the audience could not be greater. His eyes widened as if to show concern, but at that point I was afraid there was little he could do to help the situation. I was slow to respond, but eventually I managed to mouth back a "*What?*" and then looked around to see if anyone had caught the exchange.

Sophat pointed at me and then down. I followed his aggressive direction and realized he was pointing to the phone I forgot I was still clutching. Was it ringing, and in my free-floating space, had I not realized it? No, it was lit from a text message that the kid had sent to me.

SOPHAT (7:36 p.m.): WTF. YOU LOOK LIKE YOU'RE
                     GONNA DIE.

I returned to Sophat's concerned squinty eyes, weighted down by layers of furrowed brows. He was reading my mind. Of course. I felt like I was going to die.

SOMA (7:37 p.m.): I AM going to die. This is how I die.

Ma wasn't coming to the wedding.

From the stage, I could see his phone glow from my returned message. It was so visible even Dahvy's attention moved from the podium to Sophat next to her. And damn, she looked guilty, like she knew exactly what was going down and with zero power to change any of it. She had to just watch and wait it out. I must've looked real stressed too because, like magic, all three of them (including Ruben) immediately switched to smiles that stretched beyond the authentic limits of actual sympathy. Yup. These were some sad, sorry faces.

Thunderous applause echoed throughout the room. Oh no. Evie was done. My eyes broke from the fake-ass trio in the front row and moved to Mr. Lozano, inching to the stage and summoning me on. It had to be me. I was the only one left.

"*And last* but certainly not least, please welcome to the stage, Ms. Soma Kear!"

Ma wasn't coming to the wedding.

The room fell silent as the applause went to the grave. I lifted myself from my plastic blue chair and began to move toward the podium. The second I arrived, the intensity of the light hit me so hard, I could barely see anything, let alone anyone. I closed my eyes to prepare myself for takeoff.

Ma wasn't coming to the wedding.

Someone coughed.

A wooden chair squeaked from the house.

People began to murmur.

Ma wasn't coming to the wedding.

I opened my eyes again, and this time, along with the dust, I noticed red fuzzies flying all around me. The effect was surprising and kind of magical. I wondered if I was truly being beamed up. As the particles swirled and lifted, I balled up my fists, preparing for flight.

Nothing happened. No levitation. No abduction. No one to tell me what to do next.

Just a roomful of faces staring back at me, wondering if I was going to start already.

Ma wasn't coming to the wedding.

And then, in the very back, I could see Britney smiling right at me. I smiled back. I remembered. I was wearing her red shaggy jacket she'd loaned to me for protection. Instantly, I felt her arms around me. It felt like armor. Maybe I wasn't in such a bad way, after all.

Ma wasn't coming to the wedding.

I took a deep breath in . . .

And a deep breath out . . .

And I tried to speak my piece . . .

Ma wasn't coming to the wedding.

CHAPTER 28
What I Would Have Said

"What's God to you?" she said
Like she was leaving me on "read"
Asking for the room
As if even to assume

That I had a notion
About the potion
To the question
Of my obsession

That God was a man
With some ultimate plan
That only he knew
How to really break through

"What's God to you?" she said
Like she wasn't trying to tread

The intensity
Of this perplexity

As I try to understand
Even push to expand
What I think I know
As I grow, as I flow, as I break down like whoa

The idea that a dude
Was the only real food
For the appetite for meaning
As we go a-machining

"What's God to you?" she said
Like some hundred-pound lead
Understanding what it means
To break the routines

Of thinking that he's there
When it was only a prayer
And behind the curtain
Is absolutely uncertain

Or not even real
You can't even feel
But some abstract ideal
That's absurdly surreal

"What's God to you?" she said
Like even God might be dead
So what's there instead
But some person's dread

"What's God to you?" she said
Like I was trying to wed
A word that held it all
When maybe it's kind of small

Like a look across the room
When you smell a sweet perfume
Or a body dancing to the beat
When the melody's just that sweet

"What's God to you?" she said
Like I was trying to be led
To give a single word
When we live in the absurd

Or maybe I'm actually wrong
When I'm talking about a song
Because when it starts to flow
I'm sure of how we grow

To the enormity of mortality
The size of our rise

The way that we sway
And reach to teach
Ourselves as we delve
Into the questions that may be . . . God

"What's God to you?" she said
Like she saw inside my head
And searched within my heart
To show me: I'm a work of art.

That's what I would have said.

That's what I would have said if I hadn't lost my complete chill and forgot how to speak altogether. That's what I would have said if I hadn't embarrassingly hit the mic, spectacularly knocking it over into the podium. That's what I would have said if I hadn't looked out to the sea of terrorized faces in the audience and realized that every single person in that room felt uniformly sorry for me. That's what I would have said if I hadn't found out Ma wasn't coming to the wedding only moments before I stepped onto the stage.

That's what I would have said.

But I didn't.

I didn't even get a line out, a word, a syllable. The aliens had somehow hooked into my soul, exorcised that from my body, and left the remaining shell onstage to tragically fail dot com. The poem wasn't going down, and as soon as I came to realize that, I ran out of the auditorium so fast you could've probably seen one of those cartoon dust clouds trailing behind me.

"Why didn't you tell me the truth?" In Dahvy's parked car well after the finals, I yelled the question from the back seat. I couldn't bear to sit next to her. Dahvy had rightfully sent Ruben and Sophat along on their way, so we could have the sister showdown we'd been waiting for. Whatever answer she was prepared to give would be meaningless at this point. She'd lied to me. She'd embarrassed me. She'd taken away the one thing I had left—the chance to share my words.

"I just found out myself. It was so last-minute. I was reeling from what she was saying." Dahvy's voice was shaking. From the front seat, she looked beyond the windshield and onto the bricked back wall of the school. Sometimes she'd try to direct her face toward me, but never quite directly. Maybe that contact was just too much.

"And you couldn't just communicate that when I walked into the kitchen yesterday morning? You had a chance to say something."

"I was sad, Soma! I skipped out on teaching yesterday because I was *so* sad. I couldn't think straight."

"And what do you think I am?"

I couldn't stand that Dahvy was using her emotions as the reason she couldn't update me about the worst news ever. She was acting like I wasn't always aware of every anxiety she displayed. Was there ever room for me to feel anything? Would our shared reality always be guided by what she was going through?

"I know you're sad too. That's probably why I didn't say anything in the moment. I knew you were about to perform in the finals, and I didn't want to ruin your show."

"Well, good thing, because you did it anyway. Why can't you just treat me like an adult? Why don't you believe I can handle what's going on?"

"Because I'm having a hard time handling it myself!"

"Just tell me what the hell is going on with them!"

As the decibels hit their peak, Dahvy turned fully to look at me. There was no hiding now. There was only the truth. She gripped the car headrest, as if that would give her any support, and finally shared what I'd been waiting for this entire time.

"OKAY. You wanna know the full truth? Fine. Since you think you're mature enough to take it on, I'll gladly share it with you. Ba was deported, and so he's really fucking sad right now, okay? *Everyone is sad.* But you already know the guy takes meds for his depression, and he recently stopped taking them because, well, that is something none of us understand. So Ma is scared shitless because she doesn't know what to do about him. She's stalling. She's made it very clear that she is more worried about him than us—"

"That's not true!" I couldn't understand why Dahvy was using this moment to take a dig at Ma when it was clearly not her fault.

"*It is, Soma!* She should be more worried about him, because the real truth is, Ba may never come home. You get that, right? Like ever. And when you love someone like that, it destroys a person. Ma is disappearing right before our eyes, whether we like it or not."

In the driver's seat, Dahvy's twisted body was turned back toward me to drop that lovely truth. After some wild panting and staring down each other's drenched faces, Dahvy returned her gaze out onto the windshield. At this point, I was surprised the glass windows hadn't shattered. It honestly felt like they had. There was nothing else to say or do in this moment. Everything *had* changed, and we weren't looking back.

After some silence, Dahvy turned the car on, and I shared what little I had left inside me.

"I'll never perform another poem again because of you. It's all your fault."

When I got home, I ran upstairs and locked the door. I would never leave again, and people would have to unhinge the door to get me out. No, I was done with it all. I wasn't going to school. I wasn't talking to anyone. I wasn't trying to do anything but be alone. After the disastrous not-performance, I'd had my limit of human interaction, thank you very much.

Dahvy placed meals in front of my door like they did in prison, and eventually, she did inform me that Sophat would need to email me my homework assignments if I was going on a staycation that following week. Honestly, in my entire academic life, it was probably the most homework I'd ever done.

In some twisted turn of fate, doing schoolwork kept me out of my feelings. I even redid my essay for Drakos's class, regardless of whether he'd accept it or not. I sent it anyways, still keeping a bit of the Rage Against the Machine but erring on the side of . . . Vibe Against the Machine. I didn't expect a reply, but I glowed when Drakos emailed me back his approval.

Dear Soma,

Thank you for your revision on the essay. I particularly liked the lines, "What are the limits to empathy? Does it end with your family? Does it end with someone you know? Does it end with you? Or can people who legislate extend their empathy for families that are broken apart by being locked in a process? How can laws be more empathetic? How can laws be more human?"

I know your performance wasn't exactly what you planned, but just remember that so many people have failed before you. Your failure stands on the shoulders of so many. And your success will do the same. You can always imagine your life outside the prison you were born in. You can always turn the ship around. You can always redo your essay.

Sincerely,
Mr. Drakos

When I'd reworked the essay (no lie), I hadn't even put much thought into it. I took his advice and tried not to eliminate my anger but look at it for what it really was . . . an expression of the questions I wanted to ask. And it wasn't like I was dispassionate or whatever, but sometimes when you fight and fight and fight, all you have left is an ask—a plea for people to care more. To not be so selfish. To just look at their neighbors as members of the universe who are trying to get by too.

From upstairs, I could hear two sets of shoes shuffling around the kitchen. A week had passed since the not-performance, and much to Dahvy's credit (not that I was trying to give her any), she let me be. Fine, whatever, I appreciated that. I knew her go-to in situations like this was to fix everything, but maybe she'd taken a cue from the past couple of weeks. Still, every so often, Dahvy would not-so-subtly speak my name in a cloud of grumbling, and Ruben would reply in a more apologetic tone. Dahvy would then come in hard with a loud, angrier argument, followed by a long stretch of silence. The whole thing would cycle through again.

Their wedding was tomorrow, and even through the floorboards, I could feel the energy rising. Dahvy's bridesmaids bailed on the bachelorette party she didn't even want to begin with. Ruben's groomsmen *did* throw a party for their boy, but from the sounds of epic hurling echoing throughout the house, maybe the party got a little too hype. I'm sure Dahvy scolded him properly. And none of that still paled in comparison to the news of Ma not making it back in time for the wedding, promptly followed by my meteoric crash onstage. Yeah, no . . . things couldn't have gotten worse.

An incoming call lit up my phone. It was from Ma.

I hesitated. Everyone was trying to reach me, but only one person was calling me directly. If she was just going to ask me if I'd eaten yet, then I didn't need that kind of conversation either. I wondered if Dahvy had reached out to her. Maybe she didn't know.

"Hi," I answered.

"Hi, gkoun. Have you eaten yet?" I could've hung up, but I knew she couldn't help it. It was just her way.

"Yeah, I've eaten. Burnt bigh."

I figured Ma needed to know exactly what was in my current diet.

She paused. I could tell she was searching for more words. Ma was never one for small talk, so I knew it had to be coming.

"Dahvy told me about the show. How are you feeling?"

Now, this question caught me off guard. Not the premise, but the question. She was asking me how I was feeling. She didn't jump to conclusions and then make decisions based on what she expected of my reaction. No, in this moment, Ma was just asking, very simply, how I was feeling.

Here, I could've lied, but I didn't much feel like it. I wanted her to know the truth of it. I was tired of editing my response so others didn't have to worry. At this point, they probably should be worried.

"Bad. Like horrible. I completely embarrassed myself. And worse, compared to everything else that's going on, it doesn't even matter."

"Of course it matters."

"It doesn't! How am I supposed to feel sorry for myself when Ba's stuck in Cambodia, and now you are too? You didn't even tell me yourself you couldn't come to the wedding."

My throat began to tighten. I could feel my eyes stinging, and the tears beginning to well. I couldn't squeak out any more accusations.

Ma paused again.

"Soma, look. We all made a mistake. Me the most. You're grown, I know that now. I should've trusted you would be able to handle it, but . . . I was nervous. Because I love you, and I wanted to protect you."

"But I can protect myself," I replied firmly.

"You can, and you can't. But maybe I should believe a little more in the first. So, let me tell you what's going on, okay?"

Up to this point, Ma's voice had sounded a little nervous, scared, alert to whatever emergency she was sensing. But as she began to tell me facts about what had been going down the past couple of months, I could hear her become calmer, more grounded, as if she were just at home, telling me to do the dishes, telling me to do my homework, telling me to do anything. I was hooked into this emotional pivot. It struck me. Like she had to adjust to tell me what she needed me to know. Like this was what all humans did. Sometimes they had to pivot.

Ma told me everything. She told me that when Ba first got to Cambodia, he was doing okay for the most part. He'd connected with an old cousin who helped him get an apartment, and while Ba was trying to get a job, the cousin's family was helping him with money. Then he got a job as a tuk tuk driver, and after a couple of awful incidents with unruly tourists who were either drunk or didn't pay him enough, he started to slip. Ma found out he'd been off his antidepressants and was drinking. She had to drop everything and go over there to help him out. Ba protested, but there was no other option. She knew she had to slap some sense into him.

It broke my heart, because I knew Ma wasn't just doing this for Ba. She was doing it for all of us. She was the glue that kept us all together, and she'd travel thousands of miles away to make sure of that.

And it broke my heart even more knowing that I'd been responsible for some of it. If I had just picked up Ba's call, if I had just texted him back, if I had just responded to one email . . . maybe Ma wouldn't have felt this was all on her. I'd convinced myself that if I just ignored everything, including Ba, I wouldn't then have to get into my full feelings about the situation. But they weren't going away. Ma taking care of Ba wasn't going away. Ba being alone in Cambodia wasn't going away.

"And listen to me, Soma. I need to ask you a favor." Ma sounded serious.

"Sure. What is it?"

"I need you to be strong for Dahvy now. I need you to make sure she gets married even without us. I need you to be Ma and Ba for that wedding, okay?"

I didn't really understand what that all meant, but I knew Ma was asking. And if Ma was asking, there was no other choice. I had to do it.

"You know, when your dad wanted to name you Soma, I told him point-blank no. I didn't want my daughter to carry that kind of responsibility. I wanted her to be free from the burden that we as Cambodians already bear. But the more you grow up, the more I see you step into your strength, the more you ask for what you want . . . I couldn't be more wrong. You are a queen. You're my Queen Soma."

This was the coronation that I'd been looking for, but it didn't feel like one at all. I didn't know what to say. I just missed her so much. I missed them both. I wanted to cry like the monster baby I was, but I couldn't do it with Ma on the phone. She'd instructed me to be strong for Dahvy, so I had to be. With one big silent gulp, I swallowed all my emotions inside and hoped they wouldn't leave me immediately. I just needed to put them away for now.

"I got the wedding covered, Ma. Don't worry." I relayed the sentiment hoping she would feel my assurance. I understood my responsibility, and I wouldn't get stage fright here.

"Good. And hey, there will be other performances. You'll find the right time, the right place, the right moment, to share your words. I love you, gkoun."

Honestly, Ma didn't know much about my poetry. I had no idea if she had even seen that TikTok video. But I felt her words of encouragement, and I knew she was right. Even if I had royally failed, there would be a moment where I could share my truth. If I believed.

Ding!

I could barely say goodbye to Ma before receiving the thousandth text from my distressed friend this morning. I appreciated his overeager concern, but if anything, he was the one I had communicated with the most in the last week. You would think that would count for something. I scrolled back up to review his morning monologue:

SOPHAT (9:10 a.m.): Rise and shine, sis! It's Friday, and the wedding is tomorrow, sooo we gotta jump-start Soma. I have a half school day, so holler.

SOPHAT (9:30 a.m.): I know you didn't just ignore that last text because you're feeling real sad for yourself. But boop, let's boop. Should we get coffee?

SOPHAT (9:59 a.m.): K we're not getting coffee coz if we would have gotten coffee you woulda responded back to my text 20 mins ago. Don't get me bothered, Soma. Text/call/tell me that you're alive.

SOPHAT (10:15 a.m.): You're trying my patience, young lady. Can we call a friend back, pretty please?

SOPHAT (10:49 a.m.): SOMA SOMA SOMA SOMA SOMA SOMA SOMA SOMA WASTING MY

DATA ON YOU SOMA SOMA SOMA

SOMA SOMA SOMA SOMA SOMA

IT OK BC I DON'T PAY FOR IT BUT

SOMA SOMA SOMA SOMA SOMA

SOPHAT (10:52 a.m.): HOW. DARE. YOU.

SOPHAT (11:04 a.m.): comin over. don't care wut you say or

do. byeee hiii.

Ah crap. When Sophat was intent on coming over, he was already out the door. I needed to change clothes and prepare myself. I couldn't avoid the wedding any longer. I knew Dahvy needed me. The marital production was in full swing downstairs, and if Sophat barreled in throwing his extra energy around, Dahvy might actually kill him. Like actually.

I threw on a sweatshirt and slipped on some shoes. Maybe I could intercept him outside before he got into the house. I opened the door, crept down to the landing, and once again faced the eternal question of absolute avoidance or facing a little bit of the music. I peeked into the kitchen, and there sat Dahvy and Ruben at the table, busily folding programs like little elves in Santa's sweatshop. I guessed this was during one of those long pauses. I knew the drama could start up again at any moment.

Watching them now, I was sort of mesmerized. It felt strangely comforting seeing them going through the motions of their assembly line. I could almost imagine them as some geezer couple, sitting at this table for decades, talking about the weather, what so-and-so said about so-and-so and arguing about whatever didn't matter that much to begin with.

In my daydreaming, I wondered if they'd have a baby. I wondered if they'd raise their family here. I wondered if Ruben would move in, and the two of them would take over Ba and Ma's room. I wondered if Ma would be pushed to the second bedroom upstairs, across from mine. I wondered if when the baby came, Ma would move into my room, and we'd be roomies. I wondered if she'd even be here at all. I wondered if I would go to college and move far away and maybe come back for weekends. I wondered if I would just go to Middlesex Community College, stay living in my room in this house, not changing anything about the current situation because it'd already been hard enough to begin with. There was nothing wrong with sticking around, but I did wonder how I'd feel about any of it—

"Soma."

I blinked once and realized I was staring directly at Dahvy.

"You want to come down and help?" she asked simply.

I began to descend the stairs into the kitchen.

"Yeah, sure. Coming."

CHAPTER 29

What Happened?

"I'll grab us some coffee. How does that sound?" Ruben asked, not-so-convincingly-casual as he met eyes with Dahvy. Her eyes widened, confirming his request.

"You really don't have to go," I asserted, honestly feeling at this point, anything was up for grabs. Dahvy looked back at him again to send him on his way.

"Everyone could use a little caffeine. Three coffees coming right up!" Ruben stood at the table and, before leaving, handed me the piece of paper he had been currently folding into a program. "All right, get to work, Lazy."

"Who you calling Lazy?" I replied, thankful for Ruben's forever ability to cut the tension. The door closed behind him, and I returned to the task at hand. Dahvy had already resumed.

"Just one fold vertically." She demonstrated.

The programs had turned out pretty good, considering they were made on our old printer that never worked half the time. Every so often, my eyes would catch Dahvy's finished product.

Edge to edge, the corners matched perfectly. Even the result-
ing stack looked absurdly aligned. I returned to mine, and the
lines were just slightly off. Not drastically but enough to notice.
Dahvy seemed unfazed by it. She was too busy searching a way
to break the ice.

"Sophat's coming over. Sorry. Maybe he can help," I confessed meekly. I knew I had to just tell her. Maybe that would
speed up her yelling at me for being such a reject onstage, blaming her righteously for my total failure, and then bringing that
energy home with me during wedding week. I awaited her
response, as she continued folding programs.

"Okay," Dahvy replied without even blinking, unattached
to any tone whatsoever.

"They're pretty."

"Yeah, I wasn't so sure about the recycled paper, but I think
they turned out nicely."

"Saving the world and love, one fold at a time."

"Ha, we might be screwed on both fronts."

I knew Dahvy was just being self-deprecating. The outcome of the wedding might be questionable, but there was
no way this couple was a doomed situation. It was the one
certainty that I could hold on to.

"No way. You and Ruben are perfect for each other." I continued to fold as I felt Dahvy's eyes on me. I could feel the
effect of my words.

"What do you think happened up there?" Dahvy's question
was surprising but gentle, completely devoid of accusation. I

could honestly tell she just wanted to know. She kept working as if to lessen the pressure of whatever my answer might be.

"Well, you lied to me about Ma, and Ruben spilled the beans right before, so . . ."

Dahvy let out a kind of quiet laugh that was earned only by the bit of time that had passed since the epic meltdown. I figured it was easiest to be direct.

"Fair. We suck. Royally." Dahvy's confession was welcome, even if I knew there was a bigger response to share. It wasn't just those bare-bones facts that caused me to lose my cool. A silence came over the room as I gathered my thoughts.

Finally, I looked back at her, and to my surprise, her eyes were red. Like she knew it was a gamble to ask me this question, but what the hell. We'd been through it all already, so why not just lean in? I wasn't on that stage any longer, so I didn't know exactly why I lost my words. But on second thought . . . maybe I'd known this entire time. It wasn't just the recent news. It had to be the fear of more to come.

"Like, I had my rhymes. I didn't need the paper anymore. The lines fly off my tongue when I'm practicing. I said them perfectly four times the day before I got up there. But then, in that room, I looked out into the audience. I saw you and Ruben and Sophat and Britney and the other people and it was like, no offense, but none of you were Ma and Ba. And that made me sad. I even thought about what people had said to me about overcoming the moment and really performing. I even thought about what you shared about acting in plays. I thought maybe I could use the poem to have some kind of cathartic exorcism moment to get everything out—to give myself a chance to feel it all. But none of that happened. Instead, I gave in. Like in a split second my brain and my body made me believe there wasn't a point to any of it, so I just . . . stopped. I didn't make the moment. I failed—"

"You didn't fail."

"No, I think I did because I couldn't be better like you all. I couldn't be strong. I couldn't see the point to any of it."

Another silence passed.

"I'm sorry, Soma. For everything. This shouldn't be your story. Hell, this shouldn't be our story. They should be here with us. Period."

I suddenly felt my face muscles begin to tighten. Crap. My eyes were getting seriously itchy. Major crap. In this inevitable moment, I could have either run out the house like a mad person or . . . I could just let it go. CRAP, CRAP, CRAP.

Dahvy grabbed my arm. I dropped my head onto the table and let the tears slip and slide across the wooden table. If I was going to cry like a disgusting baby, I wasn't going to let anyone see it. Not even Dahvy.

"I'm sorry I didn't give you the full scope of why Ma went over there. There's no excuse. I shouldn't have underestimated you. And I shouldn't have been so brutal in the car. Hurt people hurt people."

Suddenly, I felt my head rise to face my sister. She looked like a poor, sad sucker just like me. A little prettier in her crying, but still some kind of reflection.

"I'm sorry too. For blaming you for what happened onstage. It wasn't *entirely* your fault."

Dahvy smiled back at me with tears in her eyes. In all this emotional wreckage, at least I still had a sense of humor. That wasn't going anywhere. My next question would be less funny.

"Is Ma moving back to Cambodia?" I asked her point-blank. I needed to know. If it was true, then I had to begin to figure it out. How would I be without her? How would I deal with my new reality without my mother?

"No, Soma. She's not. It's just all more complicated than any of us thought," Dahvy replied firmly. "But she is coming back."

"And Ba? Is he?"

Dahvy paused. You could tell this question was harder to avoid, more difficult to meet with the truth. But as she surveyed my blotchy face, I could see her let down her armor too. After wiping tears from her eyes, she did the same to mine.

"I honestly don't know, Soma. But not anytime soon, so we'll figure out what that means for you and me."

"I'm sorry they won't be there for your wedding," I squeaked out, knowing that this would be the first step in the "figuring out."

"We'd all be fighting anyways. No, this is probably for the better right now. At least I got you, right?" Dahvy looked at me and smiled.

I returned the smile, knowing deep down inside that this must be true. She had me, and I knew I had her.

Before we could even settle into the connection, Ruben burst through the kitchen door, followed by none other than Sophat, wearing monster shades like he was at a wake or unintentionally (actually, intentionally) trying to have people not know he was famous. Ruben dropped two coffees on the table, their lids barely on and brown liquid oozing everywhere.

"Ruben, careful! The programs!" Dahvy shouted while jumping up from the table.

"Sorry, sorry! Umm, babe, you all good? Talked things through?" Ruben shouted back with little ability to conceal whatever havoc was about to hit.

"Uh, yeah. All healed here." I offered the summary, while Dahvy transported the coffees over to the sink.

"Oh, good! That's great! Dahvy, can you and I talk about something in the living room?" Ruben looked like he was in a state of emergency.

"Why?" Dahvy turned to face him.

"Because . . . I think you should let the kids have a moment alone. Don't you think?" Ruben began to pull Dahvy into the hallway before she could even answer.

"Well, I guess I have no choice here. . . ." Dahvy's voice trailed off as she disappeared.

"Yeahhhh, no choice." Ruben was now straight-up herding Dahvy out of the kitchen, shamelessly. I was too drained to let my intrigue follow them, and besides, alone in the kitchen, staring back at me with his dang shades obstructing his face, was my Number One. A beat passed.

"Is it sunny in here or something?" I poked the bear to see if he'd growl.

"I'm in mourning, Soma, for my best friend, who I thought was deadzo since she never responded to any of my correspondences, even though I emailed her all her homework—"

"I'm sorry—"

"I mean, it's been a week, and I'm trying to support you. You know that, right?"

"I do."

"But I can't be that for you if you don't trust me."

"I know."

"So freaking trust me!"

"I freaking trust you."

"Good. I'm sorry about the lit competition." Sophat finally lowered his shades so I could look at his beady brown babies. "Looks like you suffered the same fate as I. How're you doing?"

"I'm . . . okay. A little sad and tired, but okay." After finally hearing Dahvy tell me the truth, it felt a little like a weight had been lifted. I was lighter than before.

"Well, that's good. I'm glad you all had your Oprah mome, but we gotta work on these puffy under-eyes. You're the maid of honor, after all." Sophat threw both arms at my face, like he was going to make contact. I swiftly threw up my arms in protest—

"GUH DOY MIGH!" Dahvy's voice immediately entered the space.

Uh-oh.

This was trouble.

When you invoked the mama in your Khmer cursing, you knew that it was going down.

This wasn't just something Ruben had to relay to Dahvy casually.

This was a disaster of epic proportions.

Uh to the oh.

Dahvy's stomping indicated she was on her way back to us.

"Bridezillaaa," I whispered to Sophat as his eyes got wide, preparing for her imminent arrival.

"I know it's a problem, but we'll figure it out. . . ." Ruben's voice echoed behind, obviously trying to tame the situation, but it was clear things were just about to get unimaginably worse.

"THE ACHAA IS SICK. HE HAS THE FLU. HE CAN'T DO THE WEDDING. WHAT THE HELL. SELFISH MOTHER—"

"Can't we just find another Cambodian elder to bring you out?"

"IF YOU KEEP TALKING TO ME LIKE I'M SOME DOWRY THAT SOME RANDO CAMBO'S GONNA THROW OUT TO A MAN, WE BETTER CALL IT OFF NOW!" Dahvy's rage was peaking, and it was clear Ruben wasn't going to solve this. She needed someone else. Ruben resigned and leaned back against the counter, offering Dahvy the space and time to rage on. The woman needed to let it all out so she could eventually be brought back to planet earth. "What am I supposed to do? He was the only one who was bilingual and charismatic enough to pull this off. I can't find anyone with this kind of turnaround. That's it. The whole thing is off."

Dahvy sank into a chair and aggressively folded onto the kitchen table. The towers of programs fell dramatically all around her, looking like debris from war. The heap of an Artist Formerly Known as My Sister remained silently defeated. Ruben, Sophat, and I exchanged glances, trying to confirm whether Dahvy had in fact died from the culmination of all this bad karma. At this point, it remained unclear if there was anything else to do but to fully accept the KO. Knockout.

And then a thought occurred to me.

A reckless thought.

But a thought, nonetheless.

I need you to be strong for Dahvy now. I need you to make sure she gets married even without us. I need you to be Ma and Ba for that wedding, okay?

Two thoughts. Ma's and mine.

"I have an idea, but you can't shut it down before I even get it out, okay?" My request was met with silence. Dahvy stayed a heap of sadness. Sophat looked like I was about to connect the red wire with the blue one. Ruben nodded for me to continue.

"Let me do it. I'll be your achaa. I mean, I'll be right there standing next to you anyways. Why don't I just say some stuff too? I'll do double duty. I know all the rituals, and if Sophat is going to be helping lead the groom's procession—"

"I—I am?" Sophat stammered.

"You are, and if Sophat is going to lead the groom's procession, it only makes sense for me to be on the receiving end of it. I mean, we have that chemistry, right? You're looking for charisma, we've got it oozing from our pores. Don't we, Sophat?"

"Yeahhh, but let's not talk about my flawless baby skin, okay?" Sophat looked unconvinced and maybe a little worried that I'd volunteered him for another job at the wedding.

Ruben's eyes were locked into the back of Dahvy's head, which remained unmoved by my suggestion. Honestly, I thought the idea might make her implode instantaneously, but Dahvy was stone-cold still. Maybe she had died after all.

Even though the proposal really had just popped into my head out of sheer instinct, the more I was describing it, the more I actually felt like it might work. I'd been going through Ma's albums, learning about all the wedding rituals, and like I said, bridesmaids did literally nothing besides stand next to the bride to make sure her makeup wasn't dripping and drooping. Not really my kind of business. If I could be the achaa and help emcee what was going down, maybe I could help Dahvy feel like it was worth it to actually get married—not to wait around for everything to be normal again before tying the knot. I mean, at this point, with everything that had gone down, what was "normal" anyways?

Dahvy was definitely dead. Ruben looked at us to warn us that he was going to say something, and that perhaps Sophat and I should prepare for some kind of violent reaction. We both took a step back, just in case.

"Babe, so what do you think?" Ruben asked in the gentlest

of ways, and then joined us in taking a step back. Just. In. Case.

A beat passed, and then Dahvy hit the table loudly with one palm.

She was alive, but she might come swinging.

She lifted her tear-drenched face. Her eyes looked buggy, like she had just run out of a burning house. She smiled slightly, like she was ready to let it all out.

She delivered her verdict:

"Why the hell not?"

CHAPTER 30
Dear Ba

At this point, I'm sure you've been wondering why I haven't responded to your emails yet. I should just get it out there: I'm sorry. It's not that I didn't want to email you or talk to you. I was just feeling a little freaked out. You threw me a curveball with the mode, didn't you? Like who are you? A credit card company? Stop spamming me!

I'm kidding. (Sort of.) The real real is . . . I've been scared to talk to you. When you were back here, it was like I barely thought about you. That came out wrong. It's not like I didn't care about you, but it was like when you've been with someone for so long, you sometimes don't think about them as a separate entity. You think of them as part of who you are, part of your way of seeing the world. But when they leave you, you can't take anything for granted. Sometimes now, I think of you as separate from me, and that freaks me out.

I've been sad, Ba, and I know you have been too. Can we just agree to agree that we're both sad? Everyone is sad! Since you left, I've been trying to figure out how to feel something else, but this is the truth: I'm sad . . . and I want you to know that. I know you told me I was "made for this," and while I think I know what you mean, I wonder why people have to be. Made for such sorrow. I get where we came from. I get our history. I get that yes, Cambodians were made to suffer and to persevere. But maybe we're made to just enjoy our lives too? Sometimes there's just all this pressure. I've been feeling it since day one. It feels unbearable at times. Shouldn't it get easier with each generation? Maybe that's naive. Maybe that's unrealistic. But I'm telling you now . . . I want to break the karmic cycle. I want us to find nirvana. I know that's a hard thing to say right now, but I'm feeling like I understand a little bit about my purpose now.

I'm sure you've already heard the news, but I entered this lit contest at school and for the finals round, I was supposed to perform a poem live. I didn't get very far. No edit: I crashed and burned. I didn't even get a single line out. Afterward, I felt low. Not like kind of low. But like LOW low. Think on the down-low, but much further down. The lowest of lows. I gave myself permission to feel real sorry, and when I was ready, I looked over my poem again. And I gotta say . . . honestly . . . I liked it. I liked what I had to say. Did it matter I didn't get to share it? Maybe. But also, liking your own thoughts kind of feels like an accomplishment. I'm finding my voice, Ba. I'm finding words that capture what I'm feeling. And I think there's power there. I want to use that power to help us break our karmic bad luck and find nirvana. I think I can do that.

Don't feel like you have to immediately respond to me. I sure as heck didn't with your emails. But I want you to know that just as we were made for survival, I know we were made for happiness. And I'll never stop fighting for us to find that.

—Your Kween Soma

CHAPTER 31

And Walk!

From up on my toes, I could see the line snake around the block. What. The. Heck. We definitely didn't have that many cousins. I wasn't even sure our family knew that many people, but from about nine thousand miles away, Ma had done her work building the official guest list. You could tell she was committed to making it an event, even more so now that she and Ba wouldn't be there. She wanted to make sure the couple felt celebrated, and while Dahvy would've probably traded all the non-cousins for just our parents, she was softening a bit. She understood that Ma was doing her best, and at this point, there was nothing you could do but get married, so . . . get married.

"Can you see Ruben?!" Dahvy shouted from behind as Ming Ani continued to beat her face with powder. I looked back briefly to confirm that "understated" was not the aesthetic of this wedding. More like . . . *dusted*.

"No, but Sophat's doing his thing!" I reported what I could

barely make out from my sight line, and more importantly, only what Dahvy needed to know. Peeking out the front door of our house, I could see that our newly anointed emcee was walking up and down the line of people holding platters of gifts wrapped in brightly colored cellophane, while yelling loudly through a megaphone like some kind of drill sergeant. The kid understood the assignment.

"Okay, everyone get ready for the Hai Gkoun Gomlah! Two by two, bodies facing front, cellophane looking perky, people!" Sophat's shrieking voice was quaking the entire block this Saturday a.m. We had warned all our neighbors of the event, but we hadn't quite warned them about the event that was emcee Sophat Lee . . . on a megaphone.

Hai Gkoun Gomlah is the ritual that begins any Cambodian wedding. At the house, the bride waits for her groom, who is positioned down the street with the party guests. It's supposed to recreate the groom traveling the long distance from his hometown to his love's, but nowadays, the procession just begins at a random neighbor's house. Like every custom imported from the motherland, it was another thing we worked out with what we got. And even though most of the wedding rituals were steeped in old, backward, gendered rules, still . . . there was something about seeing everyone lined up in their best temple clothes, decked out in multicolored silk sarongs and shirts, that gave me this overwhelming sense of pride. We, as a Cambodian people, were helping this couple get married, and that felt important.

I couldn't exactly make out where Ruben was, but at the front of the line, the chunky little Chum brothers were pre-emptively banging on their hand gongs, which incited Sophat to scold them, which then incited them to cry. It was going real well. Behind the boys, Britney and Evie watched on as the meltdown escalated. There was open-mouth crying, snot slinging everywhere, and impressively (and simultaneously), erratic gong playing from both boys. Sophat was beginning to look stressed as he began to ask loudly where their parents were. Presumably they were close by in the line, but in proper Khmer fashion, the community was responsible for the boys now. Britney handed off her tray of gifts to Evie and crouched down to meet the pair at their level. I couldn't tell what she was saying to them, but it seemed like some peace negotiation was being struck. Eventually the boys began to quiet down, and Sophat looked relieved. Britney had handled it. When I'd invited her to the wedding, I wasn't even sure she was going to want to hang like this after my very public crash and emo isolation, but Britney had proven me wrong again. I'd texted her, and she showed for me again. Most of my people were here, and that counted for something.

"Where is my virginal young man? Don't look at me like that! That's what Hai Gkoun Gomlah means! It's what the pro-cession is named after, so . . . can I get my virginal young man up at the front, please?!" Sophat might have been riffing a little too much on the megaphone.

Then quickly, from the middle of the line, Ruben jumped

out to the front, dressed fully in his matching gold sampot, tunic, and jacket. Just as he had asked for, the guy was blinged out, draped in matching necklaces and wearing sizable rocks on his fingers that could do damage in a fight. The golden sword he had rehearsed with earlier hung to his side, and with his entourage behind him, dude looked like he was going to battle. This was straight Cambo culture cosplay.

"I see Ruben. I think they're about to start!" I shouted back to the bridal party, trying to warn them that things were about to go down. In a smog of poisonous hair spray, the women sprayed and prayed their last wishes for their hairpieces to stay intact. A flurry of action commenced, including last-minute touch-ups, a clearing of the main living space where the bulk of the wedding rituals would happen, and Dahvy's bridesmaids incessantly checking in with her about *everything*. They'd been largely absent up to this moment, but now their energy was at max. Even to the point where when they were all talking at once, Dahvy would sometimes look at me from across the room with serious "over it" eyes. I thought it best to stay away from that main nucleus, since I was about to play the part of the achaa on behalf of my sister. I knew it was about to get weird, so I needed to look over my notes.

"You ready?" Dahvy's voice crept in from behind me. I turned to see the bride in her full ensemble. Maybe it was still the residual hair-spray particles flying all around her, but no edit: she looked like a movie star. Like a *Vogue* cover, US edition. Like a Cambodian princess. I was stunned.

"Don't ask me that. Are *you* ready?" I fired back at the bride.

"As ready as I'll ever be. It's gonna be great, by the way. No matter what happens, we got this." Dahvy placed her hand on my shoulder. She rarely used the first-person-plural pronoun, but maybe she was learning that she couldn't do this by herself. I certainly didn't want to let her down. She assumed her position next to me.

Just then, the music for "Jchow Preehm" abruptly blared outside. I looked through the window, and there Sophat was, leading the way with his portable speaker playing the processional music. The little Chums went to town on the hand gongs, and I watched as Sophat's spiky amplified voice instructed the guests to: "Walk. And walk. Walk, walk, walk. Walk. And walk. Walk, walk, walk." His loud, punctuated directions made it seem like he was coaching models for Paris Fashion Week, not processing guests at a small-town Cambo wedding. The juxtaposition straight-up tickled me.

"They're coming, people!" I shouted back, giving one last notice before opening the door to prepare for the introductions. Through these wedding transactions, it was the achaa's job to be the bride's representative. The groom would present the gifts, the guests, and a request to be welcomed into the house for the wedding, but it was only the achaa who could say yes.

Sophat parked the party at the front doorstep. He looked regal in his entirely black suit, with a set of shimmering white pearls slinking out front. The kid had decided that with all his added responsibilities, there wasn't time or space for a costume change. He was going to keep it simple and classy like Chanel. This was his little black dress.

"Okay, stop playing now!" Sophat shouted at the boys. A trickle of laughter fell over the guests, as the smaller one kept banging on his gong. Britney simply tapped his shoulder, and he immediately stopped. I mouthed, "Thank you," and Britney smiled back. I returned to receiving Sophat, who looked a bit wide-eyed and deranged.

"Hello, groom's representative! Thank you for coming," I pronounced very officially.

"Hello, bride's representative! It is an honor. We've brought you and your beautiful bride—I mean, not *your* bride, but the prince's bride—actually, she's *nobody's* bride, because what year is it and this is all a gesture, but . . ." Sophat awkwardly trailed off into some strange didactic explanation of the event. His eyes locked into me, like he was looking for some help. The kid was sweating. I motioned at him to keep it rolling, and he took a stifled breath before finally continuing. "But nonetheless, we've brought you gifts! Do you accept them as a dowry and us into your house to commence the intended wedding ceremonies?"

I looked over at Ruben, whose eyes were glued to Dahvy like a dang lovesick pup. Dahvy rolled her eyes aggressively and then smiled, as if to say, *Hey. Why not?*

Suddenly, I became overwhelmed by the sight of it all. The wedding party was looking eager and ready to go. Guests were decked out in the most beautiful multicolored jewel palette of silk shirts and dresses. They held offerings for the bride—trays of fruit, money, treats, and then some. All those smiling faces were here to celebrate our bride and groom. Despite all that had come before, we'd finally arrived at this moment. The community was here, and I felt proud to be a part of it.

I grabbed Sophat's megaphone and finally gave my resolution: "Lesssgo."

CHAPTER 32
Wedding Rituals

No one died at the wedding, and truth be told, that lowest of low bars was worth celebrating. In fact, because Sophat and I were sharing responsibilities emceeing the day, we were both able to stay on a tight schedule. Most Cambo weddings felt like one big improv game. Competing mings and boos would drag the confused bride and groom around, skipping rituals, going back, fully leaning into the remix. But because we truly had *no idea* what we were doing, Sophat and I studied Ma's photo albums and wrote down everything. We forced ourselves to follow a tight itinerary approved by our fully evolved Bridezilla Pokémon, who in a seismic turn of events seemed . . . kind of chill.

Maybe Dahvy had finally submitted to the fates. Or maybe she was in a whole new stage of grief. Or maybe she was sucking on those "yummy gummies" that Ruben had bought her days before the wedding. Ruben insisted that we all stay hush about their mysterious ingredients, but we all knew what made the gummy . . . yummy. They were doing the trick.

Sure, there were some hiccups. During the Cleansing Ceremony, couples close to the bride and groom were supposed to "trim" their hair and offer them some light pumps of perfume to smell top-rate in their new life together. At this point in the wedding (and Cambodian Ritual History 101), we thought everyone understood one was to *pretend* to groom the couple, but after a couple of crazed snipped locks, it was clear that not everyone got the memo.

Luckily, most of the follicle casualties were the fake hairpieces that Ming Ani had insisted would help Dahvy's hair look fuller. In the end, they provided a needed buffer between the bride's real hair and the guests' happy scissors.

And then, during the Red String Ceremony, while the tying of the thread is supposed to symbolize the couple's union, a fool wasn't supposed to actually tie their hands together. Guests were given two different red strings—one for the bride and one for the groom. No one was paying much attention while it was happening, but when Ruben and Dahvy tried to pull away from each other and realized they had three more ceremonies to complete, we had to violently hack them apart as our ancestors collectively groaned from their graves. Yeah, no, this was not a good omen for their marriage. Cutting the couple apart on their wedding day was a big spiritual no-no.

But still, we persevered, and Ma and Ba were able to stream most of it. I mean, they were twelve hours ahead, so they were watching the event unfold literally from the comfort of their bed. But they said they wouldn't miss it for the world, so we tried to make it happen.

Sometimes Ba would yell through the laptop, "Speak up,

Sophat! Use those resonators!" My sweet, anxious friend, who essentially had been volunteered for the job, tried to speak louder, but you could tell he was burning under the pressure. At a certain point, Sophat looked straight into the laptop and requested that our parents not backseat drive from Cambodia. Ma replied that she wasn't going to miss her baby's wedding if Sophat wasn't willing to enunciate like he was trying to become a Broadway star. "A Broadway star would hit every consonant like it. Meant. Something."

Sophat ate the request and tried to hit. Every. Consonant. I would've felt bad for my Number One if I wasn't finding the whole situation HILARIOUS. Even from thousands of miles away, the parentals were making their presence known, and no one was going to have a single thing to say about it.

When we got to the end of Sompeas Ptem, the ceremony with the golden sword, I grabbed the laptop so I could be mobile as the bride and groom made their circle around the room. Ruben took his place behind Dahvy with the sword in his right hand and the bridal flap in his left. Dahvy, looking fully royal in her outfit, led the pair around our tiny living room, as they tried to avoid stepping on the seated guests.

At times, Ba would yell out, "Ruben, faster! Don't let it drag on! Your wife is getting away from you." Ruben, already sweating in his golden suit, would hear the direction and speed up as Dahvy threw back a death glare. Ba's jokes were quickly replaced with Ma's scolding, and eventually Dahvy looked straight at me with crystal clear instructions to do what we both knew I needed to do: mute the commentary. One could only imagine what it'd be like if the voluntary sportscasters were live and in person.

Luckily, the Kears stayed quiet through most of the afternoon church wedding, or at least, I remembered to keep the mute button on. It was held at St. Anne's Episcopal Church, where Ruben had recommended I go in for a little peace.

Honestly, in all the wedding prep, I'd barely thought about the second wedding. Dahvy hadn't talked about it much, so I figured it was pretty much handled. I think she knew the Cambodian wedding would take a lot out of us, so the detour to the church would be a piece of cake. Sophat, on the other hand, was on his business, doing way more things than he had bargained for. Last minute, he and Britney offered to sing their wedding song, Rihanna and Mikky Ekko's "Stay." I mean, look, no one was second-guessing their harmonies, but it wasn't exactly the wedding vibes I was expecting for this cute little church ceremony.

As Britney and Sophat looked at each other and played their parts with some major subtext that no one asked for, I kept looking over at Dahvy to see if she thought this sexy goth act was a good idea after all. Just as the song hit the bridge, I caught Dahvy wiping tears from her eyes.

No, I knew why she'd picked the song. Maybe it'd been Dahvy and Ruben's song while they were getting serious the second time around, but the song was cracking open so much more. RiRi wasn't singing some dopey love song about how things were going to be fine. She'd been hurt. She was desperate. She was asking for him to stay. It was actually the most perfect song for this moment.

I glanced over at Britney as she was finishing the song, and she smiled back. How she was still hanging around, singing at this random wedding, looking like she wasn't totally perturbed by the whole thing, I had zero clue about. Nothing could've explained how we'd all landed in this supremely weird and glorious moment. But we had. We were all here, doing our thing.

The church ceremony concluded with the seemingly endless amount of wedding photos. To let Ma and Ba off the hook so they could finally go to sleep, we took our family photo first. Stretched across the laptop were Ma's and Ba's seriously pixelated and sleepy faces. The church Wi-Fi was doing us zero favors, and every so often their faces would freeze on Ma's closed eyes or Ba's big mouth wide open. With Dahvy and me awkwardly holding the laptop together, there was little hope to get a perfect shot in there. At this point, we knew the simple truth: there was no such thing as a perfect shot. There was only a shot.

"Now, get to bed, you two. There's no use in you streaming all the drunk, dancing Cambos," Dahvy instructed our parents, as if she were the parent herself.

"But what if we want to dance too?" Ba was throwing jokes even though he was mid-yawn.

"Bong, let the kids go. It's way past our bedtime." Ma's voice sounded tired. It wasn't like she didn't want to stick around, but you could tell she didn't want Dahvy and me worrying about them for the rest of the night. She wanted us to do our thing. "Proud of you two. Dahvy, we love you so much. Congratulations to you and Ruben—"

"We can't wait to celebrate with you soon," Ba interjected. He couldn't help himself. Even if the future remained unclear, he was going to try to be hopeful.

"K'nyum sralang el puc muh-digh." Dahvy touched the screen as if to confirm his hope.

Ma's and Ba's faces disappeared into the ether, as I exited out of the Zoom screen and closed the laptop. At the very same moment, Ruben swung by to inform Dahvy that it was now time for photos with his folks. This was the perfect moment for me to disappear for a second. I crept over to the last pew in the church and sat my sorry, tired butt down. We were almost two weddings down, with one more event to go. I had to prepare myself for a full night of reception antics. In the calm quiet, I looked back toward the front of the church, where Dahvy and Ruben were now managing a different set of parents.

Mrs. Diaz, though short and round like me, had the presence of a nine-foot-tall drag-queen goddess. She was decked out in the most beautiful purple pantsuit. She was grabbing Ruben's face and yelling at him for looking too pale. She needed to bring some blood back into his cheeks. And Mr. Diaz, or should I say Dr. Diaz, was a tall beanstalk of a man, a well-known surgeon in Boston. He wore wire frames that hung at the end of his nose and was looking like some Ivy League professor who couldn't be bothered. I watched him stand by as his wife yanked at their son, looking truly embarrassed by all of it. For once, it was nice to watch someone else's family dysfunction and know this wasn't our mess. And even still, that mess was charming and undoubtedly full of love. So maybe ours was too.

Suddenly, a flash of light caught my attention, and I turned to see the source of it. Behind and above, I spotted a little triangular stained-glass window of blue, green, brown, and yellow. In the center, the light illuminated some simple purple flowers. It was the peak of the afternoon, so the light was hitting it just right. This was the Girls' Friendly Society window that Ruben had told me was his favorite, and now I could see why. He had said maybe God was in the colors. From this vantage point, as I watched the colors spread about the church, I wondered if I believed in that too.

CHAPTER 33
Kweens

"And forward! And backward! And forward! And backward! Keep flapping those wings, birdies. Saravan is gonna make you SOAR!"

DJ So Phat Phat was in full-on instructional dance mode, as the music for saravan blasted out the speakers. All the drunk little birdies flittered across the floor. This was the dance Ruben had been practicing before, but from my view, it didn't look like the groom had gotten any better. His fully outstretched arms looked like they were going to take Dahvy out. Fortunately, she was ready on the defense, dodging Ruben's wingspan and laughing like she was playing a game.

Dahvy looked happy. Like really happy. She was dancing barefoot, her face a little red from a few sneaky sips (what a lightweight), and she was moving back and forth with the guy she loved. It was freaky to say, but . . . they were married now.

We'd gotten to the end of the night, and the remaining Hennessy-drinking boos and mings were flailing around, trying to get their last dance on. Dahvy and Ruben's wedding entourage were jumping around too, and from my chair, I may have nodded once or twice to the beat. Okay, whatever, maybe I also flapped around for a bit, but it was only because Dahvy pulled me over. Thank God I had changed out my heels for sneaks an hour ago, or there would've been no chance in hell of me dancing like these fools.

The vibe was right. Even across the way, you could see DJ So Phat Phat bopping to his track. No, this feeling was in the pocket. We'd conquered two weddings and a reception, and no one had gotten murdered . . . yet. We deserved to flap. One. Last. Time.

"Okay, okay, that was a sweet li'l Cambo mome, wasn't it? Some of you still need to work on that rhythm, but most of you were . . . serviceable. We've now reached the end of our wedding festivities—that seemed quick, right?!—but before we go, I raise a wine cooler (JK, I'm not actually drinking) to Mr. and Mrs. Diaz-Kear. And surprise, here's an encore performance to sing you out from Yours Truly! Have a good night, lovebirds." DJ So Phat Phat had finally declared his last responsibility for the night. The kid went from not being invited to the wedding to *being the wedding*, and there was only one proper way to finish it out. Hit that karaoke track!

"Want to dance?" Out of nowhere, Britney glided up next to me and asked the question, leaving me twisted.

"Um . . . yeah . . . sure," I croaked, and then gave her my hand. Instantly, I felt her pull me into her, and then I knew I must be dreaming in some alternate universe. She was leading me, and I was following, and not even the silence could make sense of what was happening.

"Did you have fun?" I asked, trying to break the ice.

"Between Sophat's emceeing and those rituals, it was definitely like nothing I've ever experienced before."

"So, we've, like, totally scared you off?"

"Yeah, BYYYE." Britney laughed and pulled away like she was jumping ship, but she quickly returned. "No, I mean, I don't know what it usually is, but it was cool to see you all make something up. Like, this is what we have and this is what we're gonna do now. I feel like people can be so scared of—"

"Change?" I asked.

"God is change. Maybe I believe that more than I believe God is nothing." Britney instantly (and solemnly) recalled our conversation about Octavia Butler's book.

"She's crawling from the crypt!"

"At least, if I believe it's change, it could be nothing too. How about you?"

"God? These are some party conversations, yeah?"

"Listen, I've got questions!"

"Clearly." We continued to dance as I searched for an honest, not totally embarrassing answer. "I guess the way we talk and think about God is it's this thing you put all your hopes and desires into. The thing you want to believe in. And right now, I'm not saying I'm God, but . . . I really just want to believe in me."

"So she's got a God complex, huh?"

"No, I—"

"I'm kidding! I totally get that. It's, like, how can you believe in anything, if not yourself, right?"

"Exactly."

"And if it means anything, I really believe in you too."

"Thanks."

I looked over at Sophat, who took a moment out of his singing to throw a pair of demonstrative thumbs-up in my direction. I quickly rotated so I could cut the connection. I hoped Britney hadn't caught on to my unrelenting friend.

"It was cool meeting your parents virtually too." I'd completely forgotten that earlier in the day in a quiet moment, Britney had chatted with my parents briefly. Ba was talking to her on the laptop while simultaneously WhatsApp-ing me on my phone on the sly. In the same breath, he was being polite with Britney while texting me foolish questions like, "So, when are y'all getting married?!" Ma was a little more reserved in her judgment.

"They got a little loopy as the day went on," I replied, trying to get a feel for why Britney was even mentioning it.

"Yeah, that time difference seems tough. But man, you and your mom are like identical."

"Really? People always say I'm like my dad."

"I guess I can see some obvious reasons, but your mom . . . she's got that deep look like, 'Who is this friend of my daughter's? And is she good enough for her?'"

"Oh, I'm sorry if she made you feel a certain way. I think she really liked you."

"No, I wasn't worried about it. I was . . . in awe of it. Like I can tell she wants to *know* people. Not the phony stuff. It's like she wants to know you, so that she can figure out how to love you. I feel like you might be that way too."

Just as Britney shared those words, Sophat's final flourish of the most extra riffs signaled the ending of the song. We both turned to watch Ariana Grande close out her stadium concert. No doubt. She was a hit.

I turned back to look at Britney, and we caught eyes . . . when I realized we were holding hands. We'd seamlessly transitioned from dancing formally to low-key clasping palms like we couldn't let go. The shock sent electricity through my entire system, and I once again became totally at a loss for what to say or do next. Instead, I just stayed there with Britney for a moment. The two of us smiled at each other, not needing to communicate much, but knowing that we'd arrived at a moment.

"I should probably call my mom." Britney lingered for a second longer.

"Yeah, thanks for coming," I responded, not able to unlock my hand just yet.

"Mind if I . . . ?" And then, before I could even fully understand what was actually happening next, I nodded in answer to Britney's question, and she kissed me on the cheek. She pulled away, we locked in the memory of the moment, and then she began to leave. "I'll see you at school."

"If I don't see you first, or whatever." Yeah, no, I had no idea what words were coming out of my mouth at that point. I was sure all my vitals had stopped working instantly. I'd gotten my first kiss (a classy one at that!), and I was feeling on top of the stars, racing around the galaxy like I was transcendent! Like nothing else mattered before this moment! Like I wasn't a falling star, but a star rising! Nothing could make me feel small in this moment! I was . . . cosmic.

When my brain finally restarted, I immediately turned to see if anyone had witnessed what went down, but the dance floor had cleared and people were on their way out. Everyone was gone or in their own way. No, to my knowledge, Britney and I had actually shared a private freaking moment, and I wouldn't have to explain myself to anyone. Bless. I watched Britney disappear beyond the front doors of the restaurant.

"Okay! Well, that's our set for the night, party people. My name is DJ SO PHAT PHAT, and I'm available for all local engagements, weddings, birthday parties, bar mitzvahs, bat mitzvahs, family reunions, and then some. My Cash App handle is '$-D-J-S-O-P-H-A-T-P-H-A-T'—so if you want to throw some change my way, make it rain."

I slid across the floor to the DJ booth and gave some love to our helpless entrepreneur.

"Do you accept booty smacks as payment?" I asked earnestly, knowing the kid liked a tap every so often, like a pat on the back. But on the butt.

"Only from you."

At the very same moment, Dahvy and Ruben rolled up with armfuls of gifts, looking like it was Christmas morning.

"We're taking these to the car. Be back in a second," Dahvy relayed as she began to move toward the exit.

"Ooh, let me help. This bride looks *tired*," Sophat replied, without even thinking of the cardinal sin he'd committed. At any point of said wedding, do *not* tell the bride she looks tired.

"Thank you, I think." Dahvy let that one go and handed off her gifts to Sophat. With Ruben leading the way, he and Sophat headed out into the parking lot. Back in the restaurant, even with the guests gone now, the multicolored sparkly lights continued to swirl about the room, set to the "Time to Go" playlist Sophat had planned for the reception unwind. Taking the cues from the lights and sound, Dahvy silently grabbed a nearby cardboard box and began bussing the tables. This was just the kind of bridezilla she was. Someone had to do it, after all. I followed suit, grabbing a nearby box too, and joined her in picking up the wedding debris.

"It was a good, weird wedding," I observed while picking up an inflatable palm tree.

Ruben legitimately picked it up last-minute at Party City to give the reception a beachy Cambodian atmosphere. While Dahvy LOVED those last-minute ideas, at that point she was too tired or too high on her yummy gummies to even protest. They'd made their way across all the tables at the restaurant.

"Yeah, not exactly what I imagined, but . . . thanks. For everything." Dahvy continued packing without looking up. I knew she meant it.

"You got it."

I quickly scanned the room to check out the damage. Most of the plates and glasses had been properly bussed, but plenty of party paraphernalia (of the non-druggy variety) were still left behind, including white envelopes with wedding checks inside, the little chocolates we'd spent so much time delicately wrapping, and surprisingly (maybe not so surprisingly), a random shoe or two. Dahvy and I combed through the tables, collecting into our boxes whatever seemed valuable, or, at the very least, we could sell for a profit.

"I'm gonna get the overhead lights. Can you get the party ones?" Dahvy placed her box by the entrance of the restaurant and moved toward the main restaurant light switches.

"Sure." I meandered toward DJ So Phat Phat's station, knowing that this whole setup he'd brought was his own doing. I'd have to tinker carefully so as not to destroy the enterprise. I pressed a button and suddenly the music stopped. Oops. Wrong one. I pressed another and the party lights were out. Simultaneously, Dahvy flipped the house lights, offering a harsh, fluorescent, your-prom-is-now-over vibe. The party was definitely at a close, and the only two party monsters left behind were the Kear sisters.

Dahvy sat down in a chair and threw her feet up on another. She then grabbed a stranded wine cooler and popped it open with ease. This whole vision of Dahvy slumped back and drinking alcoholic Kool-Aid was definitely a side of her I'd never seen before. With one big gulp, she made a cringey face that could not lie.

"Ugh, this shit is so sweet! How can Ma like this so much?"

"Ma drinks?!"

"Yeah, she gets so red, people start to worry about her. Like the Asian flush times ten. I think I'll just stick to Ba's Heinekens. You want a taste?"

I paused. I wondered if this was a trick situation where I'd be ultimately punished for falling right into her trap.

"I mean, don't pretend like you haven't drunk before." Another accusation leaving me hot!

"I haven't!" I protested.

"Yeah, right." Dahvy was not picking up what I was throwing down. But it was true! I proceeded to tell her about the one time Sophat got so wasted at Hal Moreno's house and ended up throwing chunks into the toilet all night. It scared the crap out of me. After that, I told myself there was no need to rush into poisoning my own body intentionally.

"Wow, I mean like when I was your age, I was drinking Everclear like my life depended on it."

"Deep fake!"

"I did. I was getting into all kinds of nonsense."

"Ba and Ma never got on you?"

Davy took another sip of the syrupy liquid and looked away for a moment.

"There was a lot going on back then."

It occurred to me that way back when, way before I was even around, Dahvy had her own history to contend with. She had seen an entirely different side of Ba: the side of him that went to jail, that went to court, that went to detention, that fought to get back, and now this. She'd carried all that history, and she still was able to move forward and get married. And now she was drinking a wine cooler.

"I guess some things don't change," I replied, resigned to the fact that maybe we Kear girls were just meant to go through it.

Dahvy turned to look at me and placed a hand on my face.

"Yeah. And some things change too."

I was startled by her gesture. She held on to my face for a moment and looked directly into my eyes, as if to tell me our fates were never sealed. Things had changed, and they would continue to do so. That was something I could rely on.

Then suddenly, like bile coming up from my throat, I felt an impulse to share something with her.

"Can I recite something to you?" I asked.

"Um, yeah. I guess . . ." Dahvy looked a little scared, and rightfully so. I was scared in my own right. "Do you want to wait for the guys or—"

"No, that's all right. I wrote something I wanted to say to you alone." Late last night, as I was prepping for the wedding, I found these words rattling in my brain. The couples give each other vows, but do siblings? I felt a need to tell Dahvy what was really on my mind.

I pulled out my phone so I could remember my words, and in this empty room made harsh by the fluorescent lights, I shared my most honest poem.

> I used to think that to be a royal
> You had to be completely loyal
> To the virtues of the bling ka-ching
> The money bags, the diamond ring

The class of folks who have it all
Who protect their power by standing tall
The lucky few who know their might
By holding on to their sovereign right

I used to think to be a queen
You had to be the most pristine
Apsara femme with shoulders rolled back
Sketched with a smile, as if not to attack

The kind of lady who waved at a crowd
Who didn't say much and certainly bowed
When decorum asked her to quietly submit
To the rules of royals of which she befit

I used to think to have any kind of worth
Was to only come from this elevated birth
That fate held you in the palm of its hand
And things just worked out as if they were planned

That a girl like me, who was born out of grief
Through samsara's wheel and rigid belief
That I would suffer in this life, but move on to the next
And in the new one, simplify the complex

BUT HONESTLY, LATELY. . . .
I'VE BEEN FEELING INNATELY . . .

THAT THERE'S SOMETHING ALL WRONG . . .
WITH YE OLDE CAMBO SONG . . .

I'VE BEEN FEELING LIKE LIFE IS ACTUALLY
HERE . . .
AND TO WAIT FOR ANYTHING ELSE IS MUCH
ADO ABOUT FEAR . . .
I'VE BEEN THINKING I'VE BEEN SCARED OF MY
VERY OWN VOICE . . .
AND THE POWER OF MY VERY OWN CHOICE . . .

AND HONESTLY, LATELY . . .
I'VE BEEN THINKING INNATELY . . .
THAT I MIGHT JUST BE . . . **KWEEN** . . . SO . . .

NOW I KNOW that to be truly royal
You have to be completely loyal
To the virtues of your own beating heart
As you create yourself, your own work of art

NOW I KNOW that to have any kind of worth
Your feet must be rooted in this mortal earth
That fate can hold you in the palm of its hand
But what you learn most comes from what wasn't planned

NOW I KNOW that to be truly a KWEEN
Is to learn from one with an identical gene

A sister who's been there from day number one
Who's honestly out here like she's dressing to STUN

NOW I KNOW that to be truly a KWEEN
Is to be a Cambo girl who's sometimes unseen
But works every day to keep us together
When the hits keep coming, no matter the weather

NOW I KNOW that to be truly a KWEEN
Is to be my sister, who is actually pristine
An Apsara femme who today is choosing love
And is the highest of royalty that one could speak of

SO HONESTLY, LATELY. . . .
I'VE BEEN FEELING INNATELY . . .
THAT IT'S TIME TO . . .
GET LEAN
GET KEEN
GET IN THAT ROUTINE
YO, IT'S ALREADY FORESEEN
BECAUSE
THE BRIDE IS YOUR
KHMER KWEEN

With her eyes wide, Dahvy looked at me, not uttering a
single word.

Maybe it was overly sentimental to share the poem with her,

but at this point, I didn't really care. In my journey to speak my own truth, I'd gotten distracted by all the stuff that comes with it: the imposter syndrome, the judgment, the endless feedback loop, the managing the impact. But now, all I felt was a desire to tell my sister what I thought about her. What I really thought about her now, in this moment. Sis was royal, and I wanted her to know that.

Dahvy moved forward, grabbed my hand, and looked out. My eyes followed her focus, but it was impossible to locate what she was seeing. After a moment, I stopped trying and laid my head in her lap. The wedding was finally over, and now it was just the two of us. Dahvy and Soma. The Kear sisters were closing out the show.

CHAPTER 34
The Honeymoon

It's always creeping up on me like that. Every year on repeat, I look out the window and am surprised to find snowflakes drifting from the sky, in and around the trees. Fall rolls into winter, and suddenly all the reds, yellows, and oranges turn into a single blanket of white snow. A blank canvas. A fresh start.

In my humble opinion, winter reigns supreme in ye olde New England. I know that's sacrilege to say (everyone loves THAT FOLIAGE), but for me, when the trees lose their leaves against all that whiteness, you can see it for what it really is: a contradiction. The branches bud, the leaves will grow, change colors and fall, and yet . . . a tree will always be a tree. In the winter, I felt both that change and those roots.

Ooh, philosophy. I was really feeling those metaphors this morning. In my drafty upstairs bedroom, the cold was hitting hard, and not enough sheets could satisfy me. It was messing with my brain cells. Atop my mattress, I rolled away from the window and slowly and snugly into a warm chrysalis made of bedsheets. I needed a moment before all the Christmas activities got underway. Downstairs, I could already hear multiple pairs of footsteps doing busywork like some kind of holiday jig. It would only be a matter of time before they came a-knocking.

Let them wait. I reached for my phone to check if I had any emergency morning correspondences.

BRITNEY (8:56 a.m.):   Merry Xmas, babe. Should I bring something for dinner later?

This was important romantical business. I texted back.

SOMA (9:02 a.m.):   Nope. Just your beautiful self.

Britney and I had been dating for over a month now, and while I didn't know what would happen in the future, it'd be an understatement to say . . . I was into it. Post the chaos of the competition and the wedding, we'd spent the last month just hanging out, getting to know each other, and of course making an occasional night trip over to Jack Kerouac Park. Not as much as I used to, though. No shade to the guy who recognized first the fire in my heart, who loved the madness in me, but I think I was ready in my own words to make people say "Awww!" Regardless of whether I'd utterly failed the lit contest or not, I already felt the legacy of the hometown hero in me.

BRITNEY (9:05 a.m.):   Ooh check it out. Now THIS is a collab! Can you handle it?

SOMA (9:05 a.m.):   Isn't it a little late to release a holiday
                           video?
BRITNEY (9:06 a.m.):   Bro, just click the link . . .

I pressed play, and there they were: my Number Ones, sitting at the center of the marble pillars at the park. I may have gotten flack for my obsession with the sad-boi poet, but I knew the scouting of locations was purposeful. Behind Britney and Sophat, Jack's language inscribed in the brown pillars seemed to glow against the white snow all around them. I appreciated that even now, they entertained my complicated heart tugs.

Britney counted off, "One, two, three . . ." and began to play the opening ukulele chords for "What Are You Doing New Year's Eve?" Sophat looked off into the distance with those ingenue eyes. The wintry urban composition was really working for dramatic effect. Sophat took the first verse, his voice sounding like a gentle pop diva who wasn't trying to brag. He'd get to the belt eventually, but for now, the setup was some subtle falsetto riffs. Britney joined him on the second verse, and her husky voice, which had first made me fall, was tripping me all over again. They converged on the last two verses, and it was like their voices were made to blend. His more delicate and virtuosic, and hers more soulful and grounded. It was simple: it was they who were straight social media trending. They weren't trying to be something they weren't. Even Sophat, who I'd accused of being "much" hundreds and hundreds and *hundreds* of times, was just letting it flow. It was a master class in vibes, and I was taking notes.

Honestly, something about watching it now made me realize . . . maybe I didn't need to be some poet for the profile. There was no rush. I could make my way through my own thoughts, my own language, without any of the discourse. For now, maybe I could return to just making it for me. I hadn't created any new rhymes since the wedding, but I'd get there eventually. I knew that in my gut.

Midway through, I could hear Ruben's and Dahvy's voices rumbling downstairs. I exited out of the video to let Britney know the answer to her inquiry.

SOMA (9:10am):   Yeah, too bad. Got New Year's plans.
BRITNEY (9:10 a.m.):   That's why we made it, silly.

It was true. Tomorrow, I was headed to Cambodia and would be there through the first week of the new year. We all were. I looked over at the suitcases that Dahvy had set out for me, surrounded by piles of dirty clothes. Yeah, no, I needed to do laundry and get to packing. I was sure someone would hound me about it at some point today.

The trip was actually Ruben's idea. With the new semester starting, the married couple thought they wouldn't be able to have the full honeymoon they desired, so they suggested we travel to Cambodia for about two weeks. Luckily, the school administration had been supportive about the holiday time, so we were all getting to play hooky for a bit. *Maybe* that was the only upside to having a sister who was a teacher at the school you attended and was married to another teacher who now was your brother, and admittedly, had a bit of leverage. I'd take the rare nepotistic advantage where I could get it.

Ba had mentioned it was usually best to have a longer vacation to get acquainted to the time change, but we all knew with school and life, it wasn't possible. At this point, we were all used to making things work. Any couple of days I'd get with Ba felt worth it . . . and at the same time, it occurred to me, I hadn't seen him in the flesh for almost a year now. I wondered what would it be like to be around him again. Would I know what to say? Would it be mad awkward? Would he be different now? Would I be different now? Of course we would be, but . . . would we get along?

As I was racing through all the essential Q's, my phone lit up with Ba's number, as if the guy had been eavesdropping on me this whole time.

"Merry Christmas, old man." I took the first jab.

"Easy there. Who you calling j'aah?" Ba's voice sounded joyful, even if I was marking him for being prehistoric. "Merry Christmas, baby girl. I know you have a busy day ahead of you, so we'll make it short. Besides, I'm seeing you soon anyways! What what!"

"What what! You better be showing me the spots."

"Oh, I got you. Don't you worry. But hey, thank you for sending me some of your stuff."

I'd been a little behind on Christmas gifts this year, so I'd sent the old man a couple of recordings of my poems. Somehow the events of the last couple of weeks had sort of undone the pressure of sharing. Still, I opted to audio-record them so I could just focus on the words. Listening to them back made me feel like maybe this was what I was meant to do this whole time: send them to the heart by way of the ears. The vibes felt right.

"They're all still in motion, but yeah. I hope you liked them."

"They're beautiful, gkoun. The way you use your words to express yourself. It's powerful stuff."

"Thanks, Ba." I could feel my face flush. Thank God no one was around. I could just relish this embarrassment all by myself.

"And the truth about your name—"

"Here we go . . ."

"I know, I know, I'm always telling tales about your namesake, but hear me out. The truth is, a lot is unknown about Queen Soma. She's got that mystery. So many stories have been told about her, and I think that only shows you how big the desire is for people to want to find themselves in her. For them to follow her path, her story. That's why people tell tales, right? To create a path for others. Your rhymes . . . they possess that power too. You create a path for others, and you know I'll keep following. I'll see you soon, okay? Love you, gkoun."

"See you soon, Ba."

I lay on the bed for a second with the phone against my chest. Suddenly, the faint smell of chicken, burnt garlic, and sesame oil hit my nose. It had to be buh-bah sak moin, chicken and rice porridge. Among the many Khmer soup dishes I loved, it was the one that was most familiar to me, because Ma made it basically every day for breakfast. I liked it best with a fistful of bean sprouts, a couple of squeezes of lime, mint, red chili paste, and that doughy French bread that Cambodians sometimes dunked in their sweet coffees with condensed milk, chai qua. The end product was this delicious cloudy bowl stacked with fresh vegetables and sauces that brought all the ingredients together.

When I was younger, I'd rail about having to eat soup for breakfast while all the other kids ate cereal with marshmallows. But now it was like, I needed buh-bah to start my day. I'd missed Ma's cooking and the way my nose would recognize where I was before I could even form a thought.

A second later, I could hear the creaking of the wooden stairs as a body was headed in my direction. The light hum of Christmas music played on the radio downstairs. Two knocks landed on my door, followed by a firm but gentle voice:

"Gkoun, you coming down?"

I shed the covers from my body and began to emerge to meet Ma at the doorway. She'd been here for a month now, and while it was hard to miss her at the wedding, I knew she'd come home just in time. And when we would travel together to meet Ba tomorrow, I knew that would be just in time as well.

"Coming."

Acknowledgments

To my parents, Sokhom and Monica Chum. Ba, you named me "a wonder of the world." I always thought you were lying about that translation, and honestly, it made me uncomfortable to think you created this impossible identity for me. But every day, I step into that namesake because I know you believe that I might be one. To Ma, my Sagittarius spiritual soulmate. You loved me first. You love me the most. It's from you I learned about trusting my instincts above all else . . . even if they're hot, *especially* when they are. How can a person be so strong and still so kind? You are my blueprint for being.

To my family, the Chums, the Poeuvs, the Sears, the Kissams, the Suys, the Plummers, and then some. You raised me. You fed me. You looked out after me. You argued with me. You took me to wat. You took me to church. You took me to the Renaissance Faire. You took me to the movies. You made me understand what a family was with all its joys, laughs, complications, heartaches, and endless stories. Thank you for your many teachings.

To Jakob W. Plummer. Only you know what it's like to

witness my late hours toiling, my many existential crises, my need to grasp at the ineffable. With an impeccably executed joke, you offer me the constant and true perspective: that things are so much sweeter when you laugh. I can move forward because of you. I know the extent of my love because of you.

To Page 73 Productions, you helped me write this book on the beach. To SPACE on Ryder Farm, you helped me write this book on a farm. To the New Harmony Project, you helped me write this book in utopia. To the Midwives, Emily Ritger and Thomas Murray, you helped me write this book in connectivity. Without all your many resources, spaces, stretches of time, meals, and communities, I could not have written this book. I repeat: I could not have written this book.

To my friends and in particular, Christina Michelle Watkins, Taylor Bailey, Jessica Jain, Laura Jo Schuster, Matt Hagemeier, and Tiffany Nichole Greene . . . some of you knew I was writing a book, some of you will find out as you're reading this acknowledgment. Regardless, thank you for providing me an abundance of support, care, and love. You are lighthouses, all. Thank you for showing me the way.

To Darcy Perreault, my sophomore English teacher, you were the first to encourage me to keep writing. In a time where I wanted nothing more than to fade into the background, you made me feel original. You will never know the depth of your impact.

To Merrimack Repertory Theatre, Sean Daniels, Courtney Sale, and Bonnie Butkas. Thank you for extending your artistic home to me with such grace and openness, time and time again. To Lowell, Massachusetts, including the likes of Ani Vong, Dahvy Pech (Rest in peace, my friend), Soben Ung, Sovanna Poeuv (now of Long Beach), and so many more. Thank you for showing me how a Khmer community preserves, imagines, thrives, and envisions a future that is always embracing of transformation. I hope you'll witness the beauty of your city in every nook and cranny of this story.

To my Cambodian people near and far, I create spaces for you. I pray you'll see my endeavor to honor you and our experiences. To my ancestors, thank you for every sacrifice, every brick you laid so that I might dream from this foundation. I pray you'll see me as your dream fulfilled. And to Amy Windle and Ken Washington, you're a part of that lot too. I pray you'll feel my cosmic love across the multiverse.

To Jennifer Ung, my friend and editor. How dare you suggest I write a book? How dare you believe that I could do it? I will forever be in awe of your insistence, your gentle guidance, and your vision for what books can do for young audiences, especially our people. To Monica Sok, thank you for letting us draw a spotlight on your name, your likeness, your artistry, so that we can continue to inspire generations to come. To Erin Fitzsimmons, thank you for your most perfect cover. To Mel Taing, thank you for manifesting the soul of this story in this portrait. To Thatiana So, thank you for stepping into the frame as our protagonist Soma. May every young Cambodian reader take a glance at your photo and dream of what is possible for them too. To Quill Tree Books and HarperCollins, thank you for giving a first-time novelist a chance at putting down some thoughts.

And finally, to you, reader. You are holding a dream. Thank you for helping me realize it. I wrote this for you.